THE UNLUCKY ONES

JESSICA DANIEL 14

KERRY WILKINSON

ALSO BY KERRY WILKINSON

The Andrew Hunter series

SOMETHING WICKED | SOMETHING HIDDEN

Standalone novels

TEN BIRTHDAYS | TWO SISTERS

THE GIRL WHO CAME BACK | LAST NIGHT

THE DEATH AND LIFE OF ELEANOR PARKER

THE WIFE'S SECRET | A FACE IN THE CROWD

The Jessica Daniel series

LOCKED IN | VIGILANTE

THE WOMAN IN BLACK | THINK OF THE CHILDREN

PLAYING WITH FIRE | THICKER THAN WATER

BEHIND CLOSED DOORS | CROSSING THE LINE

SCARRED FOR LIFE | FOR RICHER, FOR POORER

NOTHING BUT TROUBLE | EYE FOR AN EYE

SILENT SUSPECT

Silver Blackthorn

RECKONING | RENEGADE | RESURGENCE

Other

DOWN AMONG THE DEAD MEN

NO PLACE LIKE HOME

ONE

SATURDAY

Now

Detective Constable Archie Davey glanced away from the steering wheel for the merest moment before turning back to the road. 'You can admit it,' he said.

DI Jessica Daniel was slouched in the passenger seat and didn't look up from her phone. 'Admit what?'

'You're addicted to that game.'

Jessica frowned but didn't immediately argue the point, instead setting a small storage shed to build. It was going to take eight hours unless she coughed up some real-world money for the mobile game. The rest of her town was coming along nicely and there was little doubt she made a bloody good mayor. If the process of wielding political power in the *actual* world hinged upon a person's performance at the game on her phone, Jessica would have an entirely new career lined up. It was a shame about such pesky real-world annoyances, like elections and democracy.

She thumbed the exit button and then dropped her phone

into her lap, looking up through the windscreen to the street beyond. 'Satisfied?'

'Don't mind me,' Archie replied, 'I'm just pointing out that you're always playing that game. What is it they say? Compulsive tendencies? Addictive personality?'

'The only compulsion I'm getting is to stick my boot up someone's backside. Preferably a know-it-all short-arse who's sitting not too far away.'

Archie shuffled in his seat, making himself a little taller. He didn't reply but grinned to himself.

They sat in silence for a few minutes as Archie continued to navigate Manchester's chock-a-block streets. There were cars everywhere, *people* everywhere. It was late morning on the final Saturday before the long Easter weekend and the sun was beaming. It wasn't warm but that didn't stop the psychos ambling along in shorts and T-shirts as if it was the middle of July.

Archie slowed for a crossing as lines of people streamed across in front, their carrier bags crammed full with Easter eggs bobbing from side to side. As always, most slowed to glance at the marked patrol car, wondering if the officers inside were on their way to anywhere interesting. As per usual, they weren't. Jessica and Archie were heading back to the station for weak tea, soggy sandwiches and emails that needed deleting.

Even in the driver's seat, Archie was struggling to sit still. He often acted like he'd slept in an ants' nest, squirming and wriggling incessantly until someone told him not so politely to sit still.

'You know what I don't get?' he said out of the blue.

'How to zip up your flies?'

Archie glanced down quickly, checking his fully fastened trousers and then turning back to the road. 'What did Jesus do on the Saturday?'

It took a moment or two for the words to sink in. Jessica blinked. 'What?'

'Y'know, on the Saturday after he died. What did Jesus do?'

Jessica turned sideways to stare at Archie, wondering if he was having some sort of stroke, or a breakdown. 'You've not been up late watching those tele-evangelists again, have you?'

'I went to Sunday School as a kid and have always wondered. Jesus was crucified on Good Friday, then he rises from the dead on Sunday. Ta-da! Look who's back and all that. Let's see David Blaine beat this. But what did he do on Saturday?'

'Why are you suddenly concerned?'

'Just with Easter coming up. It got me thinking.'

'You've been warned before about thinking too much.'

Archie ignored her. 'So there's Jesus with his long hair and beard. He's giving it the whole, "Bigger than Jesus"-thing.'

'He didn't say he was bigger than Jesus, he said he *was* Jesus.'

'Whatever. Anyway, he's been nailed to the cross on the Friday and then these blokes put him in the tomb late that night. They were probably on time-and-a-half or time-in-lieu, something like that. Now, did it take the whole of Saturday for him to come back from the dead before he popped up on Sunday, or did he get his mates round?'

'You think he spent a day in his tomb playing FIFA on the PlayStation?'

'Well...' Archie tailed off as they reached a set of traffic lights. He yanked the handbrake up and then scratched his chin. 'Probably not FIFA. Maybe they had a game of cards or something?'

'*Cards?* You think he got some of the disciples round for a few hands of Texas Hold 'Em?'

'I dunno. Perhaps he just wanted a day of peace? He'd

been like a rock star all those years and he fancied a day off? Being dead's as good an excuse as any.'

'You reckon they crucified Jesus on the Friday, then he came back to life shortly after, but he hung around in the tomb all day Saturday because he wanted a lie-in?'

'Wouldn't blame him, like. It's a nightmare trying to get some peace nowadays.'

Jessica closed her eyes momentarily, wondering where this particular snippet of Davey wisdom had come from. If Archie could focus on something for longer than a few minutes, he might be dangerous.

The stream of consciousness came to an end as the traffic light changed back to green.

As Archie pulled away, Jessica glanced down to her phone, waking it from sleep mode and then thumbing through her unread emails. Most were from shops advertising various bank holiday sales, but there was one from her mum, too. 'How are you? What have you been up to? Don't you know I live a few miles away?' That sort of thing. Good job she hadn't yet figured out Skype.

Jessica read through her mother's email for the fourth time that day, wondering how to reply. The obvious thing would be to visit her mum's nursing home – but then she'd get the whole carry-on about the various illnesses that were going round the other residents. There were also the muttered asides, wondering if Jessica had met anyone nice recently; not to mention the throwaway remarks about some article she'd read concerning women's fertility being a sliding scale.

It was always the same – except, with an email, Jessica could leave out as much about her life as she wanted.

As the purr of the engine dipped, Jessica peered up to see another set of traffic lights. It was the Manchester way – lights, roundabouts, incomprehensible junctions, ropy cycle lanes that ended in the middle of nowhere. The entire transport structure had likely been designed by someone tripping on serious psychotropic mushrooms.

The engine whirred and then hummed louder as the lights flickered green and Archie accelerated. Jessica looked back to her phone, still waiting for inspiration about how to begin her email reply.

'Hi, Mum. Sorry for not getting back to you sooner, it's just that you really annoy the hell out of me and, honestly, I can only deal with that sort of thing in small doses.'

That definitely wouldn't cut it.

It was only a fraction of a second, barely a blink, when she lifted her head. There'd been a flicker of a shadow, something that shouldn't be there...

It was already too late.

BANG!

The dark silhouette of a man bounced onto the bonnet of the car and then slammed into the windscreen with a squelch and then a crunch of glass. Somebody screamed, perhaps it was Jessica herself, and then there was a squeal of rubber on tarmac. At the same time, her ears popped as the airbag exploded into her face.

There was a thump from behind, a blurring of everything and then, momentarily, silence.

Jessica touched her cheek, wiping at the dusty powder that came with the airbag.

More silence.

Her heart was charging, breathing short and sharp. She was alive.

Then the screaming started.

TWO

Earlier

Jessica eased the pool car onto the crumbling tarmac outside the row of shops and pulled on the handbrake. She flapped at a yawn and then stretched high as something in either her neck or shoulders clicked and cracked.

Archie frowned from the passenger seat. 'You're like an arthritic flamingo,' he said.

Jessica would have fired back with something hilarious except she wasn't done and a second yawn rippled through her.

'Late one?' Archie added.

The second yawn roared its way past any attempted stifling, erupting like an angry bee from a matchbox.

'It's a young person's game, Arch,' Jessica replied, eyes still watering. 'Late for me is *The One Show* and a cup of tea.' She wafted a hand in front of her face, batting away the invisible yawn genie and then nodding at the newsagent in front of them. 'I'm not even at work. When I spoke to the owner yesterday, he said he couldn't fit me in till today.'

'You had to make an appointment? He only sells papers, doesn't he? Not like he's a doctor?'

Jessica shrugged and then clambered out of the car, resting on the roof with her elbow as Archie got out of the passenger's side. 'He was robbed three times last year,' she said. 'Twice by someone with a knife, once by a bloke with a pistol. Turned out to be imitation – we found it in the bin down the road. Anyway, this year, nothing. No robberies, no shoplifting, no antisocial behaviour, no dogging in the car park round the side.' She pointed at the row of shops. 'The Lees Estate is now the most crime-free spot in the city.'

Archie looked past her, unconvinced. There was a grimy pizza place, a hardware store with the shutters up, somewhere selling butties, and the newsagent. He eyed the sandwich shop for a moment too long, saying nothing about the bacon smell drifting from beyond.

'*Here?*' he asked.

'So the stats say.'

Archie's brow rippled, his top lip curling. 'No way.'

'Yes way – and it's mine, all mine.' Jessica didn't give Archie a chance to reply as she headed for the newsagent.

It was a typical bit-of-everything store inside. There were shelves of alcohol, rows of newspapers and magazines, some spinning rack full of tat, mounds of tinned food and an ice cream freezer buzzing angrily in the corner.

The man behind the counter was tall and thin, wearing a long orange kurta. He banged a scanner gun on the counter and muttered something under his breath before looking up to see Jessica.

'Mr Murthal...' Jessica offered her hand but his frown was unmoved as she produced her warrant card. 'We spoke yester-day...' she added.

He didn't look at the card. 'I said I didn't want to talk,' he replied.

'You also said I could drop in tomorrow, which is, er, today.'

The shop owner's gaze flickered to Archie and then back. His eyebrows rose. 'Okay.'

'I wanted to check in to ask how things are going...?'

'With what?'

'Everything, I suppose. I know last year was, um... *difficult*.'

'With the robberies you didn't solve? The knives you never found? Do you know how much insurance costs nowadays? Most places won't even give me a quote. You should see my excess.'

Mr Murthal's voice rose as he spoke and Jessica waited a couple of beats for him to quieten. 'But things have been better this year?' she asked.

'No thanks to you.'

Jessica nodded. 'Right... I suppose that's why I'm here. Is there anything in particular that's changed since last year? I know there was an extra patrol put on, plus they gave you a panic button. Do you have any other ideas that might help improve things?'

Mr Murthal shrugged. 'Bit late now.'

They looked at each other, but he didn't seem interested in whatever she had to say.

'Did you get the leaflet about the new police support scheme?' Jessica asked.

He stared back at her blankly as if she'd slipped into a foreign language for a few moments. 'I get lots of leaflets,' he finally replied. 'Vote for this person, sponsor that person, "have you seen my cat?". Always with the leaflets. You want to know where they all go?'

'The bin?'

The newsagent slammed the pricing gun back on the counter again. 'The bin!'

He pointed at the bin with a flourish, in case they hadn't understood.

'Right, well... er...' Jessica turned to Archie for help but he had the look of someone who'd been caught with his pants down and laptop lid open. 'I guess that'll be all,' she added, stumbling. 'If you need anything...'

Before she could finish her sentence, Jessica grabbed a chocolate bar from the counter and fished a pound coin from her pocket. Mr Murthal slammed his scanner gun into the counter one more time and then held it over the wrapper until the machine beeped. He took her money and then handed her back a paltry amount of change.

Outside, Jessica headed along the row of shops, unwrapping the Curly Wurly with disdain as she walked. 'These used to be the size of a stepladder,' she said, 'now it's two bites and they're gone.'

'Maybe your mouth's just got bigger.'

Jessica had a bite of chocolate and caramel, struggling to think of a funny retort. She ate half the bar and then handed the rest to Archie, who gleefully inhaled the rest. She'd only bought it out of guilt.

The Lees Estate was a nest of scuffed red-brick houses surrounding a series of three- and four-storey apartment blocks that lined a paved plaza. Someone had made an effort to clean the place up at some point in its recent history, with a row of leafy trees backing onto a strip of green on either side of the square. As they walked across the tiles, Jessica felt watched. They were wearing suits in a world of three-quarter-length shorts and T-shirts. Hundreds of windows were facing the square.

'Cheap suit today, is it?' Jessica asked.

Archie tugged at the sleeves. 'No.'

'It's a bit too big for you. Looks like you're off to a christening and you've borrowed your dad's.'

Archie didn't take the bait. He was too short for most trousers, meaning he had to roll them up at the bottom or have them tailored. He'd made the mistake of buying an expensive suit that was sized especially for him. After wearing it for the first time, he'd proudly told his colleagues about the whole process one tipsy evening and wished he hadn't when everyone spent months taking the piss. He'd not worn it since.

In the furthest corner, near to an arched overhang, half a dozen teenagers were huddled astride BMXs that seemed far too small for them. Jessica's instinct was trouble, but the lads weren't even smoking, let alone getting up to anything more sinister.

Archie finished chomping down the chocolate and then sucked his fingers. When he spoke, it sounded like his teeth were stuck together. 'You hear about Funtime?' he mumbled.

Jessica gave him a sideways glare, but he wasn't paying attention. 'What's he done now?'

'He was down at the canal, where they fished that body out. He was crouched over looking at the water and Dave reckons he nearly toppled in.'

'Probably saw his reflection in the water and wondered what it was.'

Detective Inspector Franks was the other DI at Longsight Station. On paper, pay grade and to anyone with a severe brain injury, he and Jessica were equals. To those who knew, Franks had somehow been over-promoted and was out of his depth. He was the type who'd one day end up being boss to them all, a corporate sort who somehow fell into jobs.

'One of the uniforms caught him before he went arse over tit,' Archie added.

'That should be a disciplinary. Obstructing the natural order of things.'

As Jessica and Archie drew nearer, the BMXers disappeared off in various directions. Some headed through the curved alley that led towards the rest of the estate, others zipped past the officers, giving the merest of sideways looks. Aside from the gentle hum of traffic on the breeze, it was quiet.

Jessica stopped and turned in a circle, taking in the buildings. It was eerily peaceful. No faces peering down on them, no one else on the square.

'Why's everyone got their windows open?' Archie asked.

Jessica looked up to the flats and realised that he was right, or close enough. Most of the apartments had the front windows open a sliver, creating a disorientating bank of glass that was refracting the light in slightly different directions.

'No idea,' Jessica replied. 'I don't think it warrants a full investigation, though.'

'What now?' Archie asked.

'I guess I go home and you get off to the station. I'm back here meeting some community liaison officer tomorrow – whatever that means. I was trying to get a sense of the place before then, but, well... it's a housing estate, innit? Much like all the others. Bricks, buildings, kids on bikes, probably used condoms in the stairwells.'

Archie paused. '"Community liaison officer"? That sounds like a properly made-up job. He probably empties the bins or something. Why are you meeting him on a Sunday?'

Jessica shrugged. 'Don't ask me. Shift patterns? Something to do with a holiday? Fate? You know what it's like' – she slipped into her posh, corporate voice – 'we're a twenty-four-seven, modern police force. *We* don't stop because *life* doesn't stop.'

Archie groaned. 'That's not the new slogan, is it?'

'I bloody hope not.'

Jessica had taken a step in the direction of the car when a shrill, sharp whistle punctured the silence. She turned and looked up to where a man was leaning on the railing of the balcony that surrounded his first-floor flat. He had thinning grey hair and an overcoat that was far too big for him.

'You dibs?'

Jessica wondered if she'd misheard – 'dibs' was a new one on her – but Archie nodded. 'Aye, mate. You need something?'

The man took a half-step backwards, eyeing the estate and then nodding towards the door behind him before disappearing through it. Archie turned to Jessica, who shrugged, and they headed towards the stairwell.

'"*Dibs*"?' Jessica said when they were out of earshot.

'You did your time on the streets. Didn't anyone ever call you Dibble?'

'I got called a lot of things on the streets.' Jessica took the first stair ahead of her colleague. 'We got Dibble now and then – but are we really at a point where people can't be arsed using two syllables as slang?'

Archie didn't reply as they passed a heavy-looking door next to the open stairwell and then clomped their way up the stone until they were on the second level. The darkness of the steps gave way to the bright of outside as they found themselves on a straight balcony with a long row of doors on the left. The old man's was slightly open as Jessica knocked gently and then poked her head into a hallway that smelled of cigarettes being covered up by pine air freshener.

The old man was leaning against the wall. He was shorter than Jessica, his back slightly hunched. 'You comin' in?' he asked.

'Do you need our help...?'

The man turned and headed along the hallway, Jessica a little behind. Archie stopped to close the door and then followed until they all ended up in a poky kitchen. There were no IKEA granite worktops and sparkling mixer taps, instead it was pure brown plastic chic. The thought popped into Jessica's head that the kitchen fittings were likely older than she was. Sitting on the countertop was a heater that was probably even more ancient. There was a hose running from the back to the slightly open window and a funnel at the front spewing a stream of scorching air into the room. It didn't look like a gas-safety certificate would be forthcoming.

The man scratched his head, unable to make eye contact with either of them. 'What's going on?' he asked.

Archie took the lead, his Manc accent thicker than usual. 'You tell us, pal. We were just out for a wander. What's your name?'

'You're dibs, though, right?'

Archie tugged at his suit collar. 'What gave it away?'

The man smiled sheepishly, showing off a missing front tooth. The rest were a yellowy brown. 'I'm Roly,' he said.

'Constable Davey,' Archie replied, motioning to Jessica. 'This is Inspector Daniel.'

Roly peered between them, not quite making eye contact. 'Has something happened?' he asked.

'You should've had a leaflet through the door,' Jessica replied. 'We've launched a new police support scheme. It's supposed—'

Roly batted a hand. 'All the leaflets go in the bin, love. D'you know how many pizza menus I get through the door every week? *Pizza?* Who needs a menu for that? And don't get me started on "support schemes". I've been here nearly fifty years. I've seen more schemes than you've had hot dinners.' He paused. 'Cold ones, too.'

Jessica didn't know what to say. She didn't entirely disagree. It was clear no one read their leaflets and, as for various police schemes, she'd seen plenty in her time as well.

Roly slouched slightly, holding his hands in front of the volcanic heater. 'What's this one?'

Jessica glanced sideways at Archie but he'd gone quiet. She didn't blame him. 'The estate has been assigned a

Community Liaison Officer,' she said, feeling a small piece of her dying as she did so. She was a walking, talking press release. 'The idea is that everyone who lives here will have a named uniformed officer who they can contact face to face, or in private. That officer will be working with me. We're hoping to get on top of incidents before they happen.'

Roly smiled. 'One officer, eh?'

'One's better than none. Besides, that's just the front man. It's being trialled across the city. Different estates and areas will have their own officer. There will still be a full support team if needed.'

He rolled his eyes, not persuaded. Jessica wasn't convinced either but she had a corporate line to peddle. In the old days of being a constable, she might have been eye-rolling herself; now she had to play the game.

'Who's our officer?' Roly asked.

'He's named Pete. He'll be around from tomorrow. If you need anything in the meantime, I'm here...'

'You live round here?'

Jessica shook her head, so Roly glanced at Archie, who did the same.

'They say everything's better than it's ever been...'

'With what?' Jessica replied.

'Your stats. Burglaries, robbing, all that.' He paused, choosing his words.

Roly was right: thefts and reports of antisocial behaviour were up in all the surrounding districts – but at an all-time low on the Lees Estate.

'It's not that great,' Roly added, more quietly.

'What's not?' Jessica asked.

He held both hands up. 'Things are the same as ever. Lies, damned lies and *your* statistics. These little shits don't know they're born.'

Jessica could feel Archie watching her. 'What little, er... shits?' she asked.

'Kids. They're always out there making noise, hanging around. You must've seen 'em? Then there's people coming and going all hours of the day and night from downstairs. Doors going, people talking.' He breathed. 'How many people d'you see out there?' Roly nodded towards his front door.

Aside from the kids on the bikes, Jessica hadn't seen anyone on the plaza. It had been creepily quiet. Roly must've seen the acknowledgement in her face because he started to nod.

'Now you're getting it. People don't go out unless they need to. I don't care what your numbers say – they're scared.'

'Why?'

He smiled but with no humour. 'You're the dibs, aren't ya? You tell me.'

'I'm asking you.'

They stared at one another for a moment and then Roly turned to his heater, extending his hands into the cyclone of warmth.

'We can help if you tell us,' Jessica added. Roly didn't reply and it felt like the moment was gone. She plucked a card from her inside pocket and placed it on the counter. 'You've got my numbers there. My mobile's on the back.'

'Expensive to call those, ain't it?'

'You can call the station and ask for me if you prefer. If you want to talk...'

She tailed off, wondering if he might fill the silence. When he didn't, she nodded to Archie, who shuffled into the hallway. They said their goodbyes and then headed back down the stairs.

Jessica felt watched again, though there were no faces in the surrounding windows.

'That was weird,' she said.

Archie was unusually quiet. He stopped in the archway that led back to the plaza, lowering his voice. 'I grew up in a place like this,' he said quietly.

'In a block of flats?'

'A terrace – but close enough.' He nodded towards a Manchester United sticker in one of the nearby windows. 'Same people, same row of shops, same barrage of pizza menus.' He sighed.

'What?' Jessica asked.

'Roly's right. It's too quiet. Where is everyone?' He batted a hand towards the deserted plaza. 'Why aren't there kids playing football? Someone revving a motorbike? I know it's all FIFA, YouTube and selfies nowadays, but kids still go outside. When I was a lad going round the estate, there'd always be someone pumping out music. Maybe a couple arguing – something like that. The sound of growing up was other people – but here...' He tailed off, point made. They stood in the archway for a moment listening to the faint sound of traffic.

'What are you saying?' Jessica asked.

Archie shrugged. 'I don't know.' He straightened himself, pulling his tie neat. 'It's yours, all yours.' He grinned wide, back to his old self, but Jessica knew he was right. Something *was* off.

'I'll talk to Pete Whateverhisnameis,' she said, 'see if he knows anything.'

They strolled back towards the car, keeping to the edge of the housing block. They stood out enough as it was, without suiting and booting it across the central plaza.

'You driving?' Archie asked.

Jessica fished around for the keys in her jacket pocket and then tossed them towards him. 'Be my guest.'

THREE

Now

The windscreen was splintering, a slow crinkling crackle of glass. The airbag hung limply in Jessica's lap. It felt like everything had happened in slow-motion and yet it still took her a few moments to play it all back. The car had hit something... someone – who had gone over the top of the vehicle.

Jessica turned to look through the back window, but there was only a misty blur. Archie was pressed against the back of the driver's seat, eyes wide, back rigid as he stared through the cracked windscreen.

'Arch?' Jessica said.

He blinked. 'I...'

'Are you okay?'

'He, um... the man, he...' Archie mumbled something that Jessica didn't catch. He licked his lips but didn't otherwise move.

She reached to unclick her seat belt and then rested a hand on his shoulder before opening her door. The cool air flooded inside, hitting Jessica like a slap in the face. She was sweating but shivering – though these were the moments for which she'd been trained. The calm and coolness when everything around her was breaking down.

Jessica clambered out of the car and headed towards the back of the vehicle, following the long smear of red that coated the tarmac. There was no body behind the car and it took her a moment to piece together what had happened... There was no body at the back of *their* car because the Toyota behind them had also ploughed into the victim.

The second car's door was open, the engine idling as the driver stood at the side, staring towards his back wheel. He was young, perhaps still a teenager, both hands on his head. When Jessica approached, he looked through her, glassy-eyed.

'I hit him,' the driver croaked.

Jessica followed his gaze to the rear of the car. There were more splashes of blood on the tarmac, another on the silver wheel rim itself – and then one large oozing puddle around a man. He was lying on the road behind the Toyota, his neck at a right angle to the rest of his body. Witnesses were beginning to edge forward nervously, but Jessica was ahead of them, striding forward and placing a pair of fingers to the victim's neck. This wasn't a situation where resuscitation would help, where a paramedic could work a miracle. He'd probably been dead the moment Archie hit him – let alone the second vehicle.

The crowd was beginning to close in. Some people were on their phones, perhaps calling 999. Others were filming. Most were simply watching, saying nothing, probably seeing a dead body for the first time.

A siren sounded somewhere in the distance, leaving Jessica to wonder how much time had passed. Had she been in the car longer than she thought? It felt like a few seconds...

Jessica realised someone was at her side when a woman brushed past her. 'Henry...' she gasped.

The woman continued towards the body, but Jessica halted her with a hand on the shoulder. Not too firm, just enough.

She turned, staring through Jessica, doe-eyed and stunned. 'Henry...' she said, twisting back to the body and then Jessica. 'We're getting married,' she added.

Jessica put herself between the woman and the body of her very dead fiancé. 'What's your name?' she asked.

'Gillian.'

Her mouth was open and she made no effort to move around Jessica. She simply stared at the blood on the wheel. The Toyota had been recently cleaned, the rims shining and previously spotless. Henry's sticky blood was glooping into a pool at the bottom. The siren – *sirens* – were getting louder.

'Someone pushed him,' Gillian added croakily and unprompted. 'One minute we were on the pavement and then...'

Jessica turned past her, looking towards the crowd. No one was passing an invisible cordon around the Toyota and Henry's body. Jessica should really be shooing people away, except...

'Where'd they go?' she asked.

'Who?'

'You said someone pushed Henry into the road...'

Gillian did not blink, still staring at the blood on the wheel. 'They ran off.'

'Do you mean they pushed him on purpose?'

Gillian didn't reply as Jessica looked up towards the surrounding buildings, hoping for CCTV cameras. This wasn't only a time for an ambulance and crowd management – there was someone to look for. Except there were other important things to do as well.

'Did you see who—?'

Jessica didn't finish her sentence because the howling roar

of an ambulance siren cut her off. The crowd parted, allowing the vehicle to ease towards the scene. A pair of police cars were behind the ambulance and then it only took seconds for everything to change. Uniformed officers were instantly out of the cars and into action, motioning the crowd away, stopping those filming the grim scene. Witnesses were asked to hang around, paramedics attended to the body. Jessica waved over an officer she recognised, telling her that Gillian was the victim's fiancée.

With more police cars arriving and everything else under a degree of control, Jessica found herself back at the vehicle in which she'd started. She'd somehow forgotten about Archie, but it didn't look as if he'd moved. His hands were still on the steering wheel, knuckles white.

Jessica opened the driver's door and switched off the ignition, removing the keys. Archie didn't stir. Didn't blink.

'Arch?'

'He's dead, isn't he?'

'It wasn't your fault, Arch. He wasn't there and then he was. His fiancée says he was pushed. There'll be witnesses.'

'I still killed him, though.'

Jessica took a deep breath and then crouched so that they were at the same level. Archie didn't turn, hands still on the wheel. She wanted to tell him everything would be fine, except she knew it wouldn't. She levered his right hand away from the wheel and he let her. Then she held it tight, waiting for someone else to come and start asking questions.

FOUR

In different circumstances, Jessica would have been at home hunting through takeaway menus and gearing up to watch a bunch of people singing badly on television.

Instead, she was at her desk in Longsight Police Station. The day had blurred into one large mess of repeating the same story over and over. It was always strange to be on the other side of the table as she told officers what had happened in the car. She'd been watching the road while talking to Archie, peered down to her phone for the merest moment and then...

She'd not seen what had happened.

When she'd been watching the road, it had been clear, she'd glanced down and then, well... bang.

There was no way she could say that precisely, though. Not the whole glancing-down thing. She'd been looking at the road.

Definitely.

It was enough for the time being, but she'd have to speak to professional standards at some point – probably Monday – and then the *really* awkward questions would come.

One question in particular...

Archie had been packed off home in the back of a marked car. It was meant to help him out – a free taxi – but that didn't stop him looking like a criminal as the vehicle pulled away. Jessica had watched him go and he hadn't turned back. He'd barely spoken since the collision, certainly not to her.

A handful of early statements from those who'd stuck around at the scene had already been filed and Jessica clicked through the screens on her computer, waiting for the creaking system to throw up the information she wanted. It had taken long enough for the force to get itself into the twentieth century – the twenty-first was still some way off.

When the reports finally appeared, Jessica scanned the text – though there was little to enlighten her. The witness reports already contradicted each other: one woman was sure the victim was wearing a red top, someone else thought he was in a dark coat. One bloke swore blind he'd seen the victim go under the wheels of the police car – despite the obvious crack to the windscreen and what Jessica had felt sure was an undisputed fact that he'd gone *over* the car, not under it. Another witness had only seen the Toyota, not the police car that was directly in front of it. No matter what the incident, day or night, two witnesses or twenty, there were always discrepancies.

Jessica kept reading and then made a couple of phone calls, finding out that the driver of the Toyota was in hospital with apparent whiplash.

It was *always* whiplash.

Jessica could remember a time ten or fifteen years previously when nobody ever banged on about neck injuries, now it felt like the entire human race had devolved into having weaker neck joints. Where there's blame, there's a claim and all that.

The poor sod probably *did* have whiplash – but he was a

damned sight better off than the bloke who'd gone under his wheels.

From what Jessica could tell, none of the witnesses had seen Henry being pushed into the road. She'd told the officer at the scene that someone should check the local shops for CCTV – but that would take time and it was a Saturday night. Everyone in uniform would be descending upon the city centre ready for the usual barrage of drink-fuelled buffoonery. Then there'd be the arrests, the paperwork, the overnighters in the cells, the Sunday decision to charge or release, the Monday morning at magistrates' court. The faces changed but the routine never did.

When everything had calmed down by Sunday afternoon or Monday, things would start to get done.

Jessica fetched a tea from the machine in the canteen and then returned to her screen. She reread everything, searching her own memory and wondering if she was recalling it all clearly. She wouldn't be investigating the crash – not with herself being a witness as well – but there was still something there. The fact Gillian had said Henry was pushed. Jessica had heard of similar things happening before. Someone had been shoved in front of a Tube train in London a year or two before, someone in Tokyo or New York as well. The details were sketchy in her memory. Gillian used the word 'pushed'. Not an accidental nudge, not someone blundering along a pavement and stumbling clumsily.

Pushed.

It was deliberate.

Jessica found out the name of the support officer who had been left with Gillian and then got the officer's phone number from one of the constables. She texted first and then, a minute or so later, her phone rang.

It was going to be a long evening.

. . .

Gillian looked even paler than when she'd first nudged past Jessica at the scene of the collision. She was sitting in the corner of a faux leather sofa, legs curled underneath herself. There were three empty mugs on the floor at her feet. Her hair had been yanked backwards into a tight ponytail and her skin was white, ethereal in the bluey glow from the television. She was staring at a blank spot on the wall close to the screen, though not *at* it. A music channel was flickering away but the sound was down, the subtitles on. A topless young man was gyrating in a way that made it look like he had some mild compression of the sciatic nerve, while lyrics blinked onto the screen that would be sexual harassment if uttered in any other context.

Gillian continued staring at her spot on the wall, inter-locking and releasing her fingers from each other over and over. Her mother was sitting at her side, peering nervously between her daughter and Jessica. They had matching short dark hair that curled around the ears, plus long slender fingers and the same slumped pose as they each leant slightly to the left. Gillian was somewhere in her thirties, her mother perhaps twenty years older. In a good light – or bad, depending on a certain point of view – they could be sisters.

The support officer was the final person in the room, watching the television in a not-watching-the-television kind of way by glancing towards Jessica every minute or so. She was a constable, probably not long out of training. All the courses in the world couldn't completely prepare someone for how people in Gillian's situation might react. From what Jessica could see – and what the officer had told her – there'd been no tears, nor anger. She was blank.

'I've got a fitting on Thursday,' Gillian said out of nothing, turning to her mum. 'I've lost three pounds since the last one.'

Her mother clasped her hand. 'I know, love.'

Gillian turned to Jessica. 'Are you married?'

Jessica shook her head and Gillian nodding at the support officer, who was twiddling the wedding band on her finger. When she realised she was doing it, she stopped.

'Two months on Saturday,' Gillian added, suddenly keen to talk. 'I've been really organised for once. Flowers booked, car sorted. I'm in a hotel the night before and we've got this mobile hairdresser coming over. Friend of a friend thing. We're supposed to be getting mates' rates.' She tailed off. 'I wonder if I've still got my list. I'm going to have to go back through it and cancel it all.'

On top of the television was a framed photograph of Gillian on holiday with a man Jessica assumed was Henry. They were both tanned and smiling, with Gillian holding a bright orange cocktail that had a sparkly tree dangling from the top. A pool glimmered in the background, the sky beamed blue. It was a far cry from this...

'We can do this another time,' Jessica said, shuffling towards the edge of her seat.

Gillian moved quickly, looking up and catching Jessica's eye momentarily. 'No. Now's good.'

'You told me earlier that Henry had been pushed...'

Gillian nodded. 'We were on the edge of the pavement waiting to cross. There's an Easter market on, so we'd gone and bought...' She glanced towards the back of the room and then the front window. 'I didn't even realise. I don't know where I left them. We had bags. There was this German stall doing chocolate. We'd bought these gourmet egg things and I suppose they're gone. I, um...'

She gulped, blinked and then rubbed her eyes.

'It wasn't just us at the crossing,' she added, speaking more quickly. 'We'd stopped to wait for the lights and there were a few other people. It was really busy in town. We were going to walk over to the Northern Quarter to try this cake place everyone keeps going on about – Teacup something or other. It happened so quickly. One moment we were standing there waiting, the next, there was this blur to the side and then he was in the road.' She clicked her fingers. 'It was like that.'

Jessica paused, allowing Gillian a moment to gulp back another large breath. Her mother's hand rested on her knee, though the older woman said nothing.

'Can you describe the blur any better...?' Jessica asked.

Gillian bit her bottom lip hard but then spoke deliberately and clearly. 'They were wearing a dark top. I think it might be maroon, sort of a dark red. The hood was up.'

'Do you remember anything else?'

'Like what?'

'Was it a man?'

Gillian pressed back into the sofa, thinking. 'I don't know. Maybe.'

'What sort of height? Taller than you?'

She shook her head slowly. 'I don't know that either.'

'Okay – and what happened with the blur?'

'It barged into Henry's side. He was on my right and they banged into him from the other side. That's why I didn't really see it all. He fell forward into the road. It was just a flash. Next thing I know, there was the squeal of the brakes and... that's it.'

'Did you see where this person went after that?'

Gillian shook her head again. 'It all happened at the same time.' She clicked her fingers again. 'One minute we're on the pavement, the next it's too late.'

'Did the person hang around?'

Another shake of the head.

'So they ran off?'

'By the time I turned, they'd already gone.' She straightened. 'It was on purpose, y'know? Couldn't have been an accident – Henry got whacked hard.'

Jessica leant back and breathed, glancing towards the photograph atop the television once more. There wasn't much to go on. Nobody else had seen the phantom pusher and the CCTV wasn't in yet. Even if it did arrive, chances were it'd be of too poor quality to show much.

'This isn't an easy question,' Jessica said softly, 'but is there anyone who might have had a grudge against Henry?'

Gillian shook her head. 'He's not that kind of bloke. He's quiet. We stay in a lot and watch Netflix. He gets on with everyone.'

There was a momentary glance between mother and daughter – and then Gillian's mum patted her leg before removing her hand. 'There was that one thing...' she said. It was the first words of note she'd spoken since Jessica's arrival.

Jessica said nothing, leaving the silence for them to fill. She could feel the support officer glance in her direction.

'What?' Gillian said to her mum.

'Well, it is a bit odd, isn't it?'

'What is?'

Gillian's mother turned to face Jessica. 'Henry was hit by a car once before.'

Gillian shook her head. 'It wasn't her. I'd have known.'

'Known what?' Jessica asked.

Gillian stared at her feet. 'Henry's ex. She drove her car at him last year. They'd been broken up for ages, but she's nuts.'

Silence. The support officer was still eyeing Jessica from the side.

'Henry's ex-girlfriend drove a car at him?' Jessica asked.

Gillian pointed to the front of the house and the cul-de-sac beyond. 'She's called Donna. It happened out there. He said they'd gone on a couple of dates two years ago, before we ever met. Reckoned they weren't even properly together – just a trip to the cinema and a couple of meals. We kept seeing her places, though. We'd go to town on a weekend and Donna would be in Harvey Nicks. Or we'd go for a pizza and, surprise surprise, she'd pop in to pick up a takeaway or something. She ambushed him just before Christmas at the end of our drive. I was upstairs getting changed, saw pretty much the whole thing from the window. He was on the pavement and this car came at him from behind. He tried to jump out of the way but it clipped him. We called the police and that but...' She shrugged.

'Was she arrested?'

'You tell me. I've not seen her since.' Gillian gasped, taking a large breath through her nose, then turning back to her mum. 'It wasn't her, though – not this time. This was something else.'

FIVE

Jessica was parked in a pub car park at the end of the road where Gillian lived. Laughter drifted from the rammed beer garden but it was beginning to cool as the early spring evening descended. The hum of voices, of people actually enjoying their lives, reminded her that she should probably go home. Either that or find something much more fun to do with her Saturday night – but every time she thought about doing just that, she remembered the windscreen splintering. It could have been her that was driving – she'd given Archie the keys as they left the Lees Estate and, if it wasn't for that, she would have been. Would she have seen Henry stumbling into the road from the side? She'd missed him from the passenger seat.

Eyes open: Not there.

Blink: There.

As Gillian had said, everything was a blur. She'd blinked and then the windscreen had cracked, the airbags whooshed, tyres squealed. Everything had happened at the same time.

She took out her phone and scrolled through the contacts, hovering over Detective Sergeant Isobel Diamond's name. 'Iz', it read. Two letters.

Jessica pressed the button. It rang once, twice, before Izzy's voice sounded: 'Give us a minute.'

There was a splash in the background, Izzy's frazzled voice and then a muffled silence. Nothing happened for a minute or so, but when Izzy next spoke, it sounded like she was yawning.

'Sorry, I was giving Amber a bath,' she said. 'It's like a tsunami's hit. There's more water out of the bath than in it.'

'You know the water's supposed to go *in* the tub?'

'*I* know that – if only I could teach my three-year-old. She's splashing around like a three-legged poodle in the deep end.' Izzy yawned again. 'Anyway. I heard you had a worse day than me.'

'I've had better.'

'How's Arch?'

'Don't know. They took him home after the crash and I've not heard from him since.'

The sound of Izzy's breath buzzed through the phone. '*Took* him home or *sent* him home?'

'Bit of both. It's a weird one...'

'What is?'

'The bloke he hit is named Henry Taylor. I've been speaking to his fiancée. She says he was shoved into the road on purpose. Not only that, he was hit by a car driven by his nutter ex a few months ago.'

'He's been run over twice?'

'Apparently. At least there won't be a third time.'

Jessica paused, wishing she hadn't said that. It hadn't even sounded funny in her head. Izzy didn't reply – but not because of the lame joke.

'What...?' Jessica added.

'We finally got an ID for that guy from the canal. The one where Funtime nearly fell in trying to get him out.'

'What about it?'

'Someone went round to see the bloke's family this afternoon. Mark Spencer, Mark Spicer, Mark Stanley – something like that. He was down as missing and they had to tell his mum that his body had been found. I wasn't there, so I've not got the details. It was a throwaway thing – but someone reckoned he'd previously survived after nearly being drowned. Some sort of work accident.'

A pause.

'How long ago was that?' Jessica asked.

'I don't know. That's just what someone said. It's probably in the file.'

Jessica held the phone away from her ear. What were the chances of someone surviving a drowning and then *actually* drowning in a separate incident?

In Manchester.

The coast was thirty-odd miles away. They pulled about a dozen bodies out of the canal every year, but, of all the ways people died in the city, drowning was close to bottom of the pile. Unless Mark Spencer-Spicer-Stanley was a body-boarder, he would have been unlucky to nearly drown once and then *actually* drown. Coupled with someone else being hit by a car twice within a few months and something felt very wrong.

'Not much you can do tonight.'

Izzy's voice brought Jessica blinking back into the car. She put the phone to her ear. 'I know.'

'I'm in tomorrow if you want me to do some poking around,' Izzy added. 'Think the guv's off till Monday.'

'Okay, we'll talk tomorrow. Sorry for bothering you.'

'Don't worry about that. Mal's finishing off Amber's bath now. He's going to end up looking like *he's* drowned.' She paused. 'Yeah, that wasn't funny.'

They said goodbye and then Jessica sat, staring towards the beer garden. It was just about warm enough to sit out without having to wear a jacket. Not a bad evening for the time of year.

If she'd been thinking, she'd have invited Izzy out for a beer instead of talking shop. But then Izzy had commitments: a child, a husband.

Jessica didn't.

The number of friends she had without those obligations was diminishing by the year, perhaps even the month.

She took one final wistful look towards the beer garden and then turned the ignition. There was work to do.

Donna Griffin was busy watching people singing badly on television – which was precisely what Jessica probably should have been doing. Henry's former girlfriend had a mobile phone in one hand, thumb typing at a ferocious pace, as her other hand twiddled a strand of hair.

It was impressive multitasking.

Jessica couldn't type that quickly on her phone with two hands, let alone a single thumb. It was a pudgy thumb at that – although Donna's bulky frame seemed to suit her. Everything was at least in proportion. She didn't look up from her phone as she replied to Jessica.

'He was hit by *two* cars?' she said.

'Right – this afternoon.'

'That's tragic, like. Totally tragic. Like a proper... tragedy.'

She didn't sound too bothered, though she did stop typing, sneaking a glance towards Jessica and then focusing on the television.

'I understand you used to be in a relationship with Henry...?' Jessica asked.

'Sort of. Ages ago.' She was evading Jessica's stare, playing with her hair in a way that blocked her face. Her voice was girlish but had no innocence of youth. It was the type of passive-aggressive tone that might be used to tell a kid that Santa Claus wasn't real.

'How long ago?' Jessica added.

'Dunno. Ages.'

'Months? A year? Years?'

She picked up her phone again, pressed something on the side, glanced at the screen and then put it down. 'Two years ago? Three?'

'When was the last time you saw Henry?'

Donna squirmed, making the armchair creak loudly. 'Few months, probably. I'm not sure why that matters.'

'Where did you see him a few months ago?'

'Can't remember.'

'Are you sure?'

Donna's phone was out again, her thumb swishing across the screen. She peeped up to see if Jessica was still watching her but then focused back on her phone. 'Look, my boyfriend's going to be home in a bit. We're going into town for a few drinky-poos. I'm sorry about Henry and all that, but my Paul's a proper man. I don't know why you'd think I'd be interested in Henry.'

Donna was certainly made-up for a night out. Her cheeks were an angry red, her eyes painted with upward curls in the corner, lashes spidery and long.

'Hang on,' she added, holding the phone to her ear. A moment later, she tutted loudly and then banged the device onto the arm of the chair.

'Problems?' Jessica asked.

'His phone's off. Either that or he's out of battery again. He should already be home.'

'Paul?'

'Who else?' She started typing on the screen again, thumb a blur. 'He's always doing this.'

'Can we talk about Henry?'

'What about him?'

'Why did you break up?'

A shrug. 'Y'know. Things.'

Jessica kept her tone calm. 'What things?'

'He called me shallow. Can you believe that? *Me?* Just because he's into museums and art and all that, he thinks everyone should be.'

'So you broke up with him?'

Donna didn't reply, instead slamming the phone onto the armrest once more. She scratched her ear with a white-tipped fingernail.

'Look – I've got to finish getting ready. I don't really know how I can help. It's tragic and all that about Henry, but what do you want me to say? It's not like we were together.'

'I read a report earlier that says you drove a car at him.'

Donna nodded slowly, eyes blazing. She bit her lip, clenched her fists. Jessica could see the volcanic temper bubbling under the surface but, for now, she was keeping it contained. 'I've been through all this with you lot before. I told you then that it was an accident. I'd gone round his house to drop off a top he'd left at mine. I was trying to pull away and he stumbled in front of the car. They told me it was fine.'

That wasn't exactly true. From the report that had been read to Jessica on the phone, Henry had declined to make a statement to the police. All they had was Gillian's initial phone call, describing how Donna had driven the car at Henry. They couldn't do much on the basis of that and the file had been left to gather digital dust. Nobody would have told Donna it was 'fine'. The likelihood was that the investigating officer had given a quiet word, saying she should probably stay away from Henry. At some point after that, she got into a relationship with Paul – for whom Jessica had great pity – and had moved onto her next obsession.

'I was at work today,' Donna added.

'I never asked where you were.'

'Yeah, but you wanted to.'

Jessica didn't reply straight away. She *was* going to ask that. She'd not told Donna that Henry might have been pushed in front of the police car and full details were a long way from being shared. There was no particular reason for Donna to be under suspicion for anything.

'I was at work until four,' Donna added quickly. 'Loads of people will tell you that. Ask 'em.'

Jessica still didn't reply – but they were interrupted by the crunch of gravel and a van's engine growling from the front of the house. They both turned towards the window and then Donna leapt up.

'That's Paul,' she said. 'We're on our way out, so unless there's anything else...'

SIX

Jessica didn't hang around to meet Donna's boyfriend or ask any other questions. Someone would check Donna's alibi, perhaps Paul's – Donna might even need to make a proper statement – but Jessica doubted anything would be out of place. Donna seemed the sort who'd embed her talons into one poor sod at a time. Months before, it had been Henry, now it was Paul.

She was halfway home to Swinton when Jessica pulled over, parking on a side street a little off the East Lancs Road. She called Archie, waiting and willing him to pick up. When he didn't, she tried again. This time, it was answered on the third ring – except it wasn't Archie.

'Hello...?' a woman's voice said. It took Jessica a moment or two to clock that it was probably Arwen, Archie's girlfriend.

'Oh, um... hi. I was looking for Arch...'.

There was a lengthy, awkward pause. The type in which the silence said far more than actual words.

'He's gone out,' Arwen replied.

'Do you know where?'

'He didn't say.'

'Did he say anything before going out?'

'Not much – something about having a few days off. He left his phone at the flat.'

A pause, and then: 'He must've said something...?'

Another silence and then Arwen's voice sounded muffled. 'We're supposed to be watching the game.'

'What game?'

'United are the late kick-off.'

'Right.'

Jessica didn't know much about football – but the fact the city centre hadn't been riddled with red shirts meant they were probably playing away. Archie and Arwen were both big United fans. It was how they'd met, and Archie spent significant parts of his shifts trying to fiddle the rota in order to let him go to the home matches.

'He's had a rough day,' Jessica added, suddenly wanting to make excuses for him.

'How am I supposed to know that? He came in and went straight back out again.'

Jessica considered asking if Archie had any familiar hangouts – pubs or working men's clubs – but Arwen's tone warned her off.

Besides, she knew where he'd be.

The Wounded Duck was the sort of pub that could only exist in post-smoking-ban Britain. The bar was a little too high for anyone shorter than six foot, meaning most punters couldn't lean on it, instead they had to strain to get an elbow up and over. Everything was meticulously clean, with gleaming pump handles arching up from the bar that gave the servers a free upper-body workout every time they pulled a pint. Instead of the usual Australian and Belgian beers, there was an array of ales named after varying herds of livestock, plus a fancy cocktail menu filled with a host of dodgy puns that didn't quite work.

It wasn't the closest pub to Longsight Police Station – but Jessica, Izzy and co. had long since abandoned that due to the whining bores who propped up the bar, constantly banging on about foreigners and the like. The Wounded Duck was the next best thing, in much the same way that the next best thing to breaking both legs was only breaking one. The alcohol was overpriced, the servers far too young and good-looking – and the extra few inches on the height of the bar was weird.

It didn't stop them drinking there, though. A pint was a pint was a pint.

Archie had found himself a booth and was slumped by himself, cradling a pint of scorched black sheep or constipated calf. Whatever the ale of the week happened to be. Jessica slipped in opposite with half a lemonade. Obviously it wasn't *proper* lemonade from a fountain gun, it was some yellowy-green cloudy overpriced nonsense from a fancy bottle.

The football was on a screen high in the corner, the commentary mute. Archie didn't seem to be watching it anyway – but United were one-down according to the score in the corner.

'Of all the bars in all the world…' Jessica began.

She hoped for a twitch of the lips – probably not a smile but something. Archie didn't flinch.

'What you drinking?' she added.

'Dunno. That barman with the beard reckoned it was good. Still, he reckons waxed eyebrows and earrings in both ears is a good look…'

Archie's words slurred slightly into each other as Jessica gave him a watery smile.

'Left my car at the station,' he added. 'Gonna get a taxi back if that's what you're worried about.'

'I'm more worried about you.'

He supped at his pint instead of replying, peering over Jessica towards the television. 'Where's the support in midfield?' he fumed. 'We're always getting overrun in there.'

Jessica resisted her usual eye-roll that accompanied football talk. Before she realised it, he was staring at her. Staring *through* her. She shivered as he bored into her with the fire of someone who'd had his rough Stretford council estate upbringing. It wasn't often she got to see the person he could've been, the spinning top that could've fallen on one side of the law or the other. But here he was, a bristling ball of anger.

'You ever kill anyone?' he whispered.

Jessica opened her mouth, knowing the reply he expected. She should say 'no' – but it wouldn't be true.

Not really.

Not quite.

It wasn't as black and white as all that.

This time, it was Jessica staring off into nothingness. She watched a couple in a booth on the far side of the pub, legs entwined, feeding each other peanuts.

Archie sat up straighter. 'Jess?'

'It's complicated,' she replied.

Archie stared at her, softening, and then she stared back. He eventually turned away, reaching for his drink. He'd clearly not expected that response.

'Me either,' he said, probably not listening to what she'd actually said. 'Until today.'

He left it there, not getting a chance to add anything because half a dozen men on the far side of the pub leapt up from a booth, cheering and high-fiving.

Jessica turned to the television, where some blokes in red were having a near orgy on a football pitch. Either that or celebrating a goal. It was hard to tell – there was definitely some dry-humping going on.

'Don't United wear red?' Jessica asked.

Archie nodded but didn't celebrate the goal. The score in the corner read 1-1.

A few other drinkers near the windows started to boo, which led to some friendly pointing and heckling with the original bunch. Archie watched it all, saying nothing. Jessica dug into her bag and fished out her car keys.

'C'mon,' she said, 'I'm driving you home.'

He didn't move, watching the screen but not watching it.

'Arch...?' Jessica added.

'What?'

'You know there are people you can talk to.'

'A shrink? Some bloody white coat? I'm not a nutter.'

Jessica waited until his eyes finally met hers. 'Grow up, Arch,' she said.

He turned away, licking his lips and taking a deep breath.

'Have you ever been?' he asked.

'For counselling?'

'Yeah.'

'A few times. After Carrie. After Adam.'

Archie nodded. 'Do you still see someone now?'

Jessica paused for a moment, biting her lip, then she slipped out of the booth and stood. The lemonade was shite anyway. 'Let's go,' she said.

SEVEN

SUNDAY

Izzy was already at her desk by the time Jessica arrived at the station. She didn't look up as Jessica approached, some sort of radar signalling the arrival.

'Nope,' Izzy said before Jessica could say anything. 'I'm off after today. Final day of my cycle. I'm not back in till Easter Monday.'

'You don't even know why I'm here!'

Izzy peered up, grinning. She pointed at an empty space of desk next to her computer monitor. 'That's my to-do pile and nothing's going on that before I go home today. Nobody's getting robbed, no one's getting a kicking, nobody's selling knock-off pornos down the local Labour club. Nothing. It's going to be a quiet, peaceful day.'

She huffed the sigh of a person who wasn't even managing to kid themselves.

'You've got a whole week off?' Jessica said.

'Time owing.'

Jessica sucked on her bottom lip, not quite believing it. 'You've got naked pics of the guv, haven't you? "Give us a few days off, boss, else these end up on the internet".'

Izzy winked. 'What are you after?'

She didn't mention that Jessica was on a day off. She was too polite to give the 'go home' look. The 'haven't-you-got-something-better-to-do?' gaze.

'I've been looking through the overnights,' Jessica said.

'You really know how to enjoy a Sunday, don't you?'

'No one saw Henry being pushed in front of the car – not properly anyway. Loads of people witnessed the aftermath. Someone reckoned they saw a kid running away but it's really vague and they got the direction wrong.' It was Jessica's turn to sigh. 'Tell me about the canal man,' she added.

Izzy didn't need to look at her screen – she was one of those who absorbed everything around her, a human sponge for information. Someone who'd probably make a success of any career she fancied. Jessica had never asked why she'd chosen the police. It wasn't the hours or perks – and definitely wouldn't be the money.

'Mark Stanley,' Izzy said. 'He worked for a company that was hired to dredge the River Irwell for the council. They do it once every year or two – something to do with flooding. Eight months ago, he got his foot caught in something and was dragged under the water. One of his workmates hauled him out.' She nodded towards her computer. 'It's on the *Herald* website. The bloke who saved him got a medal. There's some sort of ongoing investigation.'

'By us?'

A shake of the head. 'He's suing the counc—' Izzy stopped mid-word and then corrected herself. 'Well... he was until we pulled him out of the canal.' She tapped her keyboard. 'Your other bloke's on here, too. We taped off the cul-de-sac after Henry Taylor was hit by his ex-girlfriend's car and some neighbour sent photos to the *Herald*. They did a gallery on it.'

'We didn't charge the ex, though...?'

'No – the paper seems to have more on it than we do.'

Jessica tugged a free seat across from an adjacent desk and spun gently on it, stopping herself with her feet from turning too far. 'This *is* weird, isn't it?' she said. 'It's not just me. Guy survives being hit by a car and then is run over and killed, some other bloke nearly drowns in the river and then *actually* drowns in the canal. What are the odds? It's all happened in the last few months.'

Izzy pursed her lips, eyebrows raising. 'I'm off for a week.'

'Are there any forensics back on Mark Stanley?'

'Not really – he was badly decomposed and had to be identified by his teeth. It's why it took so long.'

Jessica was gently spinning from side to side in the chair. 'You said last night that they had to tell Mark's mother we'd found the body...'

'He lived with his mum.'

'How old was he?'

'In his forties.'

'Any other family?'

'Don't think so. He's not married. There's an address in the file.'

Jessica absorbed the information and then pushed herself up. 'I'll visit her later. I've got a few other things to sort first.'

'Arch?'

Jessica nodded. 'I've got to tell him he's suspended. He'll know it's coming, but still...'

'If you're looking for a tag-along for the day, Ruth started her shifts today. She's in all week.'

Jessica had already taken a step away when she stopped to consider it. She hadn't worked much with DC Ruth Evesham but knew the constable was good at her job. She eventually opted for her first choice. 'I know just the man,' she said.

EIGHT

Jessica and DC Dave Rowlands strolled across the plaza in the centre of the Lees Estate. Rowlands had spent the past year seconded to work for DI Franks, a task that was thankless enough, even if he hadn't accidentally ended up in a relationship with Franks's daughter. It had been the main topic of conversation around the station for months, but things had gradually tailed off as new topics of gossip had come along.

There was always something.

'Are you sure Funtime won't mind? It's just—' Rowlands started his sentence for the third time since they left the station.

'Of course he'll mind,' Jessica replied, 'but don't worry. I'll sweet-talk the guv.'

Rowlands missed half a step and then hurried to keep pace. 'When have you *ever* sweet-talked anyone? *Bullied*, perhaps.'

Jessica gave him the sideways glare. 'I didn't get to where I am today without being able to twist a senior officer around to my way of thinking.'

'Didn't you once tell me you got to where you are today through bribery with chocolate biscuits?'

'Yeah, that too. Never underestimate a chief inspector's sweet tooth. As long as you're not shagging the inspector's daughter, everything will work out.'

Rowlands didn't laugh, didn't even crack a smile.

'You're no fun any more,' Jessica added but still didn't get a reply. Rowlands was fiddling with his hair instead, fingering the spikes towards the back. Even after all these years, he still looked like he'd glued roadkill to his head.

Before either of them could say anything else, there was a shrill whistle from behind. Jessica turned to see a man in a police uniform walking away from the rank of shops, Ginsters in one hand, pastry flaking to the pavement. He nodded and waved and then the three of them converged on a bench towards the centre of the square.

Police Constable Pete Whateverhisnameis was tall and thickset, a typical old-school uniformed officer from back in the days when height and a gruff voice were two of the most important recruiting factors. He was mid-thirties, about the same age as Jessica and Rowlands, but browned with the skin tone of a man who'd spent a few weeks outside of Manchester.

'Nice holiday?' Jessica asked.

Pete nodded through a mouthful of pastry and then placed his lunch on the arm of the bench, wiping his hands on his trousers and apologising. 'Scorchio,' he replied. 'I bloody love the Canaries at this time of year.'

They shook hands and then sat on the bench, Jessica in the middle, Pete with his lunch on his lap.

'Community Liaison Officer,' Pete said with a slight laugh, as if speaking to no one in particular. 'Who the hell knows what that means? They only told me about the new plans before I went on holiday. What about you?'

Jessica shrugged. 'I only found out a couple of weeks back. I'd never stepped foot on this estate until yesterday.'

'How does it feel to be one of the official faces of the community?'

Jessica laughed. 'I wouldn't worry too much. Give it six months and they'll have forgotten this whole thing. We'll be back behind our desks.'

Pete nodded, reaching for his pasty but not taking a bite.

'Do you even know what we're supposed to be doing?' he asked. 'I need a full week just to get through all the emails I've had since I went away.'

'You've not missed much,' Jessica replied. 'Everyone who lives around here's been mailed some sort of leaflet. If there's a non-urgent issue, they're supposed to contact you directly. They can do it via voicemail if they want to stay anonymous. Either that or they can email or call. It's meant to give people a name and a face to make them feel more secure about contacting the police. If you figure there's something more serious than kids peeing in the stairwells, then you can contact me.'

Pete took a bite of his pasty and sighed. 'That explains the number of emails.'

'From what I can find out, most have chucked the leaflets in the bin without even looking at them. That's what I would've done.'

Pete brushed some flakes from his lap and motioned to the far side of the plaza. 'Fancy a walk?'

The three of them traipsed around the perimeter of the housing block as Pete explained how far their area stretched. It wasn't just the set of flats, their district stretched four streets backwards, encompassing some terraced housing and the remnants of an old factory that had long since been abandoned. It wasn't massive geographically – but there were a lot of people who lived on their patch. Pete was based at the nearest police station, but it was more of a one-man band operation, an office as opposed to the vast building in which Jessica and Rowlands worked.

They completed one lap of the plaza and then started another, passing the row of shops and then a handful of flats before Pete pointed out an unmarked door that he said housed the hot water system for the complex. It seemed like he knew the estate well enough.

'You're off to a good start on day one,' Jessica said.

'How'd you mean?'

'Most crime-free estate in the city. Your bosses must love you.'

Pete snorted. 'Yeah, right. Not had a pay rise in three years. Anyway, I can't really take credit for any of it. I was here a few years ago when there were half a dozen stabbings in a month. People were suggesting all sorts of things. Some councillor wanted the army on the streets.'

'What changed?'

There was a long puff of breath. 'Nothing... not really. Back then, nobody would talk to the police about anything and it's still the same. The kids don't give you any abuse, but they don't engage either. Anytime I'm here, it feels like I'm being watched, but not obviously. No one even acknowledges me. I almost preferred the abuse.'

'There was an old guy yesterday,' Jessica replied. 'Roly.'

Pete nodded towards his flat. 'I know him. He's the exception. Had a fall last year, the poor old sod.'

'He reckoned there was a load of noise coming from the flat below. People coming and going all hours.'

Pete stopped, one hand on his hip, chewing his bottom lip. 'You must have sweet-talked him. He never says much of anything to me.'

Jessica half turned, giving Rowlands a knowing wink. 'Who lives below him?'

'No idea. I can probably find out. I know a bloke at the housing association and he gave me a resident list a few months back. Probably breaks some sort of data protection law but...' He tailed off.

'Where's the list?' Jessica asked.

'At the station. You want to go now?'

Jessica looked up towards Roly's flat, feeling watched in the exact way Pete had said. She couldn't see a soul, couldn't hear anything other than the quiet hum of traffic. At least it wasn't just her who felt something was off.

'Let's go,' she said.

The 'station' from which Pete worked was more of a large cupboard. There was a police logo on a patch of stone wall that was sandwiched between a primary school and a bike shop. Unless a person was specifically looking for it, there was no way anyone would know the unassuming door housed the local police station.

Pete had to unlock the door, with the counter at the front unoccupied and seemingly abandoned. There was a pair of desks through a side door – and that was that. Pete filled a crusty old cream kettle from a limescale-ridden metal sink and then flipped it on. He wiped clean a 'world's greatest grandmother' mug with a tea towel, plopped it next to a Mr Tickle mug and another with Greater Manchester Police's logo on the front. He leant against an oil radiator waiting for the kettle to boil. There were no windows and the only decoration was the patches of damp expanding from the corners of the ceiling. With a squint, it was almost artistic.

When they were all set with a brew, Pete unlocked his desk drawers and hunted through until he pulled out a blue cardboard folder. Jessica flicked through the pages of residents until she found the number that corresponded with the flat underneath Roly's.

'Jefferson Cass,' she said, rolling the syllables around her mouth before repeating the name. She looked towards Pete. 'You know him?'

A shake of the head. 'Never heard of him. I'd only know individual names if there'd been a problem.'

'Any idea when he moved in?'

Pete's features crinkled slightly, showing a rash of sunburn under his chin that was partially hidden by stubble. He dug back into his drawer, mumbled something Jessica didn't catch, and then unlocked a filing cabinet at the back of the office. He hummed tunelessly to himself as he thumbed through the pages inside a second cardboard folder and then handed it to Jessica.

'You've got the list from six months ago, which Cass is on – but he's not named on the old one from a year back. He must've moved in between seven and twelve months ago.'

Jessica leant back into her seat and had a sip of tea. Then she asked a question to which she already knew the answer. 'How long ago did the estate start to clean itself up?'

Pete shuffled awkwardly. 'About six months ago.'

'How bad were things before then?'

'No worse than most areas. A few problem tenants playing music late at night was a big thing. The council had to get involved with that. There were some street robberies, but we got some teenager who didn't even live round here for that. The *Herald* had a field day because a pensioner had her bag nicked at the bus stop by the shops. She tried to hang onto it and this group of lads pulled her into the road, where she was nearly run over by a bus. The newsagent had been held up a week or so before. After that, the *Herald* said this was the most dangerous estate in the city. Then the *Mail* got hold of it and everyone piled in. They reckoned it was the knife crime capital of the north, but it was never as bad as people made out.'

Jessica hadn't known all of that. 'How long ago was that?' she asked.

'About a year.'

'And now this area is almost crime-free...' She left it hanging but it was more of a statement of fact. 'Does anyone else work this patch?' Jessica motioned towards the second chair in the office, on which Rowlands had plonked himself.

'Ethan was made redundant eighteen months ago. Usual thing. Government say no front-line cuts and then promptly make loads of front-line cuts. I'm surprised I'm still here.'

'You must've been given more bodies when everything kicked off.'

'Only a couple of extra patrols – bobbies on the beat with PCSOs – that sort of thing.'

Jessica nodded. 'Bobbies on the beat' meant full officers and support officers in uniform mooching about looking busy in case anyone from the media was hanging around. It wouldn't have done much practically to lower a crime rate.

'No extra money?' Jessica asked.

'Not even a fiver for the tea kitty.'

Jessica turned to Rowlands, who sat up straighter. 'What do you reckon?' she asked.

'I reckon that as long as the crime stats stay low, no one cares either way.'

Jessica thought pretty much the same. Rowlands didn't literally mean 'no one' – he was talking about those higher up. The superintendents, the assistant chief constables, the chief constable. Their careers were made or splayed by crime statistics on their respective patches.

She supped down the rest of her tea in one. 'How do you want this whole community support thing to work?' she asked.

Pete shrugged, which pretty much summed up her thoughts about the scheme. 'I guess I'll call you if something big happens,' he replied.

'In that case,' Jessica said, 'in the nicest way possible, I really hope I don't hear from you.'

NINE

Sue Stanley lived on her own in a two-up-two-down terrace close to the university area of Manchester.

Or, as Jessica reminded herself as they were welcomed into the house, Sue Stanley *now* lived on her own. Mrs Stanley must have been picking up her pension for years, hunched with a crooked back and walking with a stick. She called Jessica 'dear' and Rowlands 'love', peeping up to the sky and muttering something about the temperature, before running through a list of hot drinks she had and then offering to slice up a fruit cake she'd made the previous day.

The living room looked like there had been an explosion in a florist. Pale yellow sunflowers were dotted across the crusty brown wallpaper, with a rainbow of blossoms on the tea-stained cream carpet. It was the type of decor an estate agent might call 'quaint', or which most others might say 'needed ripping down and starting again'.

Mrs Stanley fussed with the cushions on her armchair, first putting them behind her back, then raising them, then patting them with her hand, then eventually dropping them on a side table. She did her best to avoid the inevitable conversation until there was nothing else she could offer Jessica and Rowlands to eat or drink and her cushions were finally sorted.

'I suppose I knew something had happened to Mark,' she said eventually. 'He was always such a good boy. He'd phone home when he knew he was going to be late. Didn't like me worrying. When your woman came yesterday to say they'd identified him, that he'd been in the canal all along... well, I guess I already knew.'

Mrs Stanley gulped and then sighed. She smiled weakly, resigned to what had happened. There were no pictures of her son on the walls, only a few cheap prints of familiar paintings. Jessica recognised a boat at sea on the wall above the television, though didn't know the artist.

'Do you know why Mark might have been near the canal?' Jessica asked.

Mrs Stanley shook her head. 'He wouldn't have been – he was scared of water. Who wouldn't be after what happened to him? The poor love wouldn't have baths, only showers, because he didn't like the water covering his legs. We had quite the palaver over it all. I had to get a plumber in to fix a new shower unit.'

Jessica thought that was hardly surprising if he'd been dragged into the river as Izzy had described.

'I believe the initial accident happened eight months ago,' she said. 'Had Mark been up to much since then? Did he have many friends? Any hobbies?'

There was another shake of the head, slower this time. 'He wouldn't leave the house. I had to come up with things to force him outside.'

'Like what?'

Mrs Stanley reached to her back. 'Like when my back's bad but I need some milk from the shop – that sort of thing. I'd hide things and tell him we were short of teabags or whatever and then make him go and get some. It was the only way to get him out of bed. He'd sit around all day watching television or on his phone. He wanted to go back to work, but, when the day would come around, he'd panic and change his mind. The doctor said it was to do with the swelling on his brain, that it was perfectly normal. I don't understand it all.'

'Did he have any other injuries?'

'He couldn't walk properly on his leg.' She nodded at her walking stick. 'Even borrowed that in the early days to get around. He was a lot better, but I don't know what work they expected him to do.'

'What work *who* expected him to do?'

Mark's mother waved a hand towards the front of the house. 'The benefits lot. They reckoned he was fit to work, even though he had a doctor's note. He's paid into the system all his life and then they turn around and say he's not entitled to anything. It's wrong, isn't it? They should've seen him here when he wouldn't turn on the taps because he didn't want to get wet. How are you supposed to measure that when you're talking about illness? All he had at the end was his day in court. That's what he kept talking about.'

'What day in court?'

'It was supposed to be next week, maybe the one after. He's after compensation from the council for what happened. The solicitor reckoned they'd settle out of court, that they'd never risk putting Mark on the stand because it would set a precedent. I don't know what's happening with that now...' She tailed off, shaking her head before launching back into conversation. 'Everyone round here thinks compensation is scrounging. You hear it, don't you? "Compensation culture" and all that. They think it's someone trying it on, like with all those car crashes and the neck thing.'

Jessica did her best not to react. She was trying not to think of being in the car with Archie: the bang, the squeal and that moment of terrifying silence.

'It's not scrounging if you're right though, is it?' Mrs Stanley added. 'Mark's workmates say the safety gear wasn't working and there was this certificate that hadn't been signed. It wasn't Mark's fault what happened to him and it's not his fault he can't work. He deserves that money.' She paused, before adding a lot more quietly: '*Deserved*.'

'What actually happened on the day Mark disappeared?' Jessica asked.

This time, Mrs Stanley didn't answer immediately. She bit her lip and then chewed it hesitantly. 'I wanted beans,' she said. 'I was going to do beans on toast for tea but we had run out. I asked him to go to the shops... practically forced him out the door. He'd not been outside in a couple of days.' She looked from Jessica to Rowlands, not finishing the thought. Not having to.

'When did you report him missing?' Jessica asked.

'That night. They said they couldn't do anything because he was an adult and it hadn't been long enough. Someone came round a couple of days later, but what can you do? I know you're all busy, with the cuts and everything. That's all you ever hear – police being cut. Nurses being cut. Doctors. Firemen. Where will it end?'

Jessica smiled weakly, glancing sideways to Rowlands who returned the knowing look. They were too well drilled to discuss politics or religion in public or with strangers. The wrong thing said to the wrong person and they'd end up on someone's blog or in a news story.

'Did Mark have many friends?' Jessica asked.

'He wasn't really the sort.'

'For friends?'

A small shrug. 'For people. He didn't mix well. It was the same all the way back to school. His teachers used to comment on it when I went in. They'd say he wasn't getting on well with the other children, but it was just his way. I tried to push him out to meeting people, but he was fine doing his own thing. He didn't like the attention after he was in the paper.'

'What sort of attention?'

'It was nothing really. There was that piece in the paper about him being saved by his workmate and he thought people were always talking about him. Someone wrote a comment on the internet about it all being a compensation scam. That's one of the reasons he didn't like to go out.'

Jessica paused for a moment, thinking it over. 'I'm sorry to ask this – but was there anyone who Mark specifically didn't get on with?'

'Like who?'

'I'm not sure. Neighbours? Work colleagues?'

Mrs Stanley rocked gently backwards in her chair. She looked to Rowlands as if it was a question she couldn't comprehend. 'Only the people who'd have had to pay out if he went to court.' She paused. 'I don't really know...'

'Can we see his room?'

The older woman grunted as she reached for her walking stick.

Jessica was already on her feet. 'If you point us in the right direction...'

Mark's bedroom was seemingly untouched from when he'd left the house and not come home. There was a television and a games console on a ledge above a single bed and his clothes were neatly folded away into a dresser. Likely the work of his mum, Jessica thought. There wasn't much else to see. If she didn't know already, Jessica wouldn't have been able to guess Mark's age from his room. He could've been fourteen or forty. An anonymous man living an anonymous life in his childhood bedroom.

Rowlands was picking through the stack of games, not saying much.

'Everything all right?' Jessica asked.

He had his back to her. 'Bit too close,' he said.

'What is?'

Rowlands turned, holding out a hand to indicate the room. 'I was living at home until a few years ago. Couldn't afford a mortgage, didn't want to rent. Sometimes you wonder about how things could've gone if you'd made a different decision.'

It sounded as if he had something to add but he tailed off, the thought unsaid. Then she got it.

'You spoke to Archie,' she said.

He nodded. 'One minute you're driving along and everything's normal, the next...' He made a clicking sound with his tongue. 'He reckons they'll send him back to uniform – that they'll make an example out of him.'

'They're not going to do that.'

'How do you know?'

'Because it wasn't his fault. The road was clear and then that Henry bloke was in front of the car. He was pushed. How can that be Archie's fault?'

'No one else saw him being pushed.'

They looked at each other, but Jessica cracked first. 'He was pushed.'

Rowlands returned the game he was holding to the stack and then stepped towards the door. 'We're not going to find much here, are we?'

Jessica turned, peering at the sparse walls. No posters, no photos. The barren space of a barren life. 'Probably not.'

TEN

'I've got to get away from advertising, Jess. That place is driving me mad.'

Jessica nodded amiably as Caroline repeated the same thing she'd been saying for weeks. Probably months. Jessica couldn't remember. Caroline had a glass of wine in one hand, the bottle at the base of the armchair near her feet. She swilled the crimson liquid around the glass, waving her free hand about as if she was learning sign language. Jessica wasn't listening. She had her legs curled underneath herself on the sofa opposite and was thinking of Archie. She wondered if he was sitting at home with his girlfriend, or if he was by himself. If he was off in some drinking hole somewhere. She wondered if she should call him, if only to make sure he was all right.

'...What do you think?'

Jessica turned to Caroline, who had gulped down the remainder of her wine in what felt like a blink. It might have been seconds or minutes. 'I, um... yeah, go for it.'

'That's what I'm thinking. I *should* go back to university.'

Jessica stared at her friend. *University?* Where had that come from?

Caroline reached for the bottle of wine and poured herself another glass. It had become something of an evening ritual – an all-too common one. They grew up together in a village an hour and a bit north of Manchester and had then lived together years previously when they'd moved to the city. Jessica had been a constable and Caroline was not long graduated. After that, they'd drifted apart: careers, men and life prising them off into their own worlds. They'd go months without speaking and then end up gossiping over a coffee as if they saw each other every day. That had been the pattern for years – until recently. Caroline was now spending more nights sleeping at Jessica's house than she did at her own.

Caroline tipped the bottle completely upside down, dripping the final dregs into her glass. 'The gremlins have been drinking your alcohol again,' she said, before cackling to herself.

Jessica forced a smile, even a small laugh. Those gremlins seemed to get through a lot of alcohol whenever Caroline was over.

'No one wants to work in advertising,' Caroline continued, more to herself than Jessica. 'It's like we're not quite creative enough to be artists or writers, but we're not boring enough to do accounts, or whatever. We're just sort of... there. Even if you do something good, say a jingle, you can't tell people.'

'Why not?'

'Because then they're like, "Oh, you're the person to blame". Nobody likes advertising, what with all those pop-ups and stupid songs. If it wasn't for bankers and politicians, we'd be the most hated people in the country.'

'Right...'

'If I go back to uni, I can try to get into event management. That's what I *really* want. You've been to my parties – you know what I can do.'

Jessica continued nodding along. The only party she could

remember Caroline throwing was the reception after her wedding. That was only a little shorter than the marriage itself.

After downing the rest of her drink, Caroline heaved herself up from the armchair, groaning with effort and then reaching for her back. She muttered something about age and then headed out of the room. Caroline had always been the effortlessly thin, naturally fit one… but not any more. Whether it was the fact she was nearer forty than thirty, stress over her job, or whatever else, her waist had ballooned. As much as she hated to admit it, there was a small part of Jessica that quite liked their role reversal.

The devil on her shoulder.

When they'd hit the town as younger women, it had always been Caroline *and* her friend. When they first got jobs, Caroline had made more money, lived in a bigger place, married first. Now, that teeny, tiny part of Jessica couldn't help but feel relief that, for once, she was seemingly on top.

She hated that teeny, tiny part of herself.

Caroline returned with a tub of strawberry cheesecake ice cream and another bottle of wine. She had two spoons, but Jessica waved a dismissive hand and Caroline's smile said it all. She flopped into the armchair and set to work on her sugar- and alcohol-based supper.

'We should have a proper girly night out,' Caroline said. 'Y'know, get dressed up like the old days, head into town.'

Jessica could think of little worse. The *old* days. Drinking was a young person's game and there was were few sights more depressing than a gaggle of cackling old women with their skirts hitched up, stumbling along the gutter at three in the morning. Her time in uniform was more than enough to know that.

'I'll look at my rota,' Jessica replied, knowing that she wouldn't. If Caroline brought it up again, Jessica would *defi-*

nitely be working. That was the upside to having a job with antisocial hours. Antisocial hours meant she could be antisocial, which was fine by her.

'How's Hugo?' Jessica asked, trying to change the subject.

Caroline picked at her chewed fingernail and then delved back into the ice cream. 'Still in Sydney. He's going down a storm, apparently. What with him in Oz and Mum and Dad in Toronto, everyone's abandoned me.'

She huffed loudly and Jessica wasn't sure if it was genuine annoyance or put on for show. Caroline's boyfriend, Hugo, had a level of fame that had been increasing with the popularity of his magic and comedy show. With his tours becoming longer, Caroline was left by herself for longer periods. Jessica guessed this was why they were now spending most evenings together but didn't want to delve too deep. They weren't quite at the level of sharing everything in the way they used to.

Jessica had far too many demons for that.

'It's all right if I stay over, isn't it?' Caroline asked breezily. She said the same thing every time, even though it was never a problem.

'Of course.'

'It's just... all your friend's stuff. I don't want to be in the way if she comes back.'

Jessica said nothing at first. Of all the demons, Bex – her friend, her housemate... *former* housemate – loomed as large as any.

'I don't think she'll be back anytime soon,' she replied, unable to meet her friend's inquisitive eye. Sometimes it felt like they didn't know each other at all. They'd sit across from one another, laughing at the television, complaining about jobs and colleagues. They'd have the pretence of being best friends when, really, they didn't know anything important about each other.

There was a second or two of tension, unasked questions

with concealed answers – and then Jessica's phone started to ring. She plucked it from the side table, but the number was unknown. Usually she wouldn't answer – it was always some nonsense about PPI or someone asking if she'd had an accident recently – but it was half past ten in the evening and surely even call-centre ambulance-chasers had to finish work at some point.

'Hello?' she said.

The man's voice was croaky, hushed. 'Ms Daniel?'

'Who is this?'

'It's Roly... you said I could call.'

His voice cracked and, for a moment, Jessica thought he'd gone. She repeated his name until he spoke again.

'Can you come?' he asked.

'Is everything all right?'

'I think they're coming for me.'

ELEVEN

Roly refused to say much else, let alone dial 999, leaving Jessica to race across the city by herself. She thought about calling the station, either that or Pete – but that would have taken more time. Besides, she had little idea what was going on. There was nothing quite like turning up with a riot squad because someone was playing Cher a bit too loudly.

Jessica parked close to the row of shops and headed through to the square. Dim orange lights ringed the concrete, a hazy glow seeping into the darkness of the night. It was as serene as it had been the previous times Jessica had visited, probably quieter without the hum of daytime traffic. Jessica peered up towards the flats that towered above her, but the glare and darkness proved too much to be able to see anything. Some areas of the city – *any* city – brimmed with menace. Everyone knew the spots where it was unsafe after dark. Even the biggest, bravest officers would want others by their side before answering certain emergency calls.

Jessica felt none of that.

The shadows stretched long and dark, but there was no one lurking and waiting. No invisible threat. Jessica headed up the stairs to the second level and was only halfway along the rank when she saw the damage to the front of Roly's flat. His mucky white front door was decorated with dark spray-painted letters and a curtain was flapping gently through a gap in what should be a window. Jessica stopped outside the flat, taking it all in. The word 'grass' was clear enough on the door – and even spelt correctly, which wasn't always a given when it came to abusive graffiti. The paint had started to run, making the tail of the 'g' loop long towards the floor. As the breeze continued to tickle the curtain, Jessica peered closer at the hole in the window next to the front door. The glass was rippled for privacy, stretching high towards the gutters above, but there was now a jagged hole gouged into the left side.

Jessica tapped gently on the front door and then stepped away, peering over the balcony towards the stillness beyond. She only realised she'd been holding her breath when a billow of misty air escaped from her nose, seeping into the darkness.

She jumped at the sound of a click behind her and Jessica turned to see Roly peeping through the sliver between the door and frame. He eased it wider, looking both ways along the balcony and then stepping aside without a word.

Jessica squeezed herself inside as he waited behind the door. Her shoe crunched onto a pile of broken glass and she winced, hopping away as Roly closed the door behind them. The hallway light was off, with only a soupy deep yellow glowing through from the kitchen. The half-brick that rested against the wall was impossible to miss.

'Did you call anyone else?' Jessica whispered.

Roly didn't reply, heading along the hallway into the kitchen and waiting for her to follow. When they were inside, he closed the second door. The blinds were down and the door to the living room was also closed, leaving them entombed underneath the humming strip light above. The heater was still sitting on the counter, its long hose stretched towards the window.

'Roly...' Jessica added.

'What?'

'Did you call anyone else?'

'Just you.'

'We should call the police, they'll—'

'No!' Roly's raised voice made her jump. His next words were far quieter. 'No police,' he added.

'*I'm* police,' Jessica replied. He half shrugged, sighing at the same time. 'What happened?' she asked.

'Just kids.'

'Did you see anyone?'

'Heard 'em. That's when I called you. Then someone threw the brick. Gutless, that's what they are. They're brave when there's lots of them. Get one on their own and you'd see what they're made of.'

He spoke quickly and gruffly, a hint of the man he used to be, not the pensioner he now was.

'I know a guy who can fix the window,' Jessica said. 'We've got a company that removes graffiti, too. I'll make a couple of calls and get someone out here for you.'

He opened his mouth as if to protest but then nodded in acknowledgement. 'Thank you.'

'Is this because you spoke to us yesterday?' she asked.

'I guess so.'

'If they're saying you're a grass, what do they think you've told us?'

'I don't know.'

'But something's going on around here...'

Roly didn't answer because there was a bang from below. They stopped and listened to the merest muffling of voices before another door slammed. It felt like the entire flat was trembling.

'Is it always like this?' Jessica asked.

'It's been quiet tonight.'

'Do you know what's going on?'

'Kids.'

Jessica stood, still listening to the dampened voices. It sounded like a man talking to boys through the floor, though it was hard to tell for sure. She told Roly to wait and then crept out of the kitchen towards the front door. She clicked it open and edged onto the balcony, peering over the banister towards the plaza below.

Nothing moved.

Away from the inside of Roly's flat, everything was quiet, the voices silent. Jessica figured the joint ceiling and floor separating the apartments must be particularly thin. She moved to the end of the balcony and peered down the stairwell to the empty ground level.

More silence.

Jessica tiptoed down the concrete steps until she was in the corner quadrant of the block. She clung tightly to the shadows as she flanked along the ground-floor row of flats, ducking underneath the windows and counting the front doors until she was three or four away from the one underneath Roly's. She was about to continue onwards when a squeak from the dark left her pressed against the wall, scanning the night for the source of the noise. If it had been daytime, she'd have been exposed and in the open, but Jessica was well hidden by the gloom.

From nowhere, a tunnel of light beamed brightly from the doorway of the flat that apparently housed Jefferson Cass. The shape of two teenagers was silhouetted by the white as they entered the flat, their bikes abandoned on the ground behind them. The bikes had no lights and there was seemingly no thought to locking them. There weren't too many areas around the city where a bicycle could be abandoned without having it rehomed by an opportunistic thief.

Jessica stuck to the shadow, holding her breath and waiting until the shaft of light was again replaced by darkness. When everything again felt still, she continued moving, creeping her way along the row of flats until she was directly beneath Roly's. As her eyes adjusted to the gloom, Jessica could see that it wasn't only the two bikes on the path – there were four or five piled next to a pillar, none of them secured. They were all BMXs, the saddles low, set up for youngsters who were probably still school age.

As she rounded the bikes, Jessica realised she could hear voices. They were low, the words not quite audible, like the hum from workers chatting in an office. Jessica turned, noticing an open window behind her. Not just one – most of the windows on the lower level were open a finger-width.

There was only one that interested her.

The blinds were down, but there was the flimsiest glimmer of light creeping onto the path. Jessica kept low, sidestepping across the path until she was able to see into the flat through the crack to the side of the blind. She had to squint as her vision burned from the shift of dark to light, but there was a man standing cross-armed, facing someone Jessica couldn't see. He was tall, with a broad chest, thick arms and short dark hair – presumably Jefferson Cass. His words were lost but his voice was sharp as he growled something to a teenager who stepped into view. The lad was a foot shorter than the man, skinny with youth. They exchanged a few more words and then, from nowhere, the man lunged forward and cracked the boy across the face. Their words had been muffled but the snap of flesh on flesh boomed through the open window, masking Jessica's gasp with shock.

There was another flash of movement and then Jessica saw blood oozing from the boy's lip. For a moment, she thought they were going to square up to one another, David and Goliath, but then the man opened his arms. The boy lowered his head, wiping away the blood, and mumbled something Jessica couldn't hear. The man nodded knowingly, then placed a hand on the boy's shoulder and replied.

Jessica couldn't see what happened next because they both stepped out of view. She pressed closer to the window, but not near enough to hear anything clearly. Then a door banged loudly.

At the sound of movement from the inside, Jessica scrambled back into the shadows, sitting on the concrete in the darkness and fiddling with her phone until the brightness had been turned all the way down. The front door opened moments later and five boys emerged. They said nothing to each other, retrieving their bikes from the pillar and then hovering under the dim glow of the street lamps. Jessica had only a moment to act, but she pointed her phone in the general direction of the teenagers and snapped a couple of photos, hoping for the best.

The boys quickly disappeared off towards the shops on their bikes, leaving the row of flats still once more. Jessica crept back towards Jefferson's flat, but there was no sign of anyone through the crack in the blinds. The front door was closed.

Without looking back, Jessica hurried up the stairs to Roly's flat, tapping on the front door and easing inside. Roly was eyeing her with intrigue, though he didn't ask where she'd been.

They stood in the hallway, largely in the dark as Jessica peered down to the pile of glass near her feet. 'Is there someone you can stay with tonight?' she asked.

Roly shook his head.

'Anywhere you can stay?' she added.

'*This* is my home,' he replied firmly.

'I can arrange for someone to come over.'

Another shake of the head. 'I'll be fine. I only called because...'

He didn't add that he was scared. That was obvious.

Jessica rested a hand on his arm, wondering if there was anything else she could do. It felt like the graffiti and brick through the window was more of a warning than anything else. If someone wanted to hurt Roly, they could have done.

'You go, love,' Roly added quietly. 'I'll be fine.'

'I don't—'

'It's just kids. I shouldn't have bothered you.'

Jessica forced back a yawn, but it was late and she found her jaw snapping back involuntarily.

'Get yourself home,' he added – and this time Jessica did as she was told.

TWELVE

MONDAY

With all the money floating around Greater Manchester Police HQ at Newton Heath, Jessica thought they could have afforded a few comfortable chairs.

She fidgeted and wriggled against the scratchy canvas backrest, fighting a yawn. It had been a late night with Roly and then a ridiculously early morning. Caroline had been snoring when Jessica got home and, even with a pair of doors between them, Jessica had struggled to get to sleep. It had sounded like a rhino with blocked sinuses shuffling around her spare bedroom.

Jessica rested the back of her head against the wall and closed her eyes, wishing she was still in bed. It had been a brutally busy pair of days and the week ahead wasn't likely to provide much let-up.

She jumped as a woman's voice called 'Ms Daniel'. Jessica wasn't sure anyone had called her that in a long time. She opened her eyes, realising there were two people standing in front of her.

There was a woman in a pristine grey suit, alongside the unfortunately recognisable figure of Inspector Vincent. He'd been the last person to interrogate her when she'd visited Professional Standards and was the same cartoon of a man that she remembered. His head was too big for his body and his crooked, pointy nose was even more out of proportion. He looked like a child's drawing of a scarecrow but would give far more nightmares.

'Thank you for coming,' Vincent said, offering something that wasn't quite a smile. It looked like he had wind. Jessica creaked her way onto her feet, not bothering to point out that her attendance wasn't optional.

They all shook hands and, though the female officer introduced herself, Jessica instantly forgot her name. Meanwhile, Vincent's handshake was as limp as a sodden shred of lettuce at the bottom of a salad drawer. He led the way into an interview room and asked Jessica whether she wanted a union representative present. When she said it was fine, he settled her with a steely stare of a man whose pants were too tight. She could even see his eyes watering.

'Apologies for the short notice,' he said, not sounding very apologetic. 'As I'm sure you're aware, we've been getting a lot of questions from the media. A police car did hit a pedestrian in broad daylight...'

He tailed off, waiting for her to fill the silence but Jessica was too good at that game. Only reply to the question asked and never volunteer information.

'Have you spoken to Constable Davey since Saturday's incident?' Vincent asked. The woman next to him was taking notes and didn't look up from her pad.

'Yes,' Jessica replied.

'What did you talk about?'

'Football.'

Vincent stared at her. '*Football?*'

'We talked about the lack of support in United's midfield.'

His eyes narrowed as Jessica fought back a smile.

'Did you talk about anything else?'

'No.'

Vincent's tongue clucked against the top of his mouth. 'Take me through Saturday's events...'

Jessica spoke as succinctly as she thought she could get away with, talking about the visit to the Lees Estate and explaining her new role. Well, explaining as much as she understood about it. The woman at Vincent's side continued to take notes, not speaking or looking up.

'Why didn't you drive?' Vincent asked as Jessica got to the part about leaving the estate.

'Sorry?'

'You said you drove to the Lees Estate, with Constable Davey at your side – so why was he driving afterwards?'

'It was...' Jessica stumbled, trying to remember.

Vincent leant in slightly, remaining silent. She never quite understood what drove a person to work in Professional Standards. Things like police corruption should be dealt with. If rogue officers were in the pay of people to whom they shouldn't, there *should* be a higher body to examine things. That didn't mean she had the inclination to do that sort of job herself. Besides, most internal investigations didn't involve things as sexy as a good officer gone bad, or someone running a criminal empire from the back of a patrol car. It was boring and mundane – who'd spoken to whom and when; had a certain officer read a certain email at a certain time? Now she was trying to remember why she'd tossed a set of car keys to a fellow officer in a moment of spontaneity.

'I don't know,' Jessica added.

Vincent held her stare. He had dark, sullen eyes. Not fierce, more boring. 'You *don't know*?' he replied.

'That's what I said.'

'Why don't you know?'

'Because it wasn't a big deal. We were heading back to

Longsight – it didn't matter whether I drove or if Ar—
Constable Davey did.'

'It *did* matter though, didn't it?'

Jessica opened her mouth and then closed it again. She
wondered what his game was. Did officers really want to find
dirt on their colleagues, or was this the way he did his job?

When it was clear she wasn't going to add anything,
Vincent leant back in his chair and then purred a response.
'Perhaps you were tired?'

'I don't remember.'

He flicked through a cardboard file of papers, shuffling
them dramatically as if to prove the wallet actually contained
something official and wasn't just a pile of comics. 'According
to your rota, you weren't on shift on Saturday.'

'Correct.'

'And yet you were patrolling a city estate with an officer
who *was* on shift...'

'We weren't patrolling anything. I'd gone to speak to the
newsagent.'

'So you said – but you never intimated why.'

Jessica fought back the urge to sigh. She was a walking,
talking cliché of an officer who didn't switch off. She knew it
and now Vincent wanted to know about it, too.

'I was scouting out the estate because I don't know it very
well. I made an appointment to speak to the newsagent
because I figured he'd know the people and places. He
couldn't fit me in until the Saturday, so...'

'You had to make an appointment to see a newsagent?'

Vincent sounded incredulous, much like Archie had. She
knew it was ridiculous, but there was no way Jessica was going
to tell Vincent that it gave her something to do on a Saturday.
That she had no one in particular to hang around with and no
other plans.

'It is what it is,' she said.

He held her in his dead-eyed stare once more. The gaze of a man who'd be better suited to spotting trains or embalming bodies.

'So perhaps you were tired?' he added again.

'I don't remember.'

'But you concede that maybe you were? You'd been on a run of shifts and then were putting in a few hours on your day off. It's conceivable, isn't it?'

'I don't remember.'

He nodded shortly and then moved on to asking about the route they'd taken. He asked about individual roads, enquiring as to why Constable Davey had gone a certain way and whether she'd had any input. Jessica did her best to remember, but the truth was she hadn't paid an awful lot of attention – not to the route in any case. Each week of work involved hours of crawling from traffic light to traffic light, navigating roundabout after roundabout, until the point at which it was hard to distinguish one from the other. It would be the same for most people – one daily commute blurred into the next until it was all one long journey.

Vincent held up a hand to stop her when Jessica's story reached the traffic lights where the collision had happened.

'So far you seem to have been a bit woolly as to the exact route you were taking,' he said.

'If you say so.'

'Do you say differently?'

'I don't know all the exact roads – but I know the general route we took.'

Another short nod – except it wasn't really what it seemed. It was dismissive, as if a mere bob of the head was an eff-you.

'"*General*" is the key word there, Inspector Daniel. If you only know the *general* route you took – and we can agree that you might have been tired given it was your day off *and* you handed over the car keys to Constable Davey – then perhaps your full attention wasn't on the road...'

He left it hanging and Jessica suddenly realised what he'd been trying to do. She wondered how she'd missed it.

'I saw what happened,' she replied firmly.

'Did you?'

'Yes.'

'And what did happen?'

'The light turned green, Constable Davey moved through the junction and then there was someone in front of the car. There was no way Archie could've avoided him.'

He smiled humourlessly. 'Whether or not Constable Davey could've evaded the collision is something to be decided by the accident investigators.' A pause. 'And by me, of course.'

Jessica said nothing. Vincent waited for so long that Jessica wondered if he was going to say anything at all. He stared at her and then the woman taking notes joined in. Jessica tried not to shrink under their gazes.

'Was your attention fully on the road?' Vincent finally asked.

Jessica remembered glancing down to her phone. It had been a second – not even that – and then the shadow had been in the road. She'd said something different on Saturday, but now she was certain.

'It was,' Jessica replied.

'Your eyes never left the road?' he added.

'Exactly.'

'Did you see the pedestrian step out?'

'Not quite like that. He wasn't there and then he was.'

'What would you say if I told you Constable Davey drove through a red light?'

Jessica froze, matching Vincent's steely gaze, looking for a bluff that she couldn't see. 'He didn't,' she replied.

'And you know that because your eyes never left the road.'

'It was green.'

Another short nod. 'How would you describe his speed?'

'Normal.'

'What would you say is normal?'

'I don't know – it felt right. Like a normal speed to pull away.'

'Could you see the speedometer?'

'No.'

'Because you were watching the road...?'

Jessica wondered if Vincent somehow knew. Was there CCTV footage of her at the crucial moment glancing down? Was her white lie so bad that he'd seen right through it? She didn't know why else he'd keep pushing it.

'There was no reason for me to be looking at the speedo,' she said. 'It felt right.'

'But it's fair to say you don't know for sure how fast Constable Davey was driving?'

'No.'

'So he *could* have been speeding at the time of impact?'

'He *could* have been possessed by the second coming of the Lord at the time of impact. That doesn't mean it happened.'

Jessica bit her lip, chewing with her front teeth so hard she had to stop in case she made herself bleed. There was silence.

'I think that's probably everything,' Vincent finally said, not motioning to stand. He nodded dismissively to the door and Jessica found herself on her feet. She twisted in a half-circle, unsure if she was supposed to shake his hand or simply sod off.

'I'm, um... sorry about that,' Jessica mumbled.

Vincent gave a watery smile, lips pressed together, but said nothing.

'There was nothing Constable Davey could've done,' she added.

'Thank you,' Vincent replied, nodding almost imperceptibly towards the door once more. Jessica took one step towards it before Vincent called her back. He spoke airily, as if his final question meant nothing, even though it was the most important. 'Just one final thing,' he began. 'Do you have any sort of personal relationship with Constable Davey?'

Jessica was so taken aback that she staggered slightly, as if the earth had trembled a millimetre or two. Two-point-oh on the Richter scale. 'Sorry?'

'Constable Davey and yourself.' Vincent nodded towards the notes his colleague was taken. 'For the record. I'm asking if you have any sort of relationship away from work.'

Jessica knew she could lie – it'd be simple – one word and she was out of there. The problem was that she was fairly sure Vincent already knew the answer. If he didn't, then others did. He stared up at her expectantly.

'It's not really anyone's business,' she said.

Vincent smiled wider. 'You can understand why I need to ask. Why, if you *do* have a personal relationship, it could taint any statements you give.' He paused. 'So, once again, do you and Constable Davey have any sort of personal relationship.

She blinked and then the words came out all at once. 'Not any longer.'

Vincent gave one final, dismissive off-you-pop nod – and then Jessica was gone.

THIRTEEN

Jessica felt like a failed teacher as she straightened herself and waited for something approaching silence. The huddled mass of officers crowded into Longsight Police Station's incident room were busy putting on a symphony of bodily noises more suited to a farmyard. Jessica cleared her throat in a way that she thought might persuade those in front of her to practice shutting up, but instead it only added to the cacophony. In the end, she threw a pen at one of the uniformed officers towards the back who must have some sort of venereal disease given the vigorousness with which he was scratching his backside.

That got silence.

She peered up at the clock above the door. 'All right, it's still just about Monday morning, so let's get some work done.' Jessica stepped towards the whiteboard and started writing. She gave brief details of what had happened with Henry Taylor and the collision, plus Mark Stanley's drowning, before moving on to her main point: 'Question one – was Henry Taylor *pushed* in front of a car?' she said. 'Question two – was Mark Stanley *murdered* by being drowned? Henry previously survived being hit by a car and Mark was pulled out of a river following an accident at work. If the answer to both of those questions is "yes", then is there a link between the two?' She nodded at Detective Constable Ruth Evesham, who was in the second row of seats. She half stood, turning and leaning on the back of her chair.

Ruth was a newish constable who had proven herself almost straight away when she ended up in a secluded caravan park on the trail of a possible killer. She'd probably saved the life of Rowlands.

'We've had calls all weekend from witnesses of Henry Taylor being hit by a car,' Ruth said. 'Accident investigators and Professional Standards are examining the actual collision because we've not been able to find out for sure one way or the other whether Henry was pushed. His girlfriend, Gillian, says he was – but there's no camera footage to confirm that and no specific witnesses who saw him being shoved. We've got a couple who saw him stumbling off the pavement, though they both thought he overbalanced or simply fell. Someone else reckons he stepped voluntarily off the pavement in front of the car. Most admit they only saw the aftermath. In short, we don't know what happened. It might have been an accident, it could've been deliberate, perhaps even suicide by car.'

She nodded towards Jessica and sat down again.

'We're similarly vague with what happened to Mark Stanley,' Jessica added. 'According to his mum, he left the house to go to the local shop for a tin of beans, then he never went home. We have no witnesses of him walking to, or arriving at, the shop, no CCTV, no anything. Next thing anyone knows, his decomposed body is in the canal. Obviously, he wouldn't be the first to go for a wander and drown in the canal – and he definitely won't be the last – but the fact he previously survived being drowned was covered extensively in the local media. There's a similarity in that: when Henry Taylor's ex-girlfriend drove a car at him, that got some attention as well.

Anyone who paid attention to local news could've known their names and their stories. I'm going to set a small team to look for any other links. Both were treated at the Royal Infirmary, which is a second link. They live around a mile apart, so could perhaps go to the same boozer, or play football for the same team – something like that. Are there mutual people who they both know? So far, there's nothing obvious, but I'll nick over to the hospital later and try to have a word with someone who might remember them both. They could've been on the same ward together.'

Jessica realised she actually had the silence and attention she'd demanded. Attentions would usually start to wane, backsides would be scratched, officers would start to mutter. Here, they were actually interested.

'We can't have any leaks,' she added. 'Neither of these two cases is a murder investigation at the moment and we don't want anyone saying they are. Meanwhile, everything else continues as normal.' Jessica started to nod to certain officers around the room. 'I want some progress on the pickpocket in Longsight Market. That's three cases now and it's only down the road. We also had a second report yesterday of a flasher in Birchfields Park, so let's get that stamped on.' She stopped as a series of snorts and sniggers erupted around the room. 'All right, you know what I mean.' Jessica forced back a childish smirk of her own. 'And, no, we're not doing an ID parade of potential suspects with their willies out...'

There was a low boo – pantomime season had arrived eight months early.

'...Other than that, everyone should know what they're doing. Any questions?'

There weren't – well, no sensible ones in any case, nothing that didn't involve genitalia, so Jessica dismissed everyone except Rowlands. He checked his phone and then put it back in his pocket.

'This is like the old days,' he said.

'Not so much of the old.'

Jessica was mixing it with the smokers as she stood outside the entrance to Manchester Royal Infirmary. Her mobile was clamped to her ear as she listened to the ringing, unanswered phone. Rowlands was sitting on a low wall nearby, pretending he wasn't half-eyeing the young blonde who was sucking on a cigarette next to the bins. When he realised Jessica had caught him, his gaze shot away to the road beyond.

The call rang off, finishing with a series of beeps and a message saying it couldn't be connected, so Jessica hung up and tried once more. Three more rings and Rowlands risked a glance back to the blonde, pretending he was actually looking at something inside the hospital through the double doors. Jessica was so concerned at trying to catch his eye that she winced as the man muttered a gruff 'hello' in her ear.

'Is that Roly?' she managed.

'Aye.'

'This is Detective Inspector Daniel. I'm just making sure everything's okay.'

Roly coughed. 'Your bloke was round this morning. Did a good job.'

Jessica assumed he meant that someone had fixed his window. 'That's good. Is everything else all right?' she added.

'Been out for a paper. Can't let the bastards grind you down, can you? Might nip out to the bookies in a bit.'

'But no other trouble?'

'All quiet. Just kids, wannit?'

'Well, if you're sure... you know where I am...'

Jessica heard Roly gulp, a tiny sliver of the bravado slipping. 'Aye, I do.'

She waited to hear if he'd anything else to say, but then

Jessica realised the call had dropped. She repocketed the phone and looked up to see that the blonde had disappeared. Rowlands stood up from the wall, offering the 'all okay?' eyebrow raise.

'Where's your girlfriend?' Jessica added, nodding towards the bins.

'Oh, ha ha. I'd forgotten what it's like to spend a shift with you.'

'An absolute delight – that's what it's like to spend a shift with me. Besides, I don't think it was going to work out between you. Even if you didn't already have a girlfriend, meeting by the bins isn't the kind of classic tale you tell the grandkids.'

Rather annoyingly, Rowlands smiled, refusing to take the bait. If he wasn't going to bite back, that was the majority of Jessica's entertainment for the day gone. 'I've been onto HR and we've got two paramedics and four nurses who were on duty when both Henry Taylor and Mark Stanley were here,' he said. 'One of the A&E receptionists, too. Possibly some others.'

'Are any of them working today?'

'The receptionist.' Rowlands nodded beyond the doors to where the blonde smoker was standing next to a vending machine, jabbing at her phone. 'Her name's Melissa.'

He gave her a satisfied, smug smile.

'You're no fun any more,' Jessica replied, before sweeping into the hospital, hand outstretched towards Melissa the receptionist.

The hospital café had a nifty selection of pies, pasties, chocolate, cookies and cakes. Jessica couldn't help but feel people would be clogging up their arteries on one side of the building before being admitted to the other.

That didn't stop her picking at a meat and potato Holland's. She'd grown up assuming the pie brand was national before later realising that only the north of England had been blessed. Southerners didn't know what it was to be alive.

Melissa was on her dinner break and tucking into a cheese and onion pie with chunky chips. She was lean and athletic, likely the sort who could eat absolutely anything and somehow avoid putting on weight. Poor old Rowlands was looking mournfully at a set of green and purple leaves from a plastic tub, looking as miserable as his food.

'How's the salad?' Jessica asked.

Rowlands frowned up from his lunch. 'Leafy.'

Melissa grinned between them.

'This isn't how we'd normally interview someone,' Jessica said.

'Is this an interview?'

'More of a working lunch.'

'Ahh... the worst kind of lunch.'

This time Jessica laughed. 'Very true.' A quick glance to Rowlands. 'Is it right that you work on reception in A&E?'

'Right,' Melissa replied. 'For my sins.'

'I realise this is a bit of a long shot, but there's a couple of names I'd like to run past you.'

'What kind of names?'

'A couple of admissions from recent months—'

'You know about patient confidentiality, don't you?'

'That doesn't really come into these cases, I'm afraid.'

Melissa looked up from her food and Jessica could see the truth dawning. 'Oh...'

'Do you know the name Mark Stanley? He almost drowned in a river. One of his mates dragged him out.'

Melissa's eyes widened slightly. 'I don't know the name,

but I vaguely remember the bloke. I think his mate was on the news for saving him.'

'Does anything else jump out?'

A slow shake of the head. 'All the days blend into one. People come in and by the time you get in for your next shift, they've been discharged. It's only the regulars you come to know.'

'Regulars?'

'The same people come in once, twice, three times a week.' Melissa checked over her shoulder and then leant in, lowering her voice. 'Some of them are hypochondriacs. They have a sore throat and think it's cancer. Then there are those who are just lonely. They want someone to talk to, so they wander in and say they've got chest pains. That always gets them straight through to see someone. There are a few with mental health problems who are always calling out ambulances. They know the trigger words to say to the call handlers which gets them a paramedic. They should be getting proper help, but there's no money, so they end up here. After that, there are the drunks who you see week after week. It'll be the same for you – but Fridays and Saturdays are the worst. I bet the names we see all the time are the same ones you do.'

Jessica suspected as much – but it was going to take a fair bit of sweet-talking from the superintendent or someone else higher up to get the hospital's full admission records for any given day. Even if they could get around data protection laws, it would be incomplete information because not every visitor would be documented. Being a hospital, people could walk in off the street, have a wander around the waiting room and then disappear again.

'How about Henry Taylor?' Jessica asked.

Melissa chewed a mouthful of chip, lips pursed thought-fully. 'He got run over, didn't he?'

'Right.'

'His girlfriend was here with him saying it was his ex who did it on purpose. I thought it was one of those Jeremy Kyle things with women arguing over some bloke. You probably get one or two of them a week as well. You see it all when you do this job. We had one the other night who reckoned he tripped on the bottom stair and fell into his vacuum cleaner.'

'Fell into, as in...'

'Literally *into*. One of the paramedics wheeled him in on a trolley while the other carried the hose bit of the vacuum. I think we had to get someone from the fire brigade to help in the end.'

Jessica pulled a face. 'It wasn't a Henry vacuum cleaner, was it? Imagine that – poor old Henry just going about his business and he has to put up with that sort of behaviour.'

Melissa smiled. 'Dyson, I think.'

'I guess that's one thing.' Jessica had another bite of her pie as Melissa scooped up a couple of chips. Rowlands poked at one of the purple leaves but there didn't seem to be much eating going on. Jessica waited until Melissa had finished chewing and then continued. 'Do you remember anything else about when Henry was brought in? Was it just his girlfriend who was with him?'

'I think there was a police officer, too.'

Jessica would have to check that – but it wasn't out of the ordinary.

'But how did you come to hear that Henry's ex had tried to run him over?'

'His girlfriend was in the waiting room on her phone. I assumed she was talking to her mum or something. Then she had a conversation with a couple of people sitting nearby, then a few newcomers. I think everyone in a half-mile radius knew.'

That didn't help. Jessica glanced towards Rowlands, who nodded slightly, acknowledging the problem. They'd been wondering how someone could have targeted Henry, thinking it was probably the smidgen of media coverage. As it was, it sounded like Gillian had told half the city.

'Have there been any recent security issues?' Jessica asked.

Melissa shrugged. 'Not that I know of. You get the odd drunk shouting and swearing, but that's pretty much normal. You could ask one of the porters.'

'Any idea who was on when Henry was brought in?'

'Actually, I do. There's this guy called, well... Guy. He doesn't say much, but we usually end up on the same shift pattern. He's always around and about, helping to move beds, doing odd bits of cleaning and so on. There used to be two of them in at the same time but that changed with the cuts.' Melissa suddenly straightened, pointing towards a set of swing doors off to the side. 'That's him now.'

She waved across to the man, who first looked behind and then patted his chest before accepting Melissa was trying to attract his attention. He was tall and thin, with patchy hair that was doing nothing to cover a bald scalp which started at the top of his nose and stretched most of the way to the nape of his neck. It was more of a bald oasis than a spot. The strip lights above reflected from Guy's head as he shuffled across to them, his eyes barely leaving the floor.

Jessica introduced herself and Rowlands, which got the same sort of nothing reaction she might have expected if she'd said they were accountants. She asked if they could have a word and Guy mumbled something about an office. Jessica thanked Melissa for her help and then, after leaving her lunch tray on the cleaning rack, she and Rowlands followed Guy through the hospital's bustling corridors.

For reasons she didn't want to think about, Jessica knew the hospital better than most – but she was lost as Guy took a series of turns without bothering to look back at them. He finally stopped outside an unmarked door and started fiddling with the biggest set of keys Jessica had ever seen. Rowlands was nodding to himself, apparently impressed, but then lumbering around with a kilo of keys strapped to a belt was a very blokeish thing.

Guy still didn't look at them as he flipped from one key to the next until settling on the one that opened the door. When he finally unlocked it, he stepped away as if he'd pulled off a magic trick of which Penn and Teller would be proud.

What Jessica assumed was going to be an office actually turned out to be more of a large hole in the wall. There was a filing cabinet in the corner, a small desk, two chairs with foam spilling out of the backs, a kettle, one mug – and then mops, buckets and any number of other cleaning supplies. A crisp mix of bleach and sweat singed the air as Guy closed the door behind, dousing them in the dim light of the bulb above. There were no luxuries such as a window.

Rowlands was pressed into a corner, wedged between a pair of mops, while Guy took one of the chairs. There was so little space that Jessica had little choice other than to sit in the free seat, even though that meant every tiny movement she made had the chair squeaking like a snared mouse.

Jessica handed Guy her warrant card and he held it tight between his fingers, staring at the details on the front and back.

There was a long pause before he handed it back. 'Not allowed to talk about work,' he mumbled. The words ran into each other and it took Jessica a few seconds to figure out what he'd said.

'You won't be breaking any confidentiality agreements,' Jessica replied. 'I'd like to ask you about general things around the hospital.'

Guy didn't respond.

'Do you spend much time around the A&E department?' she added.

There was another long silence, before he muttered: 'All over.'

'What sort of things do you do around the hospital?'

A shrug this time, with a slightly shorter pause. 'Beds. Cleaning. Whatever.'

Melissa had slightly underplayed it when she said that Guy didn't say much.

'Do you help out if someone's misbehaving?'

'I guess.'

'And what have things been like recently?'

Guy didn't reply for at least ten seconds. He didn't move, simply staring at a bucket close to Rowlands' feet. 'Huh?'

'Has there been much trouble around the hospital?'

Guy poked out his bottom lip. 'Like what?'

'I'm not sure. Minor things, I suppose. Things that aren't quite right but that you wouldn't call the police about.'

It took a long time for Guy to answer and Jessica couldn't figure out if he was thinking carefully about what to say, or if he was a little slow. Perhaps the gap between their chairs contained a disparity in the time–space continuum and it was taking a while for her questions to reach him.

'Don't know,' he replied.

Jessica did her best not to sigh or sound exasperated. 'Has anyone been hanging around who shouldn't be here? Or someone being a nuisance?'

Another pause. 'Sometimes.'

'Can you give me an example…?'

The gap in space and time was seemingly widening, as it was taking even longer to get a reply. Guy eventually opened his mouth, though didn't reply straight away. He licked his lips. 'Sometimes the homeless want a roof. They sit in the corner.'

'Is there anyone who causes problems?'

'No.'

The room was beginning to feel hot from the three of them in such a cramped space. Jessica had one final thing to try but knew the payback from Rowlands would be unforgiving. Still... what else could she do?

She leant back in the chair, flicking her hair over her shoulder, waiting for Guy to glance towards her. When he did, she spoke instantly, forcing him to continue looking at her. 'It seems like you're quite important around here, Guy. You help out with security, you get patients from one place to the next, you assist the nurses and doctors, you even do the odd spot of cleaning. It sounds as if the place wouldn't run without you.'

Guy wriggled in his seat, sitting up a little straighter and running a hand across the top of his head. 'Well...'

'I'm asking *you* because I can't ask anyone else,' Jessica continued. 'I know there's a security officer or two, plus doctors, nurses, other receptionists – but *you're* the person who can't be replaced.'

Guy nodded along as she spoke. 'There was someone,' he said. No delay this time. 'She was hanging around outside the doors giving out flyers. Security moved her onto the pavement but she kept coming back.'

'What sort of flyers?'

The porter lunged with such speed that Jessica yelped backwards, thinking he was reaching for her. He didn't seem to notice her alarm as he fell to his knees, opening the bottom drawer of the filing cabinet and starting to rummage.

'Was this woman harassing patients?' Jessica asked.

'I guess.'

Guy angled forward further, exposing backside cleavage that looked like he was trying to smuggle a pair of coconuts. Particularly furry ones, which was somewhat ironic considering the lack of hair on his head. Jessica exchanged a wince with a similarly appalled Rowlands.

'When was she last here?' Jessica asked.

'A few weeks ago.'

'What else do you remember?'

Guy continued hunting through the drawer. 'One of the guards said she was called Francine. They were arguing.'

'Did you see her?'

'I guess.'

'What did she look like?'

Guy pressed back, his backside disappearing into his trousers. He had stopped looking through the drawer and was scratching his temple. 'Sort of... like Mum.'

Jessica and Rowlands shared another momentary mutual glance and it was like the old days of working together. As if they could read one another's mind. Both of them were silently saying 'huh?'.

'What do you mean by that?' Jessica asked. The thought had already occurred that Guy might well live with his mother.

'Grey hair,' Guy replied.

'Was she tall, short? Thin?'

Guy blinked and then returned to the drawer. He emerged a moment later with a scrap of paper that he thrust towards Jessica. It was A5, black type on the white background as if someone had knocked it out on a computer at home and then photocopied a few hundred. The type of cheap flyer students would give out around campus when there were drinks promotions on the go, or some dodgy election.

Jessica read the line at the top in the biggest type and then turned it for Rowlands to see. The words were in capital letters, booming out from the crinkled page.

GOD'S WILL BE DONE.

FOURTEEN

Detective Chief Inspector Lewis Topper ran his fingers across the flyer, flattening out a few of the wrinkles. He pressed back into his chair and huffed out a breath.

'Medicine defies God's will...' he read.

Jessica hummed a reply. She was on the other side of the desk in Topper's office, not quite asking for help, more letting him know what was going on. After the top line of the flyer, the rest of the text was aimed at the 'sinners' within the hospital who were using drugs and medical expertise for the heinous crime of keeping themselves alive.

'My old dad reckoned laughter was the best medicine,' Topper said.

'He wasn't a surgeon, was he?'

Topper forced back a weary smile. 'A copper. Anyway, what do you reckon?'

'The porter couldn't give many other details and the receptionist didn't really remember. I spoke to someone on security who said he'd moved this Francine woman on a couple of times in the last few months.' Jessica picked up the flyer.

'Apparently she was standing outside the hospital's main doors giving these things out to anyone going inside.'

'How did they know her name?'

'She told them. Reckoned she was a prophet sent down to do God's will.'

A roll of the eyes. 'Wonderful. Why aren't prophets ever sent down to help elderly people across the road?'

'I got the impression the hospital can be a madhouse. The security guy said she wasn't the first protestor they've had. They sometimes get an anti-abortion crowd, or the odd person banging on about budgets and politicians. It sounds like they're used to it.'

'Are you saying this Francine person is involved in whatever happened to Henry Taylor? Or Mark Stanley?'

Jessica pursed her lips. 'No... I don't know. It's an odd connection – but better than anything else we have to join the two of them. If not her directly, someone she knows? Some cultish convert to her cause? Perhaps it's nothing to do with anything?'

Topper smiled once more. '"Nothing to do with anything",' he parroted. 'That's helpful. Any idea where she might be?'

'None – and security say they don't keep CCTV for long enough. It's not much help, but she has grey hair and might look like the porter's mum.'

'His *mum?*'

'So he said.'

Topper shook his head. 'I swear this job is getting weirder...' He drummed his fingers on the desk, making his decision. 'Right – let's do whatever we can to find her.'

It had only been a few hours since they'd last packed into the incident room but this time it was easier for Jessica to get the attention of the assembled mass. The flyer had been blown up to the size of the whiteboard and was on display at the front, while every officer had a smaller version in his or her hands.

'The woman handing out this flyer at the hospital is known as Francine,' Jessica said. 'We don't know if that's her real name or an alias – but it's a start. A composite artist is currently at the hospital trying to get a proper description of her but, for now, all we have to go on is that she has grey hair. It's not a lot, but, coupled with the flyers, she sounds distinctive enough. Someone must know who she is and where she can be found. Right now, unless you're told otherwise, finding her is a priority.'

Jessica took a step to the side, expecting everyone to get moving. Instead a male voice piped up from the row of uniformed officers at the back: 'Can't we just pick her up from Deansgate?'

Chair legs squeaked as everyone turned to look at the officer who'd spoken. He was young, one of the newer constables whose name Jessica hadn't yet remembered – if she'd ever been told it. With the new recruits, it was always best to give them six months before committing to memorising a name.

'Sorry?' Jessica said.

The PC suddenly seemed self-conscious, crossing his arms and glancing nervously around the room. 'I thought everyone knew her,' he said.

'Do they?' Jessica replied.

There was a low mumble of officers agreeing that they had no idea what was going on, which only made the constable appear more anxious.

'She used to hang around the uni,' he said. 'Probably still does – but she's almost always outside The Moon Under Water.'

That brought a collective nod. Everyone knew The Moon Under Water. It was a pub, after all – and they were police officers. It would be like an investment banker not knowing the location of the nearest cocaine dealer.

'When did you last see her?' Jessica asked.

'Last night. Me and the lads were in there watching the football. Didn't know she was called Francine, but I nipped out for a ciggie and she was having an argument with some woman on the street.'

Everyone turned back to look at Jessica. 'I guess we're all off to the pub,' she said.

The Moon Under Water was housed in an old cinema in central Manchester. It was on Deansgate, a mile-long straight road with lengthy rows of shops, pubs and cafés on either side. The pub itself was a standard Wetherspoon's, full of sticky tables, cheap microwaved food and even cheaper drinks. As such, it was popular with the types who preferred liquid lunches to *actual* lunches. Liquid breakfasts and dinners too, for that matter.

According to the blurb, despite its unassuming front, it was the biggest pub in the country, possibly Europe. Jessica wasn't exactly familiar with the inside – but she'd certainly had a few drinks there in her younger, poorer days. The crowd was often an odd mix of old-timers guzzling away their pensions, students guzzling away their loans, and hen parties guzzling away their dignity. By kicking-out time, it was like the aftermath of a mass chemical attack, with survivors staggering onto the street bleary-eyed and confused.

Given the pub's prominence, Jessica and Rowlands were going for the softly-softly approach. She parked the squad car a few streets over, close to the Arndale centre, and then she and Rowlands headed towards Deansgate on foot. The streets were relatively quiet, a handful of shoppers and tourists hurrying back and forth, but no big crush of the weekend.

'Ooooh, you're *so* important,' Rowlands cooed, putting on a high-pitched voice.

'What?'

'Back in the hospital,' he said. 'When that porter wasn't saying much. All it took was for you to undo your top button, flick your hair about and tell him how important he was and he was eating out of your hand.'

'I did *not* undo my top button.'

'Did you slip him your number as well?'

Jessica started to reply and then realised that she'd fallen for it. 'If you were that concerned, you could've brought it up on the drive back to the station.'

'Touchy,' he said.

Rowlands laughed – and so did Jessica. It felt like the old days, before promotions, budget sheets and Funtime Frankie. Simpler times, before all the complications of classroom confessions.

They were on the opposite side of the road from the pub when Jessica spotted the person for whom they were likely looking. Jessica didn't know the woman and yet Francine was the archetypal nutter. She was short, with a tatty blue jumper that had probably been self-knitted. It was riddled with holes and smudges of dirt. She was wearing a knee-length skirt that showed off blotchy, hairy legs. The hair on her head was grey, straggly and a potential home for birds. She was on the pavement outside The Moon Under Water, hand outstretched as she thrust flyers towards uninterested passers-by.

She seemed the sort who'd point and shout at planes.

'Are you going to undo your top button, or should I?' Rowlands asked.

'She looks like she's been through enough without you flashing your chest hair about.'

They crossed the road together a few doors down from the

pub and then headed towards Francine. As they neared, the older woman shoved a flyer in Jessica's direction.

'Read!' she demanded.

Jessica took the page and glanced at the now familiar 'GOD'S WILL BE DONE' message at the top.

'Are you Francine?' Jessica asked.

The woman's eyes narrowed as she glanced towards Rowlands and then back to Jessica. 'You will not suppress the Lord's message,' she shouted, attracting the attention of a few passers-by, not to mention a couple of the drinkers at the front of the pub.

'I just want to ask you a few questions,' Jessica replied.

'The wicked will *not* inherit the earth.'

'I understand that – I was hoping we could go somewhere a little quieter...'

'The devil takes many forms.'

'I'm sure he does. Could we possibly just—'

Jessica didn't finish her sentence because Francine lunged forward and shunted her in the chest, sending the pile of flyers to the floor.

'Demon!' Francine shouted, finger jabbing towards Jessica. 'Demon from hell.'

Rowlands moved quickly, unclicking the handcuffs from his belt and reaching for the woman's hands.

'Demon!' Francine called once more.

Jessica straightened her top. The blow hadn't hurt, more taken her by surprise. She crouched and started to pick up the flyers.

'In all honesty,' she said, 'I've been called a lot worse.'

FIFTEEN

Despite Francine's eccentricities – which was a polite way of putting things – the custody sergeant ruled she was fine to be interviewed. Jessica thought it might be touch-and-go as to whether the mental health team might have to get involved, but Francine had apparently been coherent and clear when the sergeant had spoken to her. There was also a massive grey area when it came to people talking about religion. If a person said an unseen, probably imaginary bloke named Graham was telling them to do strange things, their mental health would be examined. If they said they were doing God's will, officers were less keen to decide they were making it up. It was the biggest get-out clause of them all.

Francine was across from Jessica and Rowlands in one of the station's interview rooms. She was wearing the same ropy jumper she'd been in when arrested, but it seemed bigger on her now. She was wrapped in it like a security blanket, as if she'd shrunk in the past hour or so. Jessica explained her rights and pointed out the recording devices, but Francine wasn't interested in anything other than chewing on her sleeve. She'd refused to even speak to a duty solicitor, let alone allow one into the room with her.

'...Do you understand?' Jessica asked after the standard introductions.

'I will not be judged by you,' Francine replied.

'You don't have to be. I'm asking if you understand everything I've just told you.'

'You have no power to command.'

Jessica took a breath, figuring that was as close to a 'yes' as she was likely to get. 'Do you know the name Henry Taylor?' she asked.

Francine stared back at her, stony-faced. 'God's will is not for Man to defy.'

'What do you mean by that?'

'The Lord God Almighty has a plan for each of us.' She paused, staring deeper into Jessica with dark eyes. 'Including you.'

It was involuntary, but a tingle licked Jessica's spine from bottom to top, making her shiver. Francine noticed, smiling for the first time.

'Is this to do with the flyers you've been handing out?' Jessica asked.

'"And He said to them, 'Go into all the world and preach the gospel to every creature'".'

'Is that from the Bible?'

'Your laws are surpassed by His. Man must pay for defying God's will.'

'How should Man pay?'

Francine's tone was calm, unemotional. As if she was talking about a trip to the shops. 'With the ultimate price.'

'I'm assuming we're not talking about the cost of a pint in the city centre – because that really is taking the proverbial.'

Francine was unmoved. Jessica waited, but the other woman said nothing.

'What is the ultimate price?' Jessica eventually added.

Francine still didn't reply, continuing to stare at Jessica.

'Do you know the name Henry Taylor?' Jessica asked once more.

No reply.

'What about Mark Spencer?'

'God's will be done.'

Jessica couldn't avoid sighing this time. She glanced up to one of the cameras above that was filming the action. Or lack of action. She wondered what Topper was thinking on the other side of the wall.

'What was God's will for Mark Spencer?'

'His will was done.'

'What does that mean?'

Francine smiled once more. She was missing a front tooth and the rest were a yellowy-brown.

Jessica continued pushing for anything approaching specifics, but it wasn't coming, leaving her little option than to give away some details herself.

'Mark Spencer was found dead last week,' she said. 'Was that God's will?'

'If it happened, then it must have been. Ours is not to question.'

Jessica continued, hoping Francine might let a shred of information slip that she shouldn't.

If she did know anything about the drowning or Mark's previous escape from the water, then she said nothing, simply parroting Bible passages. She gave no firm admission to knowing anything about him, other than cryptic statements that he deserved what he got. Under any amount of scrutiny, her words meant nothing.

Jessica eventually produced one of the flyers and placed it on the table between them. 'Why do you believe medicine is wrong?' she asked.

Francine didn't bother to glance at the document. 'If Man were meant to survive, Man would do so without such interference.'

'You'd rather return to a time where the average person died at the age of thirty?'

'The Earth is God's gift to us – but look at how we've become a plague upon the surface with our greed and sloth. At how we've multiplied, destroyed and devoured.'

Jessica glanced up towards the camera once more, feeling Topper watching. They were getting nowhere. She peered at her notes and then asked Francine where she was on Saturday afternoon – the time when Henry had ended up in front of the car – and on the day Mark had gone missing. The only reply that came was somewhat predictable. Francine said she was 'spreading the will of God'. The specifics of where she was spreading such will was harder to come by.

After twenty minutes of going in circles, Jessica called for one of the uniformed officers to return Francine to the cells below the station. Then she asked if Rowlands could nip over to the vending machine to get her a KitKat. She even gave him a pound coin. He didn't complain or take the piss, he simply gripped her shoulder for a moment and said he'd be right back.

It was becoming one of those afternoons.

Jessica had the interview room to herself for a moment before Topper knocked and entered. He gave a watery smile as he waited in the corner, leaning against the wall with his arms folded.

'Rather you than me,' he said.

'If I'd asked what her favourite chocolate bar is, she'd have said that eternal damnation comes from eating anything other than pure cocoa.'

'There's nothing on file about her, no family that we're aware of. One of the constables found out that she lives in a hostel for the homeless, but that's about it.'

Jessica wasn't completely surprised. 'Has anyone been there yet?'

'I figured I'd let you sort things out.'

'I've got a couple of things to do first, but I'll probably head out myself.'

Topper's lips were tight, something on his mind.

'What?' Jessica asked.

'You really think she pushed a grown man in front of a car? Or drowned someone else in a canal?'

Jessica shrugged. 'Maybe someone she knows...?'

'Does she seem the type with a wide group of friends?'

They both knew the answer to that.

'It could be a coincidence,' Topper said. 'Bloke drowns, someone else run over. Nothing unusual there. Nothing to say either of them were more than accidents. Happens all the time.'

'In Manchester?'

A shrug. Topper half turned to the door and then spun back with a click of his heels. 'Would you be so concerned if someone else had been driving?'

'What do you mean?'

'I think you know what I mean.'

He held her gaze for a moment too long. He could have told her to stop and move on... but he didn't.

'I'll let you know how I get on at the hostel,' Jessica replied.

Jessica was in her office, two KitKat fingers down, two to go. She closed her eyes and breathed in the silence for a few moments. Relative silence, anyway. There was always a hum of activity going on somewhere around the station.

She took out her phone and thought about spending a few minutes on the game Archie had accused her of being addicted to, before deciding against it. While thinking of the constable, she wondered if she should call him. She'd heard nothing since finding him in the pub. She decided against that, too – but it was more because she had an inkling that Inspector Vincent and his Professional Standards lot could have a look at her phone records and draw something into it that wasn't there.

She wouldn't put anything past that lot.

Instead, she flicked through the photographs on her phone, settling on the ones she'd taken outside Roly's house the previous night. The images weren't quite super 4K hyper high-definition but, of the six Jessica had taken, two showed clear enough pictures of the teenagers collecting their bikes. Of the five lads in shot, only one would be definitely identifiable, perhaps two, with a squint. Jessica zoomed in as much as she could and then unlocked the iPad that Rowlands had signed out from storage.

The Big Book Of Bastardly Shites, © Greater Manchester Police, digital edition, was a limited edition one-of-a-kind volume exclusive to GMP. The original hard copy had been compiled over many years by a collection of officers, providing a comprehensive collection of mugshots from local pain in the arses. In recent times, some unnamed hero had digitised everything, meaning witnesses and officers could quickly flick through headshots of known ne'er-do-wells.

Jessica filtered the images by area, hair colour and age until she was left with a little over thirty images of teenagers. She flipped through one after the other until she found a match. The kid she had photographed outside Roly's flat was the same one whom she'd seen being slapped across the face by Jefferson. The mugshot showed him pale-faced, pimply and skinny but with a defiant gaze. All Lynx and no GCSEs. The type whose criminal career would begin at an early age and continue until he was either banged up for good or ended up pissing off the wrong person.

Thomas Adlington was days away from his seventeenth

birthday, according to their files. Two and a bit years previously, he'd been caught with a few bags of cannabis. Nothing serious, but probably too much for his own consumption. He'd been given a conditional discharge. A year before, he'd been stopped and searched while carrying a flick knife. He'd seemingly got away with that, too, after being given a training order and having the weapon confiscated. He was neither a criminal mastermind nor a brutal danger to the public – but he was hardly an angel-faced choirboy. Either way, it was bizarre that someone who'd been caught carrying a knife had allowed himself to be slapped across the face without reacting.

Jessica searched the file for the second youth and, though the quality of her photo meant she couldn't be sure about identifying the right lad, she was reasonably confident she found the right name. If she was right, the second photo showed a seventeen-year-old who had twice been convicted for theft. The last offence was a year previous and since then... nothing.

After copying down the details of the teenagers, Jessica called Pete. He sounded surprised to hear from her, saying he was on the Lees Estate at that moment, doing his rounds. She told him the names of the boys and, though he recognised them, there was little he could add.

'Has there been any problem with gangs on bikes?' Jessica asked.

'How do you mean?' Pete replied.

'I'm not sure. I noticed a group of lads on bikes when I was last there.'

'You get that most places, though. How else are teenagers supposed to get around?'

Jessica couldn't argue with that.

'Is there some sort of problem?' he added.

Jessica realised there was no particular reason to keep what she'd seen from him. They were supposed to be working together, after all.

'Roly called me last night,' she said.

'When?'

'Late. Someone had put his windows through. He didn't want to call the police or make a big deal. When I arrived, there were kids on bikes massing underneath, in the flat you said was occupied by that Jefferson bloke.'

Pete exhaled loudly, the sound bristling the speaker by Jessica's ear. 'Is that who he thinks broke his windows?'

'Perhaps. Someone sprayed "grass" as well. I don't think they liked him talking to us.'

'But he didn't tell us anything.'

'We know that – but they don't.'

There was a pause and another sigh. 'What could he have told us?' Pete asked.

'No idea. Roly says he doesn't know anything, either. There is one thing, though – I saw Jefferson slapping one of the lads.'

Pete coughed in surprise. 'He hit one of them?'

'Hard – across the face.'

'Did the kid retaliate?'

'Not that I saw.'

There were a few moments of silence. 'I'm not sure I understand what's going on,' Pete said.

'Me either.'

'Could you ask for a warrant?'

Jessica snapped one of the KitKat fingers in half and leant back in her chair. 'For Jefferson's? There's no basis. He makes a bit of noise, kids come and go sometimes. I saw him hit someone. Why would we say we wanted a warrant? We'd get laughed at.'

'True.'

'There is something you could do...' she said.

'Go on...'

'If I have a word with your sergeant or inspector, perhaps

you could run a day of stop-and-searches? See if these kids are ferrying anything to and from that flat. Drugs, money, stolen goods – anything. If you nab someone, put the shits up them and see if someone will talk. If someone's trying to stop Roly talking to us, it has to be because there's something worth talking about. We'll visit Jefferson in the morning and I'll see if I can get you some bodies for stop-and-search.'

'You've found something out, haven't you?'

Jessica peered down at the other folder she'd been reading. The one belonging to Jefferson Cass. 'You could say that,' she replied.

SIXTEEN

Francine's hostel was an old converted house a little over the Salford border. It was close to the River Irwell to the north of the city centre, four storeys high with a patchy, unkempt front yard covered with cigarette butts. From the outside, there were no signs to indicate it was anything other than an old house in need of repair and Jessica double-checked she was at the correct place before heading along the path.

At the side of the front door was a small buzzer box with a column of five buttons. A small piece of paper had been taped to the top one, reading 'press this', with four separate strips pasted next to the others that read 'Do NOT press this'. The devil on Jessica's shoulder wondered what might happen if she pressed any of the other four, but she obeyed the instructions and only nudged the top one a single time. A grating buzz sounded from the inside, followed by silence.

Jessica waited.

And waited.

She thought about trying it a second time – or risking one of the other buttons – before a silhouette appeared on the other side of the dimpled glass. A frowny woman opened the door, offering a sideways, squinty stare as she looked Jessica up and down.

'There's no room,' she said.

'I'm not after a room.'

'What do you want?'

Jessica fiddled with her warrant card and passed it across. The woman barely looked at it.

'Oh, for crying out loud,' she said. 'Who's done what now?'

'Can I come in?'

The stare-off continued and then the woman sighed, stepping to the side and allowing Jessica to move inside.

'Do you run this place?' Jessica asked.

'I'm Teri with an i,' the woman said, not quite answering the question.

She closed the door and then hobbled along the corridor, favouring her left leg and muttering under her breath before pushing her way into a musty-smelling office. A fan was burring in the corner even though it wasn't particularly warm, with the desktop computer monitor showing a half-finished game of solitaire.

'Who do you want?' Teri asked, plopping herself into a large office chair. Her greying dark hair was piled on top of her head, pinned high with a pair of biros.

'If you're in charge, then you,' Jessica replied.

Teri's frown deepened, something that Jessica hadn't thought possible. The lines in her face were like valleys. 'Why?'

'I gather one of the people who live here is named Francine...?'

Jessica hoped for a reaction but got little other than a pouty bottom lip. 'That's right.'

'We currently have her in custody.'

'What for?'

'I can't say at the moment.'

'Well I can't share any details without a warrant. My residents rely on me to keep their privacy.' Probably involuntarily, Teri glanced towards a filing cabinet to her side that had a key in the lock. It didn't exactly scream private.

'Is there anything you *can* tell me about Francine?' Jessica asked.

'Only that she's been warned about preaching to residents. We don't do religion or politics here. It's not worth the hassle.'

'Does that mean there has been hassle in the past?'

Teri rolled her eyes, glancing quickly at the computer and making it clear she'd much rather be playing solitaire. In fairness, Jessica would rather be playing games as well.

'She was making people uncomfortable,' Teri said.

'By preaching?'

'If you like.'

'Was there a specific incident?'

Jessica knew she had the woman snared. Privacy or no privacy, Teri wanted to know what was going on with Francine. If that meant giving up some information herself, she was going to go for it – even if it did lead to a succession of rolled eyes.

Teri lowered her voice, peering over Jessica's shoulder towards the door. 'Francine upset one of the other residents.'

'How?'

'The other girl's name was Lucy. She was in and out of here over a few months but ended up living somewhere else with her boyfriend. He got drunk one night and beat her up, then finished by throwing her down the stairs. He then dragged her back to the top and did it again. Christ knows how she walked away from that. She ended up having a blood transfusion at the hospital. When Francine found out, she went to the hospital and started handing out these leaflets about how medicine was against God's will and all that. Later, after Lucy was placed back here, they had some sort of row about it and that's when I said no religion or politics.'

'Has that rule stuck?'

'More or less.'

That explained partially why Francine had been picketing the hospital, though she didn't exactly seem the shy and retiring type if it came to keeping her views to herself.

'Was anything reported to the police?'

'With Lucy? Whatever happened with her boyfriend happened off-site, so I don't know.'

'I mean with Francine.'

Teri stared disdainfully at Jessica as if she'd just punched a puppy. 'Do you have any idea what it's like running this place?' she said. 'We have one regular who believes every Sunday is going to be Armageddon. She says goodbye to everyone she knows each Saturday because she thinks she won't see them again. There's someone else who's convinced MI5 is watching our every move via satellite. He wears a colander on his head when he's having a smoke. Even some of the quieter ones spend half their time in the garden muttering to themselves. At least half the people here need mental health assessments, not an appointment with you lot. Instead, the council shunt them in here and forget about them, saying there's no money to see a doctor.'

Jessica couldn't disagree, knowing much – if not all – of what Teri said was true. 'Sorry,' she said. 'You're right.'

Teri had leant forward, apparently ready for an argument, but she pressed back at the acknowledgement. 'You're damned right I am,' she said.

'Is there anyone Francine's particularly friendly with?' Jessica asked.

The permanent frown that had been tattooed on Teri's face relaxed slightly. It was still a bit scowly, but not a full-on grimace. 'There was this bloke named Ezra who followed her around for a while. I've not seen him in ages.'

'Did he live here?'

'On and off. This is more of a halfway house. People get out of prison or rehab and come here. Either that or they're long-term homeless. The council put them here while they try to find somewhere else for them to live. No one stays here for a long time, but the same faces do show up.'

'What did he look like?'

Teri pointed upwards. 'Big bloke. Black, with a beard. He used to sit outside on the front step smoking weed. I told him to stop, that I'd call the police. He'd knock it off and head out somewhere – then he'd be back the next day doing the same thing. In the end I told him to leave. I've not seen him since.'

'How long ago was that?'

'Six weeks? A couple of months? And, no, before you ask, I didn't call you lot. I didn't tell the council either. You should see the paperwork they want you to fill in.'

Jessica gave a knowing laugh. 'If you ever want to compare paperwork, we can job swap for a day...?'

The frown lightened even further. Still no hint of a smile, but Teri's expression was almost neutral.

'Does Lucy still live here?' Jessica asked.

'She does... but I've not seen her in a few days.'

'Is that normal?'

'It's not like they have to swipe in and out. Everyone knows the door closes at eleven and opens at seven. If they're in, they're in. Emily's definitely here. She's in the garden.'

'Who's Emily?'

'Lucy's best friend. I can't promise she'll talk to you – but you can head around back if you want to ask.'

Jessica thanked Teri for her help, figuring she'd got as much as she was going to. Teri did ask if Jessica could at least give her a hint of why Francine had been arrested, but Jessica had to apologise before slipping away.

She left through the front door and then followed the path at the side of the house, emerging onto a large patch of overgrown grass. A mossy, damp fence ringed the encroaching jungle and there was a thick cloying air of pollen and wildflowers that reminded Jessica of her youth. She was so taken by the déjà vu of playing in the fields that surrounded her village that Jessica almost forgot what she was doing.

She was halfway across the grass when she realised the only thing she was heading towards was the fence at the back. Jessica caught herself as her sinuses started to clog. It felt like she needed to sneeze as she turned back towards the house.

A row of browning once-white plastic garden chairs was arranged close to a back door next to a wheelie bin and a pile of cardboard. Sitting in the end seat, knees crossed, was a waif of a girl with beehive dark hair that had knitting needles sticking out of the sides. She was wearing a flowery sundress despite the lack of sunshine, her bare feet bobbing up and down as she eyed Jessica through smoggy thick eyeliner.

'You lost?' she asked, her accent local. She was smoking a roll-up, effortlessly flicking ash into the bin without looking.

'Are you Emily?'

The girl's eyes narrowed. She was early twenties at most, perhaps younger. 'Who's asking?'

Jessica recrossed the lawn, crouching so that she was at a lower level than Emily, giving the other woman the power. 'I'm a police officer and I currently have someone named Francine in custody. I gather you might be familiar with her...?'

Emily sucked on her cigarette, her gaze not leaving Jessica. 'What did she do?'

'I can't say.'

'She knifed someone, didn't she?'

'Why'd you say that?'

A shrug. 'You know when someone goes on an axe spree or whatever? They kill loads of people and then you have them lot on telly saying how they never would've suspected it could happen. "Jeff was such a nice bloke, he wasn't that sort of person" – that type of thing. Anyway, when Francine goes on an axe spree, I'll be the one on telly saying she definitely *was* that sort of person.'

Jessica sat on the grass, feeling it flatten underneath. 'Not a fan?' she asked.

Emily flicked away the remains of her cigarette. 'You could say that.'

'I heard she was friends with someone named Ezra...?'

A nod. 'Weird bloke, didn't say much. Smacked off his tits half the time.'

'Have you seen him recently?'

'Thankfully not. He was a right nutter. Used to call us all sisters or brothers. He smelled like shite, too. He followed Francine around like she was his mum. Gave everyone the creeps.'

'There was also an incident with Lucy...?'

Emily reached into her bra and pulled out another roll-up. She licked the paper and pressed it together, then picked up a lighter from the ground and lit the cigarette. 'Right.'

'Have you seen Lucy recently?'

Emily sucked hard on the cigarette once more, shifting it from one hand to the other, examining Jessica carefully. 'She done something wrong?'

'Not that I know of.'

'Why d'you want to find her?'

'Because I'm trying to find out everything I can about Francine.'

Emily started counting on her fingers, stopping at four. 'Saw her last Thursday in town. She was waiting near the bins

at the back of Burger King. That's where they chuck everything out at the end of a shift.'

'Any idea on time?'

'Before curfew. Nine? Ten? I dunno.' She held up her
wrists. 'No watch.'

There wasn't a watch – but there was a slim, braided
bracelet with black, green and yellow stripes. It looked like the
type of thing a teenager might make.

'You've not seen her since?' Jessica asked.

'Nope.'

'Is that normal?'

Emily inhaled from the cigarette once more, lips tight.
'Luce does her own thing. She might've gone back to her fella
– 'cept he's in prison. Maybe she's visited him?'

'Four days is a long time if this is where she's living...'

This time Emily shifted uncomfortably in the seat,
uncurling one of her legs. There were brown scarred scratches
towards her ankles, pimples around her toes. She switched the
cigarette back to her original hand without taking a drag and her
gaze shifted past Jessica towards the back of the garden. 'Yeah...'

'Do you have a picture of her?'

'Do I look like I carry around pictures of people?' Emily
held her hands wide, but, in truth, Jessica didn't know. Was
there a specific sort of person who carried around pictures?

'If I ask someone to visit you here, can you help them come
up with an image of what Lucy looks like? Possibly Ezra as
well?'

Emily breathed deeply, still not inhaling. The ash at the
tip of the cigarette was flaring, starting to droop. 'Yeah.' She
thrust her wrist out to Jessica, holding the bracelet under her
nose. 'Look, she made me this and we're mates, right? That
don't mean I know where she is all the time. She does her
thing, I do mine. It ain't like your world.'

'How'd you mean?'

The young woman poked a thumb backwards towards the house. 'You think we want to live here? Gotta be in by eleven, or whatever? It's here because there ain't nowhere else. Except, sometimes, it's better on the streets, innit? At least you're making your own choices, living your own life.' She tossed the still-lit cigarette onto the ground. 'I hope she don't come back. I hope she's gone somewhere far away from this shithole where there ain't no rules about where you can and can't smoke, what times you have to be in by, who you can and can't have over.' She stood and stamped hard on the cigarette. 'Somewhere where there ain't some Jesus nutter banging on about going to hell all the time. *That's* where I hope she is.'

SEVENTEEN

Jessica was sitting in her car around the corner from the hostel. The ferocity of Emily was hard to understand, but then her world, her life, was something unknown to Jessica. She'd spent time with the homeless and even given a roof to someone who came from the streets – and she wasn't sure she knew anyone who'd rather live outside.

It must be *really* bad at the hostel.

She dialled DCI Topper's phone number and waited for him to answer. When he did, he sounded distracted and, from the background clicking, she suspected he was typing at the same time.

'What have you got?' he asked.

Jessica told him about Ezra and Lucy, adding that she wanted a composite artist to visit Emily. Hopefully someone could come up with a photo. They'd need someone to find and talk to Lucy's imprisoned boyfriend as well, if only to find out if he'd seen her. If at all possible, they could do with a warrant for Francine's room at the hostel.

Topper listened, humming along at the right moments to indicate he was listening.

'What's wrong?' Jessica asked when she finally cottoned on to the fact that he wasn't giving her his full attention.

'She's not our suspect,' he said.

'Francine?'

'Who else?'

'How do you know?'

There was a noisy click and then Topper's voice sounded louder, as if he was speaking into the receiver properly, or he'd picked up from speakerphone. 'At the same time that Henry Taylor was being pushed in front of that car, we've got CCTV of Francine handing out flyers outside The Moon Under Water. She was halfway across the city.'

'It's definitely her?'

'Yes.'

'And the timestamp is one hundred per cent?'

'Checked and double-checked. One of the bar staff remembers her as well.'

Jessica wriggled in the driver's seat, accidentally banging her knee on the steering wheel. 'We've got CCTV of a woman standing outside a pub – but we don't have anything of a bloke being pushed in front of a car?'

'I know.' He sounded disappointed, but then he'd never been convinced Francine was anything other than an eccentric in any case. Jessica wasn't sure if she believed the woman was any more of a threat, either – but it felt like there was something there.

'I'm worried about this Lucy,' Jessica said. 'She had a blood transfusion a while back, which was why Francine was picketing the hospital. Apparently they had some sort of row. Lucy's not been seen for four days.'

'We can get her on the missing persons' list.'

'It's a start – but we need to get her picture out there. If she's sleeping rough somewhere, it'd help if people know who to look for.'

'We can sort all that...'

Topper tailed off, but Jessica knew there was more, so she said nothing, waiting for him to fill in the gap.

'We can hold Francine until tomorrow,' he said, 'but I don't want to ask the super if we can have her for thirty-six hours unless we have more to go on. At the moment – if we really want to push things – it's resisting arrest and assaulting an officer. We'd need better statements from you and Constable Rowlands if you want that to stick.'

'No chance,' Jessica replied.

'That's it then. It's not that she *might* have been involved with pushing Henry Taylor in front of the car, she *definitely* wasn't. She might be avoiding questions, but we can't hold someone for that either.'

'She could be working with someone – that Ezra bloke.'

'Perhaps – but we don't know what he looks like and we don't know where he is. Plus you're done for the day.'

Jessica looked at the clock on her dashboard, realising her shift had finished twenty minutes previously. She knew Topper was right about everything else, too.

'All right,' she replied.

Topper sighed, as if he'd expected a battle. 'Good,' he said. 'The night team will do what they can and then I'll try interviewing Francine myself tomorrow. Perhaps she'll talk to me?'

'Ten quid says she doesn't.'

A pause. 'I don't gamble,' he said.

'I'm not surprised – you know what they say about Scots and their money.'

Jessica didn't quite catch the reply. But she did hear the word 'off' before she hung up.

Jessica sat on one side of the table half eyeing the vending machines in the far corner of the room. She didn't like to look too closely at the man across from her, even though the smallest part of her found him mesmerising.

Perhaps it was a larger part of her?

She didn't want to think about it, so she continued to look at the vending machines instead, eyeing the chocolate bars, crisp packets and soft-drinks cans, trying to figure out what everything was by colour and shape alone.

'It's nice to see you again,' the man said.

There was noise all around them, a low murmuring as couples chatted back and forth around the room. The atmosphere was odd, not quite the visiting room of a prison but not the natter of a casual café either. The windows weren't barred, the guards not standing rigidly by the doors, batons at the ready. There were a couple of men near the doors, however, sitting and chatting with one another, keeping half an eye on what was going on around them. There were only half a dozen patients dotted around the room having conversations, but the casualness meant Jessica always felt far more on edge than she ever did visiting a prison.

'Is it nice for you to see me?' the man asked.

Jessica's eyes flicked to him and then away again. 'You *are* kidding?'

'I don't know. I never asked you to return. Don't get me wrong, I'm not upset that you're here – but it was your choice to come. Well, to come *back*. I know you wanted something the first time, but what about the time after that? And the time after that...?'

He tailed off and, without looking at him, Jessica knew he was smiling. She didn't know the answer to his question. Why *was* she there?

'Do you want something?' he asked.

'I don't know.'

'I can talk about my week if you want? It's a bit limiting being in here all the time, but I read what I can.' He continued babbling about some philosophical book he'd been reading but Jessica had switched off, trying to figure out if the top right packet of crisps was prawn cocktail or smoky bacon. She couldn't make out if the foil was pink or brown because of the glare.

She blinked back into the room when she realised the man across from her had gone silent.

'You're not listening to me, are you?' he said.

Jessica refocused on him, disgusted yet exhilarated, too. Ambivalence was the proper word. Two contrasting emotions that were both true. She wondered if that was why she returned month after month.

'Maybe I should go?' the man said.

Jessica shook her head.

'There's no point in me sitting here chatting if you don't want to say anything,' he replied. 'This is, what, visit number six? Six months in a row you've been coming here and you're saying less every time.'

Jessica totted up the months in her mind. He was right – it was six months since she'd first visited Ashworth Hospital to ask Randall Anderson for help with a case. He'd provided it, too. After that, there was no reason to return.

Except that she had.

Six times now.

He'd been counting.

'This isn't because I tried to kill you, is it?' Randall said. He gazed at her with the endless blue eyes that had once attracted Caroline as his girlfriend. For a moment, Jessica remembered being introduced to him for the first time, when she and Caroline were sharing a flat together. He hadn't just tried to kill Jessica, he'd gone after Caroline, too.

If anything, he was better-looking now, a little under six feet tall, his head shaven, his build lean and athletic in jeans and a tight T-shirt. The familiar spiky tattoo clung to his bicep, bulging slightly as he tensed and untensed his muscle.

'I thought we agreed not to talk about that,' Jessica said firmly.

'I'm just making conversation. You weren't saying anything. What do you want to talk about? Have you got some juicy case on the go? I'm always looking out for your name when we get to go online, but I've not seen anything recently.'

Jessica tried to ignore the fact that he was apparently googling her regularly. 'You know we don't talk about my work either.'

'So what do you want to talk about? You requested visiting time with me, remember?'

'Are you religious?' Jessica asked.

Randall pressed back in his seat, flexing his arm muscles, perhaps without meaning to. 'Not really.'

'Faith's a strange thing for me. I've seen it twisted and used to push a person's own aims, but then I've also seen belief do great things for people. Make them want to change their lives and be better. Even if God doesn't exist, if someone *believes* he does and then does something good with their life, isn't that a positive thing?'

It wasn't the sort of thought Jessica would have felt comfortable telling someone she knew. Perhaps that was why she kept coming back.

Randall took a moment, apparently thinking carefully about his reply. He scraped his chin with his thumb. 'Are you saying the only reason they'd do something worthwhile is if they think they'll go to hell if they don't? Seems like a pretty shoddy reason to be good, if you ask me.'

Jessica didn't reply because she didn't know what to say. She went back to peering at the vending machine, concluding it definitely was prawn cocktail on the top row. She was suddenly hungry for crisps.

'What do *you* believe?' Randall asked.

'I don't know.'

There was silence between them and Jessica could feel him watching her.

'My doctor likes it that you're visiting,' he said.

'Why?'

'He used the word "cathartic". I think he likes using it with patients. He says there's been a big improvement in my demeanour. I'm not quite sure what he means by that, but if he's happy, then everything's easier. He said the fact I was willing to help with your prior investigation, coupled with the fact that you've continued to visit, shows that I'm evolving.'

'As opposed to what?'

'Well, *de*volving, I suppose. He says a lot of things.' Randall paused to lick his lips. 'I wonder if I could ask you something.'

'What?'

The word blurted out before Jessica had thought it through.

Randall waited for her attention to shift. He was relaxed, unthreatening. It looked practised, almost certainly was. 'If I were to come up for release at some point, do you think you might vouch for me? You might have to talk to a doctor, or some panel. I'm not entirely sure.'

Jessica knew she should be angry. She stared at him, willing the volcanic rage to explode, but it wasn't there. She felt... nothing. Not fury, but not pity, either.

'You've got some nerve asking that,' she said, though not harshly.

'I know. But you came to me, remember – and I'm speaking entirely theoretically. If you once thought I was some uncaring monster, you can't still believe that to be true if you're visiting so regularly...?'

'You killed four people. You tried to kill me. You tried to kill Caroline. Do you *really* think I want you out of here?'

He nodded meekly, his fingers pressed into each other, creating a diamond between his two hands. 'I can't go back in time, Jessica.'

'Would you? If the option was there, would you go back and change things?'

Randall pressed his fingers harder together, but he seemed momentarily rattled. He shunted back in his chair, glancing towards the guards by the doors. 'I'm not sure anyone's ever asked me that before. They talk about not being in control of one's actions – or of remorse. Some around here say they don't recall their crimes, but I remember everything.'

He bit his lip, making a low humming sound. It might have been acting – probably was, considering Jessica didn't trust him one tiny bit – but Randall did genuinely seem to be thinking about his reply.

'You want me to say I would take it back, don't you?' he asked.

'I want you to tell the truth.'

A nod. 'I don't think I would. You have all these people banging on about how they don't regret anything they do because it makes them who they are. It's a very selfish way of thinking – because our actions affect others. That's like saying you don't care how you've hurt others because it's made you the person you are. All me, me, me. But I probably *do* feel like that. I regret being in here... but what happened all those years ago sort of got it out of my system. I suppose that makes me selfish... but at least I can admit it.'

Jessica realised she was staring. She was looking for the signs – a twitch of the eye, a sideways glance. She was as sure as she could be that, at least in this moment, he was telling the truth.

'You killed four people but don't regret it because it "got it out of your system"?'

'You asked. I don't have those urges any longer, so – yes – it *is* out of my system.' He paused and there was the merest hint of a smirk in the corners of his lips. 'How is Caroline?'

'That's none of your business.'

'Are you still friends?'

'That's none of your business, either.'

'Does she know you visit me?'

Jessica could sense the amusement in his voice. 'What do you think?' she replied.

'I think that's going to be an interesting conversation.'

Randall was smiling, not trying to hide it any longer. Jessica wondered if he had been toying with her the whole time.

'I've got to go,' she said, pushing backwards in her chair and standing. Randall didn't move, his smile fixed.

'See you next month,' he said.

Jessica had already said 'yes' before the possibility of saying 'no' had crossed her mind. She bobbed on the spot, caught between two worlds – the real one outside and this construct – then she headed for the door.

EIGHTEEN

TUESDAY

If DCI Topper had taken Jessica's bet about whether Francine was going to speak to him, her money would've been safe. By the time the chief inspector emerged from the interview room, he had the look of a man who'd been chained to a radiator for a few nights and then waterboarded until he ended up confessing to something he'd not done.

He staggered into the adjacent office where Jessica had been watching the action through the video cameras and then slumped into a chair, mopping his brow with his sleeve.

'Now *that* was funny,' Jessica said.

'I'm glad one of us found it amusing.'

'I think my favourite part was when she called you the demonic spawn of Satan. You should put that on your business cards.'

Topper continued wiping his head and then dried his hands on the back of the chair before giving Jessica a 'you-didn't-just-see-that' raise of the eyebrows.

'We're going to have to let her go,' he said.

'Isn't there a way to get her detained under the mental health act? Something like that?'

Topper shook his head. 'I'd have more chance of having *you* detained. Aside from something of an obsession with the Bible, they're not going to find anything wrong with her.'

Jessica let the snidey crack go. 'Lucy's still missing,' she said. 'Emily helped us get a picture of her, but there's no sign. That's five days now. She's got long blonde hair and is younger than most of the homeless community. Someone should recognise her – but we're not getting much coop-eration.'

He nodded in slow acknowledgement. 'Is there anything else that links the bloke who drowned to the one who was run over?'

Jessica turned away slightly. 'No. There's nothing at all. No clues to how Mark ended up in the water, or to how Henry ended up in front of the car.' She paused. 'Have you heard anything from Professional Standards?'

'Not a peep.'

'We're a bit short-staffed...'

Topper snorted. 'If you think I have any sway over if or when Constable Davey will be allowed back to work, then you've really misread the situation.'

Jessica already knew that. 'Sorry, guv.'

They both stood. 'What's next?' Topper asked.

'I'll brief the team to let them know we're releasing Francine, otherwise we'll keep at it. We nabbed that pick-pocket but we've not arrested the Birchfields flasher yet. There was a burglary a few streets over last night and a few calls about kids letting off fireworks in Platt Fields. It's all go. I've got to head off to the Lees Estate to meet with my Community Liaison Officer.'

She might have been wrong, but Jessica thought she might have seen the merest roll of the eyes from the chief inspector. 'How's that going?' he asked.

'Still the most crime-free estate in the city. Hooray for me.'

Topper eyed her over glasses he wasn't wearing. 'Let's hope it stays that way.'

Jessica and Pete were sitting on one of the benches towards the edge of the paved plaza that was overlooked by the flats on the Lees Estate. Uniformed officers were out in force on the surrounding streets, stopping anyone who looked remotely iffy. It had taken a couple of favours, some muttered remarks about 'intelligence' and some serious good faith, but Jessica had been on a run of getting into people's good books and this was the pay-off. If the officers could find some drugs that were being smuggled around the estate, then all the better.

Pete stared off to the flats beyond and then glanced sideways towards Jessica. 'Jefferson Cass has previous?'

'He used to live in Leeds,' Jessica said. 'I couldn't find it at first because it's under the name "Geoff" with a "G". I don't know if Jefferson is an alias, or if that's his real name – but it's definitely him. He got six months a couple of years ago for a series of assaults. Put some poor sod in a coma.'

Pete ruffled his hair and puffed out a breath. Suddenly the drop in crime that coincided with Jefferson's arrival had a whiff of suspicion about it. 'Anything else?' he asked.

'Not really. There's nothing on his record since then. I guess he upped sticks from Yorkshire and moved here.'

'By himself, though. Hardly anyone makes that sort of move on their own. They bring their wife, or girlfriend – or they're moving to be closer to family. If you were by yourself, you'd have to be moving for a reason.'

'Precisely.' She pointed towards the ground-floor flat on the far side of the quadrant. 'Shall we go and have a word?'

The first thing Jessica noticed about Jefferson Cass was that he was wearing flip-flops. He opened the door and then leant against the frame, eyeing her and ignoring Pete. He was in loose tracksuit bottoms, with a tight vest that showed off a physique that wouldn't be out of place on the set of a super-hero movie. He was tall and stubbly, with a smile that could have a certain type of woman – or man – swooning at thirty paces.

'All right, darling,' he said by way of greeting, not sounding particularly northern. Jessica flashed him her warrant card but he barely looked at it before returning his gaze to her. 'You want to come in?' He angled over his shoulder towards the inside of the flat, which wasn't what Jessica had expected. Hostility and obstruction was all well and good – an open invitation into someone's home without asking was rare.

There were half a dozen locks on the inside of the front door, including one that faced the wrong way – blocking the hinge side rather than the edge that would swing open.

Jessica and Pete trailed Jefferson inside, following a hallway until they emerged into a living room. The place was minimalist and spotless, a snapshot from an IKEA catalogue. There was a low cabinet at the front of the room with a flat-screen television, a games console and tall surround-sound speakers. Aside from a pair of sofas, that was it. No photos, no decorations, no ornaments. The walls were plain white, the carpet a spotless coffee colour. Jefferson was quite the clean freak. The window at the front was open a fraction in the same way it had been when she'd been snooping the other night.

Jefferson plopped himself into the centre of one of the sofas and stretched his arms wide so that he was taking up the entire space.

'What's with the locks?' Jessica asked.

'Can't be too careful, can you?' A beat and then: 'There's a lot of you around today. Something going on?'

Jessica continued standing. 'Nothing in particular.'

As she spoke, Jessica suddenly had the sensation of being watched. She could feel Pete's attention was lost and turned, following his gaze towards the back of the room. The blind was rippling gently, presumably because of the open window behind. Jessica was about to turn back when she noticed the large glass tank running from the back corner towards the centre of the room. At first she thought it was for fish – except there was no water, no obvious movement.

Then she saw it.

Not just it. *Them.*

Coiled at the bottom of the tank, spaghettified into one another, were at least three snakes. One was browny-grey, thick like her wrist. Another was red with black stripes, one more albino white and yellow. They weren't moving much, but the gentle way they curled and writhed was plenty enough to give Jessica the creeps.

When she turned back to Jefferson, he was grinning. 'They're friendly,' he said. 'You want to hold one?'

'I'm all right,' Jessica managed.

'Sure? They don't bite. Well, not often.' He winked at her and Jessica wasn't sure whether he was joking. She didn't want to find out.

Pete took a step away, even though there were already a good couple of metres between him and the tank.

'Snakes get a bad rep,' Jefferson said, still amused. 'They're the best rodent control going in their natural habitat and there's all sorts of medical research about uses for their venom. Fascinating things.'

Jessica turned between him and the snakes, thinking she'd rather have a trap and some cheese to deal with any potential mice she might come across.

'I'll take your word for it,' she said.

Jefferson clapped his hands together loudly. 'So... how can I help, officers?'

'There have been a few reports of antisocial behaviour from around the estate,' Jessica said. 'You're not being accused of anything, but it looks like you've got the ear of some of the local kids, so we were hoping you might be able to shed some light...?'

'What sort of antisocial behaviour?'

'I don't particularly want to go into specifics.'

'Who says the local kids listen to me?'

Jessica nodded towards the front window. 'No one in particular – but when I was out for a walk around here the other day, there were a pile of bikes outside your front door and I saw some lads coming out...'

Jefferson's smile had slipped, his eyes narrowing until he caught himself. He flashed a set of whitened teeth at her. 'I s'pose a few of the lads like coming over to check out the vivarium...'

Jessica resisted the urge to look at the snakes once more. She also didn't believe a trip to 'check out the vivarium' was high on many young people's list of things to do – unless that was some sort of euphemism of which she was unaware.

'How long have you lived here?' Jessica asked.

'Why?'

'Indulge me.'

Jefferson weighed her up with a pout of the lips. 'Nine months or so.'

'Any particular reason you were drawn here?'

'Somewhere to live, innit?'

'But why here *specifically*?'

Jefferson fiddled with the pocket of his tracksuit bottoms, then reached inside and took out a mobile phone. He checked the screen and then put it away again. 'No particular reason.'

'Perhaps you're unaware of this, but the Lees Estate used to be a problem area. It was called the knife crime capital of the north. People were being mugged, the newsagent round the corner was robbed multiple times, some poor old pensioner was dragged into the road because some kids wanted her bag. All sorts of nasty things. And then, a few months ago, it seemingly all stopped...'

Jefferson nodded slowly. 'That's good, isn't it?'

'It is – but crime is up in all the surrounding districts. Not by much. A couple of per cent here and there. Barely noticeable.'

He checked his phone again. 'I'm not sure I understand what you're getting at...'

'It's just the lack of crime on *this* estate and the slight rise in crime in the surrounding areas directly correlates with the time you moved in. Coupled with the fact you seem to have the ear of the local youths and...'

'And what?'

'Some might say that's a bit of a coincidence...'

Jefferson shuffled on the sofa and, for a moment, Jessica felt sure he was going to launch himself upwards towards her. His forearms flexed, but then he relaxed back further onto the sofa, pearly whites on show again. 'You sound like an intelligent person,' he said.

'Not according to my old school reports.'

'Have you heard of correlation coincidences?'

Jessica shook her head.

'Fascinating things,' Jefferson added. 'For instance, do you know the best way to stop global warming?'

Jessica stared at him, wondering whether to play along. 'Go on,' she replied.

'Become a pirate.'

Jefferson burst out laughing, an emotion shared by neither of the officers. Pete was too preoccupied in keeping an eye on the snakes.

'It's true,' Jefferson added. 'Back in the early 1800s, the average global temperature was about fourteen degrees. At the time, there were around thirty thousand pirates. That was all they did, sail across the oceans and rob other ships. Two hundred years on, there are almost no pirates, but the average global temperature is about sixteen degrees. That's fact. So it must be true that, if we want to fight global warming, we need more pirates on the ocean.' He finished with a theatrical 'arrrr'.

Jessica folded her arms.

'Not impressed?' Jefferson continued. 'How about this: what internet browser do you use?'

'What has this got to do with anything?'

'If you use Internet Explorer, you're raising the murder rate. In 2006, Microsoft had an eighty per cent market share with Internet Explorer and the number of people murdered in America was about 17,000 people a year. By 2012, Internet Explorer's market share was around thirty-five per cent and the murder rate had dropped to 14,000. There's a direct correlation – Internet Explorer causes murder.'

'That doesn't prove anything.'

Jefferson snapped his fingers, finishing by pointing at Jessica. 'Ah, so there we go. You said it yourself – these correlations don't prove anything.'

Jessica wanted to come up with a smart reply, but it was hard to argue. She had no idea if his statistics were correct but was hardly in a position to question them. He continued smiling, knowing he was steps ahead.

'You've got it all wrong,' he said. 'I'm a normal bloke enjoying the surroundings.'

'I don't know many fully-grown men who spend their time hanging around with teenagers.'

'Who says I spend time hanging around with teenagers?'

Jessica looked crookedly at him. There was little else she could do that didn't make it sound like she'd been staking out the flat. 'Why did you move from Leeds?' she asked.

'Change of scenery.'

'You seem to be fitting in well.'

'What can I say? I'm a people person.'

Before Jessica could say anything else, there was a knock at the door. Jefferson shot up from the sofa and peered through the crack in the curtains. His discomfort disappeared as quickly as it had arrived, a momentary slip, but he winced. He was soon smiling again as he turned back to Jessica.

'You'll have to excuse me,' he said, ushering both her and Pete towards the door. When he opened it, there was a teenager on the other side, his bike dumped on the path behind.

The youngster took a step forward: 'Bizzies all over, they —' He looked up, noticing Jessica and Pete, before jumping back quickly. 'Oh,' he muttered.

Jessica peered from Jefferson to the newcomer, missing whatever look she felt sure had passed between them. 'Problem?' she asked.

The teenager stared at Jefferson, not replying as he continued to back towards his bike.

'Nice meeting you,' Jefferson said, offering his hand for Jessica and then Pete to shake.

'Let me leave you a card,' Jessica replied, digging into her pocket. 'I'm sure you've seen the flyers. This is all part of a new community engagement project. If there's anything you'd ever like to talk about, you know where we are.'

NINETEEN

Jessica and Pete walked quickly away from the flat, not looking back. It felt to Jessica as if they were being watched the entire way across the quadrant. Unseen eyes from above and behind, spying on their every step. They only stopped at an empty bus stop after passing the row of shops. Jessica rested on a broken bench and Pete followed, leaning on the side until it creaked ominously, as if the entire structure was going to come crashing down. The frame had recently been painted, but that couldn't hide the outline of the scratched graffiti underneath.

'I think you just kicked a hornets' nest,' Pete said. He seemed nervous, shuffling from side to side. Jessica also noticed that his tan was already fading, despite being home from his holiday for barely a few days. The Manchester curse. He towered over her, but it felt like she was looking down upon him.

'I prefer *stroked* a hornets' nest,' Jessica replied.

'That's worse.'

'How is that worse?'

'At least if you kick something, you can run for it. If you're stroking it, you're right in the middle of the action.'

Jessica nodded. 'Good point.'

Pete shuddered, a full-on head-to-toe tremble. 'Those snakes...'

'Not your thing?'

'Gives me the creeps. Why would you keep something like that in your house? Like those nutters who have tarantulas. I'd lock 'em up.'

'The snakes or the owners?'

'Both – chuck in the tarantulas for good measure.'

Jessica went quiet as a bus started to slow. She shook her head and the driver gave a thumbs up, before speeding away.

'It felt like he'd been waiting for us to come knocking,' Pete said.

'Perhaps not *us*, but yes. All that bollocks about pirates. I got the sense...' She tailed off, unsure how to put it into words.

'I got it, too,' Pete said. 'Not just that he knew we'd be coming – but that he knew why and what we'd ask about. That we wouldn't be there with battering rams and a warrant – that it'd be softly-softly, like we wanted his help.'

Jessica waved away a second bus, deciding that it wasn't the best of places to hold an impromptu police briefing.

They were sauntering back towards the shops when a pair of uniformed officers emerged from around the corner. There was a taller man with a much shorter woman. She was slim, he was big, as if they'd been paired together for maximum comedy value.

The female nodded towards Pete and they went through the muffled series of 'all rights' that counted for introductions.

'Found much?' Pete asked.

The female officer answered: 'Not even a stolen pack of gum. What is it with kids today? If we'd done this a few years ago, there'd be nicked CDs, some knock-off movies, the odd porno, someone would have a flick knife. Bloody hell, what are they teaching them in school nowadays?'

In the distance behind the uniformed officers, Jessica spied a couple of lads on bikes zipping onto the quadrant. They were standing tall on their bikes, the saddles low as they pedalled furiously. The teenager from outside Jefferson's was nowhere in sight.

'Have you checked the kids on bikes?' Jessica asked.

'We've pulled over all sorts, but it's like we've been searching a bunch of nuns. We'd have found more stolen goods if we raided the desks at the station.'

That was a given – no officers dared bring personal items into work because, if it wasn't nailed down, it would disappear quicker than a superintendent at the Christmas party when it was his round.

The four officers looked to one another, none of them quite sure what to say. Were they finding nothing because there was nothing to find – or because the collective crime community who lived on the Lees Estate were too smart for them?

As Jessica was about to suggest it was time to go, a woman strode up to them, pushchair out in front like a snowplough. She coughed loudly and the officers parted, allowing her to continue along the pavement, even though there had been plenty of room to go around.

'You done yet?' she hissed.

'Sorry?' Jessica replied.

The woman paused when she was level with Jessica. 'You lot hanging around all day, pissing everyone off? Always the bloody same.' She wagged a finger in Jessica's direction. 'You fitted anyone up yet? Planted drugs, or whatever? That's what you do, ain't it?'

'I don't think anyone's looking for trouble,' Jessica said.

'Yeah, yeah. I've seen it all before. *Heard* it all. You don't know what you're messing with.'

It didn't sound like a threat, but the choice of words was odd. 'What *are* we messing with?' Jessica asked.

The woman huffed noisily. 'People won't stand for this,' she said. 'We don't go shitting on our own doorsteps round 'ere.' With another loud exhalation, she shunted the pushchair forward and stomped off along the road. Jessica hadn't even noticed if there was a child in the seat.

The female officer watched her go and then nudged the other uniformed officer with her elbow. 'With a welcoming manner like that, she should answer our phones.'

Jessica stared after the woman, wondering if they – if *she* – had gone too far. It wasn't like they'd called in a host of warrants to batter down doors – but stop-and-searches could be murky ground. It was far from the first time police had swarmed an area to stop suspicious-looking locals in the hope of finding drugs, stolen goods, or something else that'd look good in court – but the Lees Estate had been quiet for months.

She wondered why she'd instigated it. Roly was part of it, especially considering the brick put through his window. Someone wanted to shut him up, even if he didn't know what he was supposed to be keeping quiet about. Then there was the mystery of Jefferson appearing on the estate from nowhere and having the power to slap a teenager across the face without retribution. Even without the near instantaneous drop-off in crime on the estate, things felt wrong. And wasn't it odd that the stop-and-searches had come up with nothing? She hadn't expected a few kilos of heroin to be knocking around in someone's coat pocket but a kid with a nicked phone was almost guaranteed.

As Jessica gazed into nothingness, she realised she was definitely being watched this time. A pair of lads were sitting on their bikes outside the newsagent, passing a cigarette between them. Each had a phone in their hands, but one of them was staring directly at her. She recognised Thomas Adlington from the photo she'd snapped outside Jefferson's flat. He was the youngster who'd been slapped.

Jessica muttered 'excuse me' to her colleagues and then edged between them, heading to the newsagent. She expected the boys to scarper, but one didn't notice her as his thumb flashed across his phone screen, the cigarette dangling from the corner of his mouth. The other – Thomas – looked down quickly at his own phone as she approached.

'Shouldn't you two be at college, or something like that?' Jessica asked.

They both looked up together. 'Oh, give over,' the second lad said. 'Your lot have already turned us over once.'

'Turned you over?'

Thomas's friend was short and stumpy with ginger hair and freckles that were merging with his pockmarked acne scars. He was eighteen at the most, likely a year or so younger. 'Empty your pockets, show us your arse crack, all that,' he said. 'You've got a load of fags working for ya. I know my rights.'

Jessica peered between the two of them. 'Go on then,' she said.

That confused the gobby one. 'Go on, what?'

'What are your rights? Name one.'

He glanced towards Thomas, hauling his bike up straighter so that he was leaning over the handlebars. 'Um... Wi-Fi...?'

'You think that generations fought at an unimaginable cost of life, all for the unarguable and irrefutable purpose of allowing you access to the Internet without a cable?'

She was pretty sure she lost him at the word 'unimaginable'.

Big-mouth glanced down at his phone and then told her to 'do one', before bolting along the pavement on his bike. Thomas was left standing by himself, one foot on the pedals of his own bike when Jessica gripped the handlebars.

She nodded at the reddened bruise that cupped the top of his cheekbones. 'Where'd you get that?' Jessica asked.

Thomas scowled back, his eye ever so slightly closed from the swollen skin. 'None of your bizness.'

He pressed down on the pedals, shooting forward, though Jessica held tight to the handlebars. He could either run her over, or stop.

He stopped, scowling defiantly.

'If something's going on around here, you can talk to someone,' she said. 'Doesn't have to be me, doesn't have to be in person. I can give you a number. No one will know it was you.'

Thomas was an inch or two taller than her and stared down, unblinking. 'Piss off, yeah?'

He jolted forward and this time Jessica had no option other than to let go of his handlebars. A quick blur of legs later and he was off on the pavement as well.

Jessica headed back towards Pete, who was standing by himself, the uniformed officers having sodded off to find lunch, peace, spiritual enlightenment, or whatever else.

'Do 'em for riding on the pavement?' Pete asked, not really meaning it.

Jessica cocked her head, wanting to smile but not feeling particularly jovial. Off to the side, not far from the bus stop, stood Jefferson Cass. She wondered how long he'd been watching, or if he'd somehow materialised out of nowhere. He saluted them casually using a single finger to his temple – and then spun on his heels, striding away down the road.

TWENTY

Jessica was on her way towards the station when the traffic started to back up. It wasn't uncommon for Manchester's central roads to be crammed full of vehicles stop-starting their way to oblivion – but for early afternoon on a Tuesday, it felt unusual. Jessica eased into one of the inside lanes and waited, watching the other drivers around her. As the traffic moved forward a few car lengths every minute or so, there was the usual mix of those switching lanes for no particular reason, realising they were going nowhere fast and then silently fuming. Others were darting for the side streets, skipping onto the wrong side of the road for a short period, no doubt to emerge on a parallel route that was equally rammed.

If ever there was a true test of the nature of man, it was how an individual reacted to traffic jams. Either that, or a slow internet connection.

The traffic lights on the corner close to Manchester Arena were in Jessica's sights when her phone started to ring. She reached for it instinctively, pressing answer, speakerphone, and then dropping it into her lap in one go.

'I'm stuck in traffic,' she said.

Rowlands' voice fizzed in and out. What with 3G, 4G, 5G, or however many Gs the phone networks happened to use, none of them could seemingly come up with a situation in which two people could have a phone conversation with any degree of clarity.

'Where are you?' he asked.

'In traffic.'

'Yeah, but where?'

'Somewhere near Victoria. Has there been an accident in the centre? I bet it's a lorry, isn't it? It's always a lorry. Or a taxi.'

'Not quite...' Rowlands sounded hesitant.

'What?' Jessica asked.

'A woman's jumped from the top of the NCP near Whitworth Street. Proper pavement pizza stuff.'

'Christ's sake, Dave.'

There was a small pause. 'Sorry...'

Another moment of silence – and Jessica realised why he'd called her. It wasn't a friendly neighbourhood traffic update.

'Where's Francine?' Jessica asked.

'Released a bit before lunch. Time was up and we couldn't hold her any longer. I thought you knew?'

Jessica told him that she did. That didn't make it any better though. 'How long ago did this woman fall?'

'The call came in about half-hour ago.'

'You said "jumped".'

'Sorry?'

'You said she jumped from the car park. Did someone see her?'

'I don't know, Jess.'

Jessica thanked him for the call and hung up. The traffic lights in the distance were green, but nobody was moving anyway. Whitworth Street was perhaps fifteen minutes on a good day due to the myriad of one-way streets – in this traffic, it'd be triple that. On foot, it wouldn't take much longer. Jessica dumped the car in the nearest side street and then started striding towards the city centre.

As she crossed the junction by the Arena, Jessica could see backed-up traffic in all directions. Horns were honking, engines idling. No one was moving.

She hurried over the railway lines at the side of the Arena, passing The Printworks and National Football Museum, then darting underneath the elevated tunnel that linked Selfridges to the Arndale Centre.

Shoppers were continuing about their business, oblivious to whatever had gone on across the city. The traffic was unmoving wherever she went.

Market Street was heaving with shoppers bumbling from the shopping centre to the rest of town, bags overflowing with Easter Eggs. Piccadilly Gardens was even worse, crammed with a host of pop-up market stalls and creaking trams. Jessica was never quite sure when the schools and colleges broke up for various national holidays – but it was a pretty good bet they were done for a couple of weeks, given the number of young people hanging around. A group of goths were gathered on a corner close to the green, heads bobbing in conformist unity as they shared a set of headphones. Not far from them, a group with placards was banging on about some war, or politicians in general. Jessica was never quite sure. There was always something to protest. The clash of cultures, colours and sounds gave the square a carnival feel. There was even a set of monks in orange close to Burger King handing out flyers.

Manchester in all its glory. There was a place for everyone.

Except Liverpool fans, of course.

Jessica cut through along Sackville Street, but as soon as she reached Whitworth Street, it was clear to anyone that something had happened. Police tape stretched across the junction with Princess Street, with a single officer standing in the centre of the road, feverishly waving drivers in the opposite direction. Small huddles of people were gathering on the pavements on either side of the road, pointing, gaping and speculating towards the scene beyond. Some were on their phones, either taking photos or searching social media for a clue about what might have happened.

A second officer crossed towards them, waving in the general direction from which Jessica had come, muttering something about there being nothing to see. Well, except for the three ambulances, four police cars and general gathering of emergency services a little further along the road.

The uniformed constable in the middle of the road turned away from the traffic as Jessica approached, giving her the standard 'move along' nod and point that was days one and two of training. Verbal commands were day three. She showed him her card and he examined it, apologising and lifting the tape for her to pass under.

Pizza.

Rowlands and his idiotic joke had Jessica thinking of the horrors ahead as she passed between a pair of ambulances, emerging close to the entrance of the car park, where the bright white sheet on the corner of the road beamed out as brightly as a lighthouse in the night.

That was all there was.

Officers and paramedics were standing in a semicircle a little away from the scene, apparently not entirely sure what came next. If no one was attending whatever was under the sheet, then that could only mean one thing...

Jessica caught the eye of the crime scene manager, an officer she recognised from the Bootle Street Station. He was older than her, attractive in a winding-down-to-retirement way, talking to one of the paramedics. Both had the wide-eyed looks of people who'd seen something they'd rather forget.

'Do you know who's under the sheet?' Jessica asked.

The officer looked from her to the sheet and then turned away. 'A woman, probably young. ID might take some time.'

'Not pretty?'

He shook his head. 'You could say that.'

'What happened?'

The man puffed out a long breath and then nodded towards the cordon with Oxford Road. 'I'm not sure. Sounds like we had a jumper. A few witnesses hung around.' His eyes darted upwards, Jessica's following. The top of the building looked a long way up.

'Can I see the body?' she asked.

He raised an eyebrow. '"Body" is probably pushing it. I wouldn't recommend that anyway – there's not a lot to see. Nothing much identifiable.'

Jessica tried to remember what Emily had told her back at the hostel. Lucy had survived being thrown down the stairs a couple of times, and now, not long after she'd gone missing, a woman had died in a fall that was even higher. Proof of nothing, and yet...

'Was she wearing a bracelet?' Jessica asked.

The officer glanced towards the sheet once more. 'I'm not sure you'd be able to tell.'

The paramedic was standing nearby, listening. 'Some sort of friendship thing?' she asked.

Jessica turned and nodded. 'Black, green and yellow?'

The paramedic sighed. 'My daughter's always making them with her friends. I was the same at that age.'

The crime scene manager's frown lines had deepened. 'What have I missed?' he asked.

'I think I know who your body is,' Jessica replied.

TWENTY-ONE

The junction of Whitworth Street and Oxford Road next to the train station was usually one of the busiest in Manchester – but not for the moment. Police tape stretched across from the Palace Theatre to the hotel and three uniformed officers were moving along anyone who stopped to gawk between the police cars.

Completely out of place compared to everything else that was occurring was a woman sitting in a deckchair in the corner entranceway to the hotel. She was sipping a cup of tea, saucer on her lap, three shopping bags at her feet, contents spilling onto the floor. She was bundled up in a bonnet and jacket, even though it wasn't particularly cold or wet. Still, she was probably a local – a person could never be too careful when stepping into the Manchester weather. Sunshine one minute, hurricane the next. Jessica had no idea where the tea had come from, let alone the deckchair. The woman said her name was Mary – and that she'd seen everything.

'I can't believe it,' she said for the third time as Jessica crouched nearby.

'Where were you?' Jessica asked.

Mary nodded through the entranceway onto the street. 'On the other side of the road. I was by the bus stop about to cross over when I, well... I don't know. You don't normally look up, do you?'

She looked to Jessica, expecting an answer. Jessica offered an assuring nod.

'I just had this urge,' Mary added. 'Like something deep down inside. Do you ever get that when you feel like you're being watched? Or you get the shivers when it's not cold. My old mum said it was someone walking on your grave. I never quite got that.'

Jessica continued nodding, not quite sure what to add.

'Anyway, I had this feeling that I should look up, so I did. Maybe I heard a noise, or something?'

'Did you actually hear a noise?'

Mary stopped to sip her tea and scratch her chin. She fought back a yawn for good measure, looking drained, stunned – which wasn't a surprise, if the finality of Lucy's demise was as bad as the crime scene manager had indicated.

'I don't know... maybe. I don't know why else I would've looked up. I don't remember.' She clicked her fingers. 'It was like that.'

'What did you see?'

'A woman. Blonde, long hair.' Mary pointed upwards. 'There are four or five levels of the car park with these rails across the front. I walk down here a few times a week, but I've never noticed them before. Never look up, I suppose. I thought it was strange.'

'What was strange?'

'Just that she was there...' Mary paused. 'Actually, it was stranger that I noticed. I wondered if people were often up there looking down and it was only now I'd noticed someone. People down here were carrying on as normal, crossing the road, driving and all that. There was just this moment where I looked up and it felt like she was staring at me.'

'Did she say anything?'

Mary shook her head. 'I don't know. Doubt I'd have heard if she did.'

'Was there anyone up there with her?'

The woman stared at Jessica for the first time properly, blinking and then turning away once more. 'I don't think so.'

'What happened then?'

Mary gulped down a final mouthful of tea before replacing the empty cup on the saucer. Jessica took it from her and laid it on the tiled floor. Mary shook her head. 'One minute she was up there and then...'

Jessica waited, but there was no elaboration. The whites of Mary's eyes blazed wide and bright. 'I know it's hard, but I really need you to tell me what you saw,' Jessica said.

'She jumped,' Mary said.

'Over the barrier?'

A nod. 'I think I blinked. One minute she was standing behind the barrier, the next she was over it. There was this sort of whistle and it was like slow motion. I remember her falling, looking at the pavement and thinking someone should catch her. There was no one there, though – and then I thought that she was going to hit the ground. After that, well...'

Mary held her hands wide, which summed it up.

After making sure there was an officer to sit with Mary, Jessica headed back onto the street. It was eerily quiet with traffic diverted away from the scene and pedestrians avoiding the area. Another police car had joined the other four – but it was a little late for that. Jessica crossed the cordon and followed the pavement until she was level with where a series of screens had been erected to block the view of any morbid passers-by. She found the bus stop where Mary had been waiting to cross the road and peered up at the car park. It was housed in a clean, red-brick building, with a central pillar that had three large NCP letters pinned to the side. One half had four rows of balconies climbing upwards, the other three. Each row would be a parking level, with the highest of the seven directly above the police screens.

Jessica stepped backwards away from the bus stop, giving herself the widest angle possible to see from where Lucy had fallen – but she knew it was too steep for anyone to know for certain that Lucy was by herself. She might have been – but equally there could have been someone – perhaps more than one person – standing behind her, concealed by the angle. Someone would already be collecting CCTV from the car park – but it would never be that simple. There would be fire escapes and black spots in the coverage. If someone wanted to get in and out unseen, they would be able.

Jessica sat on the bench underneath the bus stop and called Topper.

'Tell me the jumper isn't someone we know,' he said, not bothering with a traditional hello.

Jessica told him about the pair of bracelets Emily and Lucy apparently shared. About the blonde hair. 'It might be a coincidence but, well...'

'What's it like over there?'

'I didn't look myself – but it doesn't sound good. One of the witnesses says she blinked and then the woman was falling. She didn't see her jump and didn't see anyone else on the scene.'

'Could just be a jumper...?'

'Could be...' Jessica didn't have to say much to make it clear she didn't believe that for a moment. 'Have we got someone trailing Francine?' she asked.

'Give me a minute and I'll get you a location.'

The line went quiet as Jessica watched a small white van edge towards the scene. She didn't know who'd be inside but it would be some sort of clean-up crew. Within a couple of hours, it would be as if nothing had happened. She pressed against the glass behind and closed her eyes, listening to the distant sounds of the city. Manchester was as quiet as she could remember.

Jessica only knew what Lucy looked like because of Emily's description, but she tried to picture the young, blonde woman standing against the railings high above. Could Francine have been behind her, somehow forcing her to jump? Or someone else?

Assuming it was Lucy who had fallen, the pattern was becoming distressingly clear. Henry Taylor killed by a car; Mark Stanley drowned – and now Lucy dead from a fall, after previously surviving plummeting down the stairs at the hands of her ex-boyfriend. The boyfriend was still very much behind bars, which at least ruled him out.

Until the body was officially identified – which might take a day or two – there would be no full-on investigation into what had happened. That gave Jessica and her team a little time to crack on before the media got involved. Francine had been released – but that didn't mean Topper couldn't authorise someone to trail her.

Jessica jumped as Topper's voice fizzed from her phone. 'Francine's on Deansgate,' he said. 'She headed straight there after being released. She's been handing out her flyers by the pub as before.'

'Was she there when Lucy fell from the car park?'

'Apparently.'

Which meant this was another incident for which Francine had an alibi.

'Where's our bloke?' Jessica asked.

'Café across from The Moon Under Water. He reckons he's dying for a wee.'

'Pfft – he needs to get creative if he's going to get by in this business.'

'Fine, but we're busy enough as it is without one of my constables bursting.'

It took Jessica ten minutes to get from Whitworth Street to Deansgate. The roads were still backed up, though it was an hour since Lucy had fallen from the car park and the message was beginning to get around that the city centre was best avoided.

Jessica found the constable sitting in the window of the café directly across the road from The Moon Under Water. He recognised Jessica, bolting to his feet, his knees angled in.

'Thank God you're here,' he said. Before Jessica could reply, he was half wobbling, half running towards the back of the café.

Jessica took his seat, rearranging the three empty coffee cups and peering across the road towards the pub. She shielded her eyes from the glare, hunting across the distant faces of those sitting outside. Some were eating, others simply enjoying an afternoon pint.

There was no sign of Francine.

The constable took a few minutes to return from emptying his bladder. He was still drying his hands on his trousers as he slipped in across from Jessica. When he offered his hand for her to shake, she raised an eyebrow and he sheepishly withdrew it with an apology.

'Where's Francine?' she asked.

'She went into the pub a couple of minutes before you got here.'

Jessica squinted across the road once more. There was still no sign of Francine. 'How long was she outside?'

'She walked here from the station. I guess the flyers were

among her possessions when we nicked her because she was handing them out to people she passed and then she set up shop here.'

'Have you been watching her the whole time?'

'First time she left my sight was when she went into the pub.'

Jessica checked the clock above the counter. 'She was definitely here an hour ago?'

'One hundred per cent.'

After needlessly checking the time once more, Jessica and the constable sat in silence watching the pub. Two minutes passed and Francine hadn't re-emerged. Three minutes. When five minutes had gone, Jessica couldn't wait any longer.

She crossed the road, passing under The Moon Under Water's awning and heading inside. There were high stools and tables on both sides and a small carpeted staircase heading into the main part of the pub. Inoffensive pop music tinkled in the background, largely drowned out by the chatter. Jessica felt something icky clinging to the bottom of her shoe as she continued ahead to where there were many more tables and people. Given the day and time, even Jessica was surprised by how packed it was. There were people of all ages and ethnicities piled around the tables and the air smelt of chips. Cheap chips at that.

Jessica moved slowly through the crowd, checking the faces. Francine didn't seem the type to sit around chomping down a burger – but it was hard to see where else she might have gone. Constable Need A Wee might have bladder issues but he had at least had the willpower to keep an eye on where Francine had gone.

Illuminated signs led the way to the women's toilets, but, after entering, Jessica immediately wished she could be somewhere else. The smell was somewhere between bitter lemon and roasted dog poo, more of a solid than a gas. She poked her head back outside and took a breath of fresher air before heading back into hell.

The first toilet stall was out of order, the rest unoccupied. Jessica nudged the doors just in case, but there was nobody hiding.

Back in the main part of the pub, Jessica walked around the tables until she was certain Francine wasn't inside. She was about to head across to the café again when one of the servers, a young woman, asked if she was all right. Jessica flashed her warrant card discreetly and said she was looking for someone. She started to describe Francine as the server nodded along. Francine was a familiar face.

'Have you tried the toilets?' the server asked. 'She comes in and uses them most days. It's supposed to be for customers only, but the manager said to let it go because it'll only cause an argument.'

'She's not in there,' Jessica said.

The server shrugged.

'Have you ever seen her with a man?' Jessica asked, fishing around her pockets for the composite image of Ezra. 'He's tall, apparently. Six foot something stupid.'

The server narrowed her eyes, looking at the image of Ezra and then nodded. 'Ages ago.'

'Not recently?'

'I try to ignore her when she's outside. Or inside for that matter.'

'Probably sensible.'

Jessica thanked the server for her time and then headed back to the toilets. The stalls were still empty – but there was a window at the back that was unlatched. Jessica pushed herself up using the radiator pipes, levering the window open and staring out onto the empty back alley.

If Francine had been inside, she was long gone now.

TWENTY-TWO

WEDNESDAY

Jessica had never quite got around to silencing her phone while she slept. Over the years, the various ringtones had been an intermittent alarm as someone requested her presence in the early hours.

A strange sense of awareness gripped her as she rolled over and answered her phone. The clock read five minutes past four, which was too early by anyone's standards. Even milkmen would still be having a kip at this hour, assuming they still existed.

'Is that Inspector Daniel?' Roly's voice asked as Jessica answered.

'What's wrong?' Jessica asked.

And then he told her.

The Lees Estate felt as quiet as ever under the glare of daylight. There was no sign of kids on bikes or militant mums with pushchairs as Jessica and Pete stood on the walkway outside Roly's flat. The glazier was using some sort of cutting tool to remove the remaining glass from the window next to the door. He turned to Jessica as he lowered an angled slice of glass onto the ground.

'Your mate must've pissed someone off,' he said.

Jessica gave a thin-lipped smile of acknowledgement as he held open the front door for her and Pete. They headed along the hallway, stepping over a scorch mark that was etched into the carpet, then moved into the kitchen and poked their heads into the living room. The television was still on the small display cabinet, Roly's row of vinyl records untouched. Nothing smashed, nothing apparently stolen.

'He was outside when he called me,' Jessica said quietly.

'What time?'

'Four. He was sleeping when someone put his windows through. He got into the hall and then there was a bang. I think someone threw a firework inside.'

'Little shites.'

'He reckoned it was safer outside than in. Called me from the alley next to the bookies. I picked him up and he's in my spare room. Argued about it the whole way over – didn't want to be a burden and all that – but he was out like a light within five minutes of getting his head down.'

They headed back to the kitchen and rested against the countertops. In the corner, Roly's heater burred and rattled like an ancient fridge. The exit hose was still draped through the small corner in the window.

'Is he...?' Pete started.

'He won't report it and I didn't want to argue with him,' Jessica said. 'I'll get the fingerprint lot down here later, but I'm not expecting much. He seems happy to talk to me, but won't make any official statements. He's scared, and I don't blame him.'

'Shall we knock downstairs? Even to ask if Jefferson heard anything?'

Jessica shook her head. 'I've got another idea.'

. . .

After leaving the Lees Estate, Jessica called Roly to ensure he was making himself at home in her spare room. He was more concerned about imposing himself, insisting he'd be out of her way by lunchtime – even though Jessica said she was at work anyway. Following that, it was back to business.

Francine hadn't been seen at the hostel, or anywhere else, but Rowlands had compiled a list of the churches in and around central Manchester. They went from place to place, small hall to Gothic palace, showing photos of Francine to vicars and parishioners, each time getting an all too familiar shake of the head.

They'd been trying for two and a half hours when Rowlands pulled up outside St Benedict's, a few streets over from the hospital. It was modern, yet somehow dated at the same time. The red-brick spire and bell tower were in perfect keeping with the surrounding area, but it felt like it belonged to another time, as if the design was fine but whomever had built it had used the wrong bricks.

No matter how many she met, Jessica always had a picture of vicars being old and greying – but the priest of St Benedict's couldn't have been much older than mid-forties. He had dark hair with a matching beard and was wearing jeans with his more traditional white collar. More of a wannabe hippy than a man of God. When Jessica and Rowlands pulled into the empty car park, he was busy rewriting the times of service board at the front of the church. Jessica had expected the usual 'sorry, can't help you', but he told Jessica to call him Matthew as he nodded along when Rowlands showed him the photo of Francine.

'I'm almost certain she was here at Christmas,' the vicar said. He waved across to a woman who'd been repotting some flowers a few steps away and introduced his wife, Victoria. She was wearing a flowing summer dress with specks of soil dotted along the front. She had slightly reddened apple cheeks, her reddy-blonde hair in a bun, about as English as it came. Victoria looked at the photo and agreed with her husband.

'Wasn't she the one who—' She didn't finish the sentence because Matthew jumped in.

'We don't turn people away here, but she was very vocal during the Christmas sermons,' he said.

'How do you mean?' Jessica asked.

Matthew turned towards the church and beckoned them inside.

Jessica and Rowlands followed the vicar and his wife along the central aisle until they reached the pew at the front. There was a large cross and altar on a raised dais, fairly standard stuff, Jessica reckoned. Quite churchy.

Matthew sat on the steps in front, next to his wife, inviting Jessica and Rowlands to sit on the pews so that they were facing each other.

'She sat right at the front,' he said. 'Where you are now. At Christmas, we get a lot of new faces, people who only come once a year. That's fine, obviously – it's always like that – but it means I try to give a different type of sermon. Something a little friendlier to those who aren't used to hearing from the Bible. I was talking about the traditional nativity and how certain things could be metaphors. That the stable everyone knows about wasn't necessarily a stable. How the star that was followed by the wise men might not have guided them in the way people traditionally believe.' He glanced to his wife, smiling. 'I think I even mentioned *EastEnders* at one point. It just sort of... popped out. It was going all right – but then the woman in your photo jumped up and screamed that I was telling lies to everyone. That I was a false prophet.' He forced a laugh. 'You expect a bit of heckling if you're on at the Comedy Store, but not when you're giving a Christmas sermon. I asked her to calm down, but she was screaming and shouting, then she ran out the back, saying I was going to hell and taking everyone else with me.'

'She pretty much said the same to me,' Jessica replied.

Matthew smiled thinly, though he didn't dispel the idea that Jessica might well be on the way to underworld. 'It's fair to say some parishioners prefer the more traditional Old Testament fire-and-brimstone sermons,' he added.

'Was that the first time you'd seen her?' Jessica asked.

'As far as I know.' Matthew turned to his wife, who flattened the front of her skirt against her knees.

'Our doors are always open,' she said. 'We get the odd lost soul, but I don't remember seeing her before... or since.'

'That was my next question,' Jessica said.

The couple turned to each other, each offering a small shrug at the same time and then laughing softly about it.

'We've not seen her since,' Matthew confirmed.

Jessica turned to Rowlands, who produced the picture of Ezra from a cardboard wallet. He handed it to her, but she didn't turn it over.

'Was Francine with anyone?' Jessica asked.

'No,' Victoria replied.

The vicar turned to her, frowning slightly. 'I thought...'

'What?' his wife asked.

'Aside from the heckling, that's the biggest reason I remember her. There was this tall man next to her. I assumed they'd arrived together.'

Jessica flipped around the photo and held it up, asking if that was the person with whom Francine had been sitting.

Matthew nodded slowly. 'I think so. He might have had a shave when I saw him. He was massive. Six foot something.'

Jessica handed the photo back to Rowlands, who filed it away. By height alone, Matthew had just described Ezra.

Neither of them had ever seen him, yet it felt like he was consistently in the background.

'Did he say anything when Francine stormed off during your sermon?' Jessica asked.

Matthew shook his head. 'I don't think he said anything at all.'

'Have you seen him since?'

'Only that one time.'

'I know this might be a silly question,' Jessica said, 'but do you have any idea where either of these two might be?'

Matthew shook his head. 'Sorry.'

TWENTY-THREE

The heater in Roly's flat might well have had health hazard written all over it – but Jessica had to admit it was warm. The blind in the kitchen was down, but there was a small hole that Roly must've cut, allowing the hose from the deathtrap heater to hang through the open window. There was probably a hole in the ozone layer directly above the block of flats.

Jessica was sitting at the kitchen table, fingers wrapped through the chipped handles of a mug of tea, listening to the silence from below. If Jefferson and his younger friends were out to cause havoc that evening, then it was all quiet for now.

'It's all gone to shite,' she said quietly.

Archie rocked back and forth on the chair opposite. He was wearing jeans and a dark top, his hair ungelled, not looking too much like the sharp-suited lad about town he so often appeared to be when he was on duty.

'Francine's missing,' Jessica continued, 'Mark and Henry's deaths are unsolved – and Lucy's probably dead too. We didn't get confirmation back yet.'

'This is what happens when I'm off,' he replied with a small smirk. 'Are you absolutely sure they're all linked?'

Jessica shook her head. 'Nope. The guv said as much earlier. He asked if we were making connections because we wanted to see them.'

'Are you?'

'Not on purpose. There *is* a connection from Francine to all the victims, especially given what she says on her flyers. It might be nonsense – but, if it is, we've not found out anything else. Lucy *might* have jumped from that car park, Mark *could* have drowned by accident – and Henry *might* have stepped out in front of you. When you take it all together, though, it doesn't feel right.'

Jessica realised Archie was staring down at the table. She shouldn't have mentioned the collision.

'You been busy?' she asked.

'Being paid to sit at home – that's the dream.'

'I thought the dream was Davey triplets who'd dominate the United midfield for a generation?'

Archie winked. 'Aye, that too. I'm surprised you remembered.'

'You bring it up at least twice a week.'

'True.'

There was a clunk from the flat below and they both went silent. Thirty seconds passed, a minute – then it was quiet.

'So, this Roly bloke's staying at your house...?' Archie said.

'Right.'

'He's definitely got the better end of this house swap. Aren't you worried he's going to trash the place while you're here?'

Jessica waited for a moment as the heater glugged noisily, before resorting to its more usual hum. 'I wasn't until you brought it up. He was busy watching a *Countdown* repeat when I left.'

'*Countdown* fans are the worst. They get overexcited when they get the conundrum, next thing you know they're rioting.

They're well known for it.' Archie grinned to himself, but when he realised Jessica wasn't rising to it, he slumped back into his seat. 'We going to do this all night?' he asked.

'You can go anytime you want. I only invited you over so you didn't spend all night sitting around watching Babestation.'

Archie nodded towards the living room. 'I bet you can get Babestation here. Channel nine-hundred and something.'

Jessica gave him the glare.

'So where is this Francine and Ezra?' Archie asked.

'If I knew that, I wouldn't have wasted a day going around churches asking questions. We found a few parishioners from Saint Benedict's who remembered seeing both of them at Christmas – but no one's seen them since. You'd think the general public might remember a great big black bloke hanging around a fiery old woman who bangs on about hell and death, but apparently not. We've spoken to a few more people at the hostel, but no one wants to talk to the police. No one admitted to knowing where either of them are – but a couple reckoned Ezra used to sit at the bottom of Francine's bed while she slept.'

'Sounds normal.'

Archie climbed up from the table, crossing to the sink and washing out his mug. He opened the cupboard above the heater and then worked his way around in a clockwise direction.

'Can't believe there's no biscuits in the place.'

'I'm guessing getting the biscuits in wasn't high on Roly's list of priorities when they put his windows through.'

A shrug. 'Have you ever known an old person who doesn't have a packet of fig rolls knocking around?'

'What are you on about?'

'Both of my nans were mental for them. They'd get a couple of those tins of Danish biscuits at Christmas too – then they'd be in the cupboard for months. They never ate any themselves, but every time I went round, they'd be shoving them down my throat. That wasn't so bad, but after they run out, it was always fig rolls. Disgusting bloody things – like someone vomited, froze it and then wrapped it in a biscuit. They should be banned.'

Jessica grimaced. 'I have no idea why I invited you over.'

Archie plopped himself back at the table, empty-handed. Jessica had wondered whether it was a good idea to invite him to sit in Roly's flat with her for the night – but it wasn't an official operation anyway. At some point, one of them would go to sleep on the sofa while the other waited up in case there was another attack. If they moved quickly enough, they'd be able to catch a perpetrator or two. The front door was on the catch and it would only take a few seconds to reach the balcony from the kitchen.

'How did you go with Vincent?' Jessica asked.

'He says my suspension has to remain until at least the end of the week. He kept saying I must've been speeding or distracted. Reckoned there were witnesses – but it takes a bull-shitter to know a bullshitter – and he was full of it.'

There was a loud, sharp screech from below – probably a chair being moved – and they both went silent and listened. Another minute or so passed and then Archie continued, quieter than before.

'If you're not officially here and I'm not officially allowed to work, then what are we doing?' He nodded towards the quadrant. 'It's not to admire the view.'

Jessica finished her tea and crossed to the sink, placing the mug inside. 'You really want to know?'

Archie shrugged in the non-committal way she expected.

'Roly reminds me of my dad,' Jessica said, not quite able to look at Archie. 'He's this proud old bloke who doesn't want to ask for help. He doesn't have any kids or grandkids to look after him and all he wants to do is live out his days quietly. Instead, he's got this lot making life hard for him.'

Pity.

That was the short version of why they were there.

'What are we going to do if we do catch someone?' Archie asked.

'I'll say I was visiting Roly and was on hand.'

'Even if something happens at four in the morning?'

'Stranger things have happened.'

Archie turned away, making it clear he didn't think there were that many stranger things that had gone on than a woman in her late-thirties hanging out with a pensioner at four in the morning. He was probably right – but they'd deal with that if and when they needed to.

Beyond that, Jessica knew it wasn't only about Roly – it was the mystery of whatever was going on around the estate. Crime never simply went away, no matter what they tried. She'd never known a stop-and-search campaign that had thrown up nothing. It was easy enough to turn a blind eye because the stats looked good, but that was the easy thing to do. The corporate thing.

Archie turned back to the table, catching Jessica's attention and nodding towards the floor. 'You spoken to him?'

'Jefferson? He didn't give much away. There's something about him I can't quite place. He's too cool, too calm. It felt like he knew exactly what I was going to ask.'

'You know what's good for cocky so-and-sos like that? A good knee in the bollocks.'

Jessica rolled her eyes. 'Teach you that in training, did they?'

Archie winked at her. 'Learnt that back in primary school.'

Jessica didn't doubt it. He'd grown up in an area much like this and his speciality was the arm-round-the-shoulder, 'come on, mate, haven't you had enough?' technique. He'd calmed a fair few situations that Jessica doubted she'd have been able to control by herself.

He also had a darker side.

She remembered the field on the edge of the city and a man mercilessly beaten when he couldn't defend himself. He might have deserved it, but still...

'You must have a theory,' Archie said, disrupting Jessica's thought process. She'd been in that field, watching on in exhilarated horror.

When she blinked back into the room, she realised Archie was staring at her. The casual look suited him. Less puffed-up chest and tensed biceps, more normal bloke.

'I don't know what to think,' she said.

Archie grinned. 'C'mon, Jess. I might be cursed with dazzling youthful good looks but I wasn't born yesterday.'

She laughed, not meaning to. 'There was this angry woman the other day who said something about people round here not shitting on their own doorstep. I reckon Jefferson's got all the gangs on the estate doing jobs for him. The difference is, he makes sure everything they do happens away from here. They might rob or deal drugs – whatever it is they're into – but they police themselves to make sure it happens elsewhere. It's why the crime rate here is practically zero, yet it's marginally up everywhere that surrounds here. It's not enough to put a big hole in the crime stats, just the right amount so that no alarm bells are going off at HQ. Plus it means everyone who actually lives here has a happier, quieter life.'

'Except Roly.'

'Well, yes...'

'If that's all true, then why's Jefferson so special? I remember being a kid and if some old-timer had told me and my mates what to do, we'd have kicked off.'

Jessica shook her head. 'He must be offering something they can't get themselves.'

'Like what?'

That was a question she couldn't answer, not for sure. 'Money, I guess,' she said. 'If some old-timer had offered you a few quid a week to do jobs for him, you wouldn't have kicked off then, would you?'

'Guess not.' Archie sucked on his cheeks, making a loud clucking sound, like an asthmatic chicken. Jessica forgot all too easily how annoying he could be. Just when she thought she could do with a few minutes' peace, he continued talking. 'Why don't you just stop all the kids?' he asked.

'Good thinking, genius.' Jessica jabbed her forehead with her finger. 'Why didn't I think of that? Oh, wait – I did.'

'All right, Miss Sarky Pants.'

Archie was grinning, possibly because he'd got the reaction he managed so often. He knew how to press her buttons.

All of them.

'We didn't find anything,' Jessica said. 'Stopped all the kids on bikes – and anyone else who looked a bit shifty. Not so much as a stolen pen.'

'There must've been someone carrying around a joint or something?'

Jessica shook her head. 'Cleanest estate in the country.'

There was a bang from below – a door opening and closing, quickly followed by a second. Muffled voices drifted up through the floor, though the specific words were impossible to make out. Jessica stood slowly, careful not to scrape the chair on the floor, and then crept into the hallway. She eased open the front door and looked both ways along the balcony.

Nothing.

There was another scrape from below.

Archie edged past Jessica, pressing towards the barrier and then peeping over the top towards the darkened plaza. He turned and stepped backwards towards Jessica, out of sight from anyone below.

'There are a couple of bikes down there,' he whispered.

Jessica nodded and then pulled Roly's door closed behind her before stepping as quietly as she could along the balcony, following the path until she was at the stairwell. Although it was dark outside, a dim bulb clung to the wall above the stairs, casting a hazy glow around the enclosed space. There was no alternative, so Jessica moved as quickly as she could without making a noise, jogging down the stairwell until she was on the ground level, swallowed by the shadows, close to the heavy-looking door.

Archie pressed in at her side as they moved closer to the position where Jessica had seen Thomas being slapped by Jefferson a few evenings before. A handful of lights brimmed from the flats around the plaza, pinprick snapshots of life, but, for once, Jessica didn't feel watched.

She froze as a *creak-creak-creak* sounded from somewhere nearby. It was only a couple of seconds before its source became apparent. A silhouette on a bike materialised from the dark, skipping underneath a street light and then approaching Jefferson's door. Instead of dropping his bike, the youngster hopped off and then knocked gently. Moments later, the door swung open and he wheeled his bike inside.

Jessica and Archie stood in silence for a few moments as the door closed, sealing off the slim corridor of light that had spilled onto the concrete.

'That was weird,' Jessica whispered.

'Why?'

'Because Jefferson is some sort of clean freak. He doesn't seem the type to let people wheel their bikes in and out.'

Neither of them spoke for a few moments, each fixed to their spots inside the shadow.

'What do you want to do?' Archie asked. He was so close that his words tickled Jessica's ear. She shivered and he noticed, touching a hand to her hip.

She batted him away. 'I don't know.'

They stood in silence, looking towards Jefferson's door. Jessica was about to move further along the walkway to try to get a peek through his window when another soft squeaking cut through the night. Jessica felt Archie tense behind her, knew something was about to happen a moment before it did.

A second lad on a bike glided into view, his dark shadow sending long shapes across the path. He was heading for Jefferson's door – but Archie swooped, stepping out of the darkness and away from Jessica. He clamped a hand on the teenager's shoulder, making the lad jump and gasp.

'What the—'

'What's your name?' Archie asked sternly.

'Who are you?'

Archie reached into his pocket and Jessica knew the mistake he was going to make a moment before he did. He flashed the lad his wallet, quickly repocketing it before anyone could have a closer look. His warrant card would have been confiscated when he was suspended.

Archie told the boy it was an official stop-and-search and, for a moment, Jessica feared the worst. The lad stood up on his heels, showing off that he had a few inches on Archie. She thought they'd square up properly – but then the boy stepped away, arms out.

'I'm clean,' he said.

'What's your name?'

'Steven.'

'Steven what?'

'Carpenter.'

Archie should have a form ready to go that would accompany the search, but Jessica knew he didn't. She was glued to her spot in the shadows, hoping the lad had nothing on him. At least then he'd go on his way.

The teenager turned out his pockets voluntarily, listing

everything he was carrying. A phone, a wallet, headphones, an ID card that might or might not be dodgy... nothing out of the ordinary.

Jessica breathed.

'C'mon, pal – you think I was born yesterday?' Archie was sneering, chest puffed out like a preening peacock.

The lad bobbed on his heels, standing even taller. 'What? You've already checked me once. You gonna try up my arse or something?'

'You wish.'

Jessica sighed silently, willing Archie to shut his mouth and step away.

'C'mon, big man,' the lad taunted. 'What you gonna do now? You know I'm clean.'

Archie glared at the youngster, fists clenched. Jessica knew he wouldn't hit the kid. Well, she was pretty sure.

Out of nowhere, Archie lunged forward unexpectedly. Not grabbing Steven, instead reaching for his bike.

'Hey, whatcha—'

'Shush,' Archie hissed, surprisingly polite.

The lad was quiet as Archie ran his hands across the handlebars and then the bottle holders. It was hard to tell for sure because of the light – but it looked like a mountain bike, heavy and cheap. A Halford's special. He pressed the tyres hard and then spun the front one, making it creak.

'You should get that to a bike shop,' Archie said. The boy didn't respond.

As Archie's shoulders dipped, Jessica could almost see him thinking. Hear the cogs turning. She knew him too well.

It took him both hands and a grunt, but Archie flipped the bicycle upside down, giving the whole machine a shake before returning it to the ground, right way up.

'Aye, aye...' he said, digging into his pockets and emerging with what looked like a penknife. 'Good job I carry a set of hex keys with me, isn't it?'

'You can't do that, man.' Steven was nervous, the air was tingling.

'You wanna bet?'

Archie fiddled with something at the base of the saddle and there was a soft squeak, then – in one swift movement – he popped the saddle and seat post off the bike and handed it to Steven.

'You all right there?' Archie asked, brash and smug. The teenager said nothing as the bike was tipped upside down once more so that the hollow seat tube was facing the ground.

Nothing happened.

Then there was a series of small, sliding plops, one after the other, five in all, each small bundle of rolled-up money slipping into the light.

'Wow,' Archie said, resting the bicycle on the ground and peering down at the haul. 'Now what would a kid like you be doing with so much money hidden in a bike frame?'

TWENTY-FOUR

In a flash, Steven had his phone in his hand, the bright white light illuminating his face from below. Jessica thought it'd be a bit late now to make a call for help or send a message to his mates. But Steven didn't try. Instead, he calmly tapped the screen, loading some sort of app.

Then all hell broke loose.

A shrill, searing howl burst from the device, wailing like a neurotic car alarm. Archie leapt towards Jessica, covering his ears, but she was crouching involuntarily, hands clamped to the side of her head in an attempt to block the sound. It was so loud, so bone-rattling, that it felt like she'd gone momentarily blind. Steven was a muddled blur as he scrambled on the ground to retrieve the money. Archie watched on uselessly, hunched at the waist. His lips were moving, but she could hear nothing other than the blazing roar of the phone.

It took Jessica a moment to realise that she'd moved. She was no longer hidden by the shadows, she was standing close to the street lamp a few steps from Archie. Steven was staring at them both, the bundles of money cupped in his hand.

As quickly as it had started, the noise stopped as he repocketed his phone – but it was too late.

Jefferson's front door was open and half a dozen lads had emerged. Steven had dropped his saddle back into the frame and started to pedal away, not needing to say anything because it was already clear what had happened. Other doors were opening, too, residents wondering what all the noise was about.

Or already knowing.

Jessica recognised Thomas among the group of youngsters – but he was the only one. More shadows emerged from the dark – not only from Jefferson's place but the surrounding apartments as well. A dozen lads. More.

Lots more.

Archie made the first movement: backwards, not forwards, stepping away from the street lamp towards the stairwell.

It wasn't just teenagers, there were adults – men and women. Big and small. A snapshot of the community surrounding them.

'You lot,' someone said. A woman, gruff and annoyed.

'Knew this would happen,' someone else added.

Archie continued moving towards the stairwell, Jessica at his side, but there was nowhere to go. They were trapped in the corner of the buildings, the only way out being up – except that only led to the next level of flats. Sooner or later, they'd have nowhere to go.

Jessica reached to her belt and unclipped the airwave radio. It was how the police communicated using their own frequency. Safe and secure, apparently.

And it had a shitstorm button.

That wasn't the official name, of course – but that was what many called it. If an officer was in the middle of a shit-storm, he or she could press the button and the silent call would go out. There were no flashing lights, no loud sirens, just a call to HQ letting whomever was on duty know that an officer was in trouble.

Something fizzed over Jessica's head, cannoning into the wall behind and exploding in a shower of something hard.

She jumped, edging closer to Archie, not that he could do much. Jessica was sure he'd jumped as well.

Jessica pressed the shitstorm button.

The crowd continued to move forward, not rushing but edging Jessica and Archie further into the corner.

Whump!

Something else smashed into the wall behind them, crumbling on impact. Jessica turned and squinted into the shadows, eyeing the pile of rubble just behind. It had been half a brick.

'Shite,' Archie muttered.

'Help's coming,' Jessica whispered.

'I don't think they'll be quick enough.'

Archie ducked as something zipped past where his head had been. Another brick. It smashed into the wall and crumbled.

'What now?' he said.

Jessica continued edging backwards, further and further, until they were at the mouth of the stairwell. Faces were concealed by the shadows beyond, but menace rippled through the night.

'*Always wanted to smash up a copper.*'

'*Dibs on the dibs.*'

'*Here piggy, piggy...*'

The only way to go was up – except there were footsteps echoing down the stone steps from above.

Nowhere to go.

Jessica turned from side to side, back against the brickwork, feet on top of a small mound of rubble. She fumbled along the wall, stepping sideways, hoping there might be a gap in the ring of people that was closing towards them. Archie followed her lead – except there was no opening, only someone sneering from the darkness.

'Backup is on the way,' Jessica announced as forcefully as she could. Her voice cracked in the middle of the sentence.

'Too late for you,' a shadow replied. It felt like the person meant it.

Jessica had been vulnerable in the past, but most threats were empty. Pathetic and easy to laugh off.

Not now.

Jessica fumbled for Archie, missing and scratching the wall instead. She stumbled over another pile of rubble, almost falling to the ground as something whizzed past her ear.

There was no point in putting on a brave face any longer: she was terrified.

TWENTY-FIVE

The fear gave Jessica a strange sense of clarity. It was like time had slowed and her vision was now pure and crystal. She suddenly realised her hand wasn't on the brickwork any longer, it was on the anonymous heavy-looking door she'd passed every time she'd visited Roly's flat. The front doors that led into each individual flat had a large glass panel front and centre, with a separate window to the side. This was different. There was one thick sheet of metal, its front blue but scratched heavily, with a small porthole window towards the top. The metal was cool as Jessica pushed against it. There was a creak, a moan – and then it swung inwards.

Jessica grabbed Archie's arm, almost falling inside as she dragged him into the deeper darkness. They had moved too quickly for the approaching crowd to act and Jessica heaved the door closed behind them, pressing herself against it and hoping it might hold. She knew it wouldn't, not with just their weight against it, except it didn't need to. Something thick dug into her back and she turned to find a large, lever-down bolt. Archie saw it at the same time, lifting it with a grunt and then swinging it into place with a solid clunk.

She breathed.

The voices on the other side of the door were muffled – but the anger was clear as something thudded into the door.

'Smells of shite in here,' Archie said.

Jessica turned, taking in the room. There was a dim orange bulb above, draping a slender amount of light across a downward slope towards four enormous boiler tanks in the corner. Pipes ran up the walls and the ceiling, disappearing off in all directions.

A fist pounded into the porthole of the door through which they'd escaped.

'Bit tight, wasn't it?' Archie added. He was smoothing down his top, trying to appear as if he'd been in control the entire time. His way of coping, Jessica supposed.

'Too tight,' she replied.

'Bit of fun, though, innit?'

He grinned.

Jessica didn't.

'There's nothing fun about what just happened,' she replied.

'It'll be all right. Backup on the way, this lot will nick off, we're in the clear.'

'We're *not* in the clear. You performed an illegal stop-and-search.'

'Don't think he'll be reporting it anytime soon. Besides, we know now where they keep the money. Probably drugs as well. No wonder we didn't get anything in the searches – we were looking at the kids instead of their bikes.'

Something clattered into the porthole, not a fist this time. Something more solid. Jessica jumped, though the glass held firm.

For now.

'We've got to get out of here,' Jessica said.

There wasn't much light, but they moved past the boilers

into the shadows. In the near silence, the scrapes and moans leaking from the dark sounded ominous. Jessica told herself it was just the pipes, the sound of hot water bubbling around a hundred crumbling flats, but that didn't stop her jumping as something *creeeeeeeeeeeaked* close to her ear.

There was another loud bang from behind, the sound of splintering glass bouncing around the walls and pipes. The porthole wasn't likely to last much longer and then someone with a long arm would be able to open the door.

Archie was using the light from his phone to show the way. It felt like they were heading further downwards, the passage narrowing until the corridor turned sharply to the left. Jessica was somewhat sure they were now underneath the flats. The corners were littered with dust, sand and other rubbish. There were faded crisp packets, a chocolate bar wrapper, a condom. The ceiling was low, not much taller than Jessica, with a series of pipes brushing the top of her head. It was getting hotter, too, sweat pooling behind Jessica's ears, curving across her chin.

Another bang splintered from behind, the porthole glass likely shattered.

Archie led the way, the beam from his phone glimmering back and forth. Jessica watched his heels, trying to keep up. She only realised he'd halted when she clattered into his back.

'Why'd you stop?' she hissed.

He shone the light from his phone up and down, making it obvious.

There was a door.

Archie pressed down the handle and pushed – but nothing happened. 'It's stuck,' he said.

'You're just weak.'

Jessica shoved down the handle herself, rearing back and ramming her shoulder into the door. There was the merest amount of give – but nowhere near enough for it to open.

They both stopped at the sound of voices from behind.

The words were lost but the low tone of men's voices echoed along the tight corridor.

Archie was running his finger across the grain of the wood. 'I don't think it's locked,' he said. 'It's just swollen.'

'So put your boot through it.'

He didn't need telling twice.

Archie stepped back, ushering Jessica out of the way and handing her his phone. He then stomped forward, crushing the sole of his shoe into the part of the door closest to the handle.

If it wasn't so serious, Jessica would have laughed as he bounced off, ending up on his back like an upturned tortoise. His legs waggled as he tried to right himself.

'Will you stop pissing about and break the door down?' she hissed.

The voices from behind sounded nearer.

Archie clambered back to his feet, brushing down his lap and taking a run-up. His foot crunched into the door frame once, twice. Each time, he wobbled but managed to keep his footing. At the third attempt, with a crunch of splintering wood, the door finally flew open.

'Your kids aren't gonna play for United with technique like that,' Jessica scolded. She dashed around him, shining the light ahead and following the corridor as it started to slope up once more.

The height of the passage was increasing once more, the pipes arcing left and right until they burst into a hallway. It was barely a cupboard – but there was a light above and some sort of electricity panel pinned to the back wall. On the other side was another metal door with a porthole at the top.

It wasn't locked.

Jessica handed Archie his phone, shrugged to tell him she didn't have a better idea, and then edged the door open, poking her head through the gap.

It took her a moment to realise they were halfway along the row of flats. The stairwell was a short distance away, the light from within illuminating the shadows of the crowd. She could just about see that the door to the boiler room through which they'd escaped was open. People would be following.

She pushed ahead, whispering Archie out onto the plaza as she closed the door as quietly as she could. There was no easy way back to Roly's. Between them and the row of shops – not to mention her car – was a dotted line of street lamps.

'What do you reckon?' she asked.

'I reckon our lot should pull their sodding fingers out.'

'We can't wait here until they do. Want to run for it?'

Archie peered past her towards the lights and the shops. 'I'm like a bloody greyhound when I get going. They used to call me Whippet Davey.'

'Are you sure that was a compliment?'

'Well, I—'

Archie didn't get to finish his sentence as a cry erupted from towards the stairwell.

'There!'

Jessica didn't need a starter's pistol to know it was time to move. She ran in a straight line across the plaza, flying across the paving slabs and then sprinting over the grass. She could sense Archie nearby, but he either got off to a slow start or she was quicker than him.

A low light glimmered from the row of shops, with Jessica's car parked on the street beyond. The keys were in her pocket and they had such a lead that there was no way anyone could catch them before they'd reach the car.

She felt good, confident... until a set of figures stepped out from under the stairs at the back of the shops. There were six or seven of them, arms by their side, blocking the way. Jessica missed a step as she slowed, stumbling and risking a glance behind to see that they were being chased.

There really was nowhere to go this time. Shadows ahead, shadows behind. No doors or stairs – only the exposed openness of the plaza.

Jessica slowed until she was walking. Her chest was tight from the burst of acceleration. She and Archie were only twenty or thirty metres from the shops and the figures in front were no longer shadows. She recognised Jefferson's tall, slim shape in the centre, a handful of lads on either side. The group that had been chasing had closed to a similar distance, sandwiching them in the middle

Trapped.

Jessica opened her mouth to say something, to reason that this was madness – but she didn't have to because Jefferson spoke first.

His arms were folded.

'Time to go home, lads,' he said. His voice was strong, crisp, authoritative. The teenagers at his side turned to look at their commander and Jessica realised *everyone* was watching him. The centre of attention. The only show in town.

'Seriously, fellas,' he added. 'Haven't you got homes to go to?'

Nobody moved... but only for a moment. Jessica turned to see the shapes of the residents disappearing back towards the shadows, their feet clip-clopping across the paving slabs. Doors clicked open and closed, curtains fluttered, watching eyes returned to their televisions.

Then the spinning blue lights of their overdue saviours flooded the estate.

Superintendent Jenkinson rubbed the bridge of his nose, finishing with a pinch that made his eyes water. He blinked, then sighed, putting on a show as he turned sideways to DCI Topper. Jenkinson was the exact type of copper with whom Jessica had always struggled to get along. He was a lifer, the type whose father had been in the force. Probably his father's father, too. His life plan would have been laid out from the day he was born. Convention dictated he must have spent some time in uniform in the distant past, but Jessica doubted it was long. He'd have been earmarked for a top job and then quickly removed from anything that involved dealing with the public. All he needed was a half-decent short game and he'd have been cracking balls around the golf course with the bigwigs of Greater Manchester Police in no time.

For good measure, he rubbed his forehead and sighed one more time.

They were in Topper's office on the upstairs level of the station, Jessica and Pete on one side of the desk, Jenkinson and Topper on the other. Topper hadn't looked at Jessica since she'd walked in, his eyes firmly on his computer monitor. Pete was shuffling with nerves.

'Let me get this straight,' Jenkinson said. He wasn't shouting, but he wasn't far off. 'You're assigned to monitor the most crime-free estate in the city and, within a week – a *week*! – there's been a riot...'

He stared at Jessica.

'I wouldn't exactly call it a riot,' Jessica replied.

'Don't get smart with me, *Inspector*.'

'Sorry, sir. I was just clarifying.'

Jenkinson leant forward, nostrils flaring. He was likely furious at having to be at work before midday. 'If you wouldn't call it a riot, what would you call it?'

'A differing of views...?'

Jenkinson's head was bobbing up and down manically. 'You use the emergency button to bring the wrath of God down upon that estate – and you call it a "differing of views"?'

'It was, admittedly, a *large* differing of views.'

The superintendent continued nodding, though his bright purple cheeks and the bulging vein in his neck didn't seem to indicate that he was agreeing with her. Jessica glanced quickly at Topper, who was wearing an expression that screamed for her to take the bollocking and stop being a wise-arse.

'And you were there with a suspended officer?' Jenkinson continued.

'I wasn't *working*,' Jessica replied.

'So what were you doing?'

'It's sort of... complicated.'

Jenkinson was now nodding at such a furious rate that Jessica wondered if his spinal cord had been partially severed.

'*Un*complicate it.'

Jessica risked another look at Topper, who was doing everything he could to tell her to shut her mouth. His lips were clamped together, eyebrows raised, giving it the full-on mind-planting act.

Shut up, he told her through thought alone.

'I think there's a reason why crime on that estate is so low,' Jessica said.

'Is there now...?'

'I don't think it's because of anything we've done.'

'Well that's good to hear. We invest resources, train officers, launch awareness campaigns – and any success is down to others. That's wonderful news.'

Jessica remained silent.

'Go on,' Jenkinson urged.

'Pardon, sir?'

'Why do you believe crime is so low on that estate?'

'I think there's someone who lives there acting as a sort of protector for the estate. There will always be troublemakers anywhere – but he makes sure any problems happen *off* the estate. It's why the crime rates in the surrounding area is slightly up. They look out for their own and stick up for one another. He's got the kids doing jobs for him – drugs, thefts, whatever. Everything happens away from where they live but the proceeds end up back at home. They're not robbing the rich to give to the poor, they're robbing from anyone who doesn't live there.'

Jenkinson stared at her. He'd somehow managed to turn even purpler, as if he was auditioning for a role in a Ribena commercial. 'Of course, you have full and irrefutable evidence for this...?'

'Well, we – *I* – found money on a kid last night. It was hidden in his bike frame. Hundreds, probably thousands.'

The superintendent clapped his hands together. 'Excellent. You have someone in custody?'

'Not exactly, sir. He sort of... got away.'

'So, even though you *weren't* on duty and the suspended

constable with whom you were working also *wasn't* on duty, you found money that is likely the result of either theft or selling stolen goods. You then managed to let the suspect go...?'

Jessica risked another glance at Topper, who had a face of thunder. She wondered if he feared having another officer suspended. His anger only helped fuel the fury that was building within her. There was a time and a place for bollockings – and it wasn't the morning after she'd been more scared than she'd ever been.

'Sorry, sir,' she said. 'I didn't *plan* to let him go – I was busy trying not to get the shite kicked out of me. It's not my fault backup took a couple of lifetimes to arrive.'

She felt Pete tense next to her. He'd not even been there, yet it must've felt like he was getting a kicking as well.

Jenkinson rose slightly from his chair, not quite standing but on the way, as if he was doing squat thrusts. Or needed a poo. 'Excuse me?'

'There's a pensioner who lives on that estate, has done his entire life. He's had his windows put through twice in a matter of days. He's scared out of his mind and I was *trying* to help.'

'Look how well it went,' Jenkinson said.

Jessica took a breath, hazarded another glance towards Topper. He was sitting back in his chair and had given up.

'I want to arrest Jefferson Cass,' Jessica said.

Topper answered before the superintendent. 'On what grounds?' he asked.

'Suspicion of handling stolen goods.'

'Based on what?'

'An anonymous tip.'

Silence.

Jenkinson stared between Topper and Jessica. He spoke firmly and slowly. 'I want to be absolutely clear about this,' he said. 'I don't care what you do – I honestly do not – but if this comes back to bite either of you, then do *not* expect anyone from the senior management team to cover your behinds. We do things by the book here. We do *not* support rogue operations or rogue officers.' He focused on Jessica. 'Do you understand?'

'Yes, sir,' Jessica replied.

Topper nodded, which was seemingly good enough for the superintendent.

Jenkinson was still nodding and Jessica wondered how much longer the bollocking would continue. It had to peter out sooner or later.

If she was honest, Jenkinson had a few things to learn. Chief Superintendent Aylesbury was far better when it came to pouring shite all over people's heads. He built up great big buckets of the stuff and then climbed up a few storeys before hurling it all over those below him. He was better at swearing, too. It couldn't be a proper bollocking without a few F-words thrown in, perhaps the odd C as well. If Jenkinson wasn't using the F-word as a noun, verb and adjective in the same sentence, then he really wasn't trying.

Before Jenkinson could ramble on for any longer, the phone on Topper's desk started to ring. He glanced to the superintendent for permission and then picked it up. He waffled through a series of 'yes', 'right', 'okay' and 'I see' replies before he put the phone back on the receiver and turned to Jessica.

'There's been an incident.'

TWENTY-SEVEN

The air smelt of overdone barbecue. Someone had squirted on half a bottle of lighter fluid, incinerated a dozen burgers, nearly lost their eyebrows – and then eaten the remains and given themselves food poisoning.

It was like that – but worse.

The fire marshal led the way, Jessica behind him, Rowlands behind her. The charcoal crackled and crumbled underneath, but, more than that, everything squelched. Uncountable litres of water had been jet-powered into putting out the inferno, but it was far too late to save the kitchen where it had started.

Whenever Jessica visited the scene of a fire, it was hard not to remember the arsonist she'd helped catch a few years before. Impossible to forget waking up and seeing the smoke spiralling across the ceiling above her head.

She blinked the thoughts away as the marshal's big heavy boots clumped across the sooty, soaking remains of what had once been a chair. They were in what was essentially a large caravan that had been converted into a mobile food van. It had been parked on the edge of an industrial estate for the night when someone had set it on fire. He pointed towards the back of the space, where a clock was high on the wall, scorched black claws licked onto the paintwork below.

'The fire started at the back door,' the marshal said. 'Someone sealed it closed, tipped petrol over it and then wham.' He clapped his hands together and Jessica jumped. She had done a lot of that in the previous few hours.

Jessica stared towards back of the van. If the marshal hadn't pointed it out, she'd have struggled to know it had been a door. It was now just a seared, roasted hole in the wall.

The marshal turned and pointed towards the only window. It was wide but not tall, stretching across the top of the sink. The glass had warped, melting, resetting and melting once more. It looked liquefied, even though it was solid.

'That's where we found the body,' he said. 'I think she was trying to escape through the window, but it had been nailed shut. Either that or she was trying to get water from the taps. The pipes had been disconnected – but I'm guessing she didn't know that.'

Jessica gaped across the horror. The doors underneath the sink were crusted to black. She could imagine the heat building, the fire raging, the crackling and popping that would inevitably follow.

'Poor girl must have been terrified,' she whispered.

'Aye.'

Rowlands was in a daze. He ran a hand across the crispy window frame before pulling it away, realising what he was doing.

'What about the body?' he asked.

The fire marshal was a burly bloke. Big shoulders and thighs, probably a rugger bugger at weekends, the type that'd be called a gentle giant by the tabloids. He scratched his chin and turned to the side.

'This place is a deathtrap,' he said. 'Wood panels, cheap

_n. Whole place would've gone up like a bloody fire-work. By the time we got here, most of it had already gone. Poor love didn't stand a chance. There wasn't much left by the time we got in.'

Jessica stared down at the near circular spot on the floor where the charcoal had been cleared. She presumed that's where the victim had been found.

'I know the bones have gone off to be identified,' she said, 'but what exactly was it you found?'

'Not me,' the marshal said. 'One of the lasses, Chrissy. Bloody hell, you know of anyone who reckons women shouldn't be in the service and I'll show them her. She was first in. She found the necklace. 'Twas pretty much the only thing recognisable.'

Jessica gulped a breath of salty, sticky air and took one final look at the patch of clear floor. 'I've got to get out of here.'

Eve and Alastair McDonnell had been married for longer than Jessica had been alive. Within moments of meeting them, she could guess their life story. Both born in Manchester, child-hood sweethearts, married as teenagers, pregnant a little after, settled on a housing estate they never left. In other circum-stances, they'd likely finish each other's sentences and squabble over who'd left the tap dripping. They reminded Jessica of her own parents... of times gone by.

Eve nodded sadly, her voice cracking. It had been a long day. 'It was definitely Tiff's necklace,' she said. 'We bought it for her eighteenth.'

She was sitting in a rocking chair and turned to her husband in the recliner. The television remote sat untouched on the arm. He nodded along, agreeing but not able to confirm it.

'Can you do something for me?' Eve asked.

'Of course,' Jessica replied.

'There was this girl earlier, a police officer. I can't remember her name, but she was lovely. Sat with me and helped Ally up the stairs. Can you thank her for me? I meant to, but then they took us into the room to identify the necklace and it slipped my mind.'

'I'll make sure she knows.'

'It's nice of you to call,' Eve added. 'I know they said the results on the bones are going to take a little while, but it's definitely Tiff's necklace. I'd recognise it anywhere. She wanted the one that had the spinning heart in the middle. It's better to know, isn't it?'

It sounded as if that was the type of thing she'd been telling herself since her daughter went missing ten days previously.

Better to know.

The words stuck in Jessica's head. She had thought the exact thing when her friend and housemate, Bex, had gone missing. Now, even though she knew Bex was safe, she wondered if she'd been better not knowing what happened.

'I know you've been through this before with other officers and I'm really sorry for asking,' Jessica said, 'but is there any chance you could tell me about what happened to Tiffany three months ago?'

'Do you think that's something to do with what happened?'

'I don't know.'

Eve nodded, even managing a small, sad smile. 'If you want to know exactly what went on, you'd have to talk to Tiff's friends. I've probably got their numbers somewhere – I know a couple of the mothers. She'd gone to a party at someone's house. She said she was sleeping upstairs when it happened.' A pause. 'She didn't say so, but I think she'd had a bit too much to drink. You know what it's like when you're young.'

There was a flicker, the tiniest glimmer of something close to a mischievous smile. It disappeared almost as instantaneously as it had appeared with the realisation that her daughter would no longer get to experience those rebellious nights.

'Do you know what happened?' Jessica asked.

'The fireman said someone dropped a cigarette on the sofa. They tried to put it out but everything went up so quickly. No one realised Tiff was inside until they were on the lawn and someone asked where she'd gone. She was unconscious, but one of her friends carried her out. He was on the front page of the *Herald* – they called him a hero.'

Jessica vaguely remembered the story. Officers at a different station would have investigated the fire – but the story of the teenager who'd run into a burning house to save his friend had been all over the news. The word 'hero' was overused, but, in this instance, Jessica figured it was probably correct.

'Was Tiffany okay afterwards?' Jessica asked.

'She spent a day in hospital and had minor smoke inhalation. She didn't go out for a week or so afterwards, but I think it was more the shock than anything else.'

Jessica asked Eve and Alastair if either of them knew of any link to the hostel or St Benedict's church, but both parents shook their heads. Jessica would assign an officer to talk to Tiffany's friends.

'What happened on the night Tiffany disappeared?' Jessica asked.

Eve glanced to her husband, but he was content to listen. 'She was out with her friends. They'd gone to some pub in the centre and then she'd got in a taxi to come home. That was the last they saw of her.' She pointed towards the window. 'The driver said he'd dropped her at the end of the road – he remembered the top she was wearing – but she never got here.

The neighbours didn't see anything and we'd long been in bed. That was that.'

She sighed, eyeing the window longingly, as if her daughter might come tootling along the path at any moment.

Jessica hadn't known about the taxi driver, but it would be in Tiffany's missing persons' file. Someone would have checked the timings, plus verified the driver's story. Now Tiffany's charred body had been discovered in a food truck on the edge of the city, everything would need to be looked at again.

'They say seven hundred and fifty people go missing every day,' Eve said.

Jessica realised the older woman was watching her.

'Sorry?' she said.

'That's what I read,' Tiffany's mother continued. 'You think it's just the person you know. A child, a friend – whatever. You wonder why the police can't find the people who go missing, then you realise it's because so many disappear.' She bit her bottom lip. 'Seven hundred and fifty people every day. Where do they all go?'

Jessica could only offer a thin-lipped smile. Almost all of those seven hundred and fifty were found.

'How do they decide who goes on the news?' Eve was staring directly at Jessica.

'I don't know.'

'Sometimes you see these men and women on the TV, or in the papers. Or the kids that go missing. There are these big appeals asking if anyone's seen them. I thought that's what would happen with Tiff – but there was nothing.' She touched Alastair on the arm. 'We put up a few posters, but no one called. No one even knew she'd gone.'

There was a long, awkward silence in which Jessica struggled to know what to say. She didn't know the answers any more than Tiffany's parents.

Jessica showed them pictures of Francine and Ezra but was met by two shaking heads. Someone was going to have to ask Tiffany's friends the same questions, with Jessica as sure as she could be that they'd get the same replies. Then there was the taxi driver, anyone in the pub who might have seen her – and so on. It would be a big job.

By the time they were back at the car, Rowlands had already found the news story on his phone. He read it out loud as Jessica drove – but it was only three lines before the story revealed the road on which Tiffany had lived. Anyone could have found her – especially given the carelessness of most people when it came to protecting their own privacy on social networks.

Jessica asked Rowlands to oversee going back over everything they had in regards to Tiffany's disappearance.

Neither of them mentioned the obvious.

Tiffany had survived a fire, only to die in another one three months later.

TWENTY-EIGHT

After arriving back at the station, Jessica gathered her crew in the incident room and assigned a team to try to figure out what had happened with Tiffany. There was firstly the disappearance and then how she'd ended up in a scorched food truck. With the fire service's investigation ongoing, answers would not arrive quickly. Everyone already had their own assumptions anyway. After Henry Taylor being hit by a car, Mark Stanley drowning, Lucy falling from the car park and now the fire, there was too much of a pattern.

There was something else, too. A still from a CCTV camera on one of the lower floors of the car park from where Lucy had fallen showed a large black man exiting through a fire escape ninety seconds after the incident. It was only a side view and grainy at best – but the man looked similar to the description and composite image of 'Ezra' that Teri had given at the hostel.

With all that in place, Jessica found herself back in the interview room, this time with a different face on the other side of the table.

Jefferson Cass sat impassively, his eyes never leaving her. He was dressed as casually as when she'd seen him before – in tracksuit bottoms and a vest. He'd refused the offer of a solicitor – either his own or a free duty lawyer. Nonchalant and as confident as could be.

'Busy day?' he asked.

'Six months,' Jessica replied.

'Sorry?'

'Assault occasioning Actual Bodily Harm – yet you got six months. Not a bad sentence. You must've had a good solicitor.'

Jefferson was wearing a slim hint of a grin. His gaze never shifted from Jessica. 'If you say so.'

'Two counts of cannabis possession. Community service for common assault. Six points on your licence. Pretty good for a thirty-one-year-old.'

'Thank you.'

'It wasn't a compliment.'

Jefferson didn't reply, didn't shift at all in his seat.

'What brings you to Manchester?' Jessica asked.

He grinned white and wide. A dentist's dream. 'The weather.'

'Not enough rain in Leeds?'

Jefferson shrugged, still smiling.

'There's a lot of new stuff in your flat,' Jessica said. 'I take it your credit card bills will stand up to scrutiny. Definitely no stolen goods in there...?'

He said nothing, leaving the pause to hang.

'Well?' Jessica added.

'I didn't know you'd asked a question.'

'Something's happening on the Lees Estate,' Jessica said, still not quite a question. 'Something rotten.'

'Is it?'

'You're at the centre.'

'Am I?'

'Why do all the young people who live there listen to you?'

'I wasn't aware that they did.'

Jessica had to turn away, unnerved by Jefferson's unflinching stare. He was better at this game than she was, unworried by being in an interview room. He pressed back into the chair, splaying his legs as if lounging with a beer in front of the television.

'We stopped a young lad outside your flat the other night. He was about to go inside. There was money stored in his bike frame – thousands of pounds. Why was he taking it into your flat?'

'Who says he was?'

'Me.'

A shrug. 'Ah well, if you say it's true, then it must be.'

'Why was he taking money into your flat?'

'I don't know who you're referring to – but *if* someone was about to knock on my door and they had some money on them, then I have no idea. Why don't you ask this mysterious "young lad"?' Jefferson made bunny ears, glancing towards the camera and then quickly back to Jessica once more. 'I assume you questioned this phantom "young lad"?' More bunny ears.

Jessica had the strangest sense that their roles had been reversed and she was being questioned.

'You've got these kids working for you,' she said, trying to regain control.

Jefferson did nothing except smile.

'They sell goods on your behalf and then return your cut hidden away in their bike frames.'

'Do they now?'

'Crime is non-existent where you live because you make sure they operate in the surrounding areas.'

'Is that right?'

'You know we'll find the money, don't you? We'll get a warrant and go through your flat.'

'Sounds like fun. What are you going to do when you don't find anything? I hope you clean up afterwards. I like everything to be neat and tidy. If you're going to make a mess, it'd be really nice if you could put everything back where you found it.'

Jessica had already started her next sentence but she stopped mid-word. They stared at each other, but Jessica knew she was going to blink first. She pressed her chair backwards and then stood, heading out of the interview room and closing the door behind her. She leant against the wall, feeling the cold, hard surface on her back, taking a deep breath and closing her eyes. When she opened them, DCI Topper had appeared. He had his arms behind his back, a plod on duty. Some habits never died.

'You didn't expect anything else, did you?' he said.

Jessica didn't know what to say, so she said nothing. In truth, this *was* the outcome she'd expected, even though she hoped she was wrong. She wanted Jefferson to know that she was on to him, except she wasn't sure that was true. He felt a step ahead of them and she was definitely missing something. Probably more than one thing.

'Send him home,' Topper added.

'We're not going to get a warrant, are we?'

'I can't believe you're even asking that. He shouldn't be here.'

'You must see it.'

'See what?'

Jessica rubbed her eyes, squeezed her nose, trying to make the words form. 'I don't know... something. He knows how to talk to us, knows what we're going to ask.'

'He's probably seen a few interview rooms in his time.'

Topper might be right – the career criminals did often

have their own way of dealing with police – but it felt like more than that.

'Can you do it?' Jessica asked.

'Do what?'

'Send him home. I don't think I can take looking at his smug face any longer.'

TWENTY-NINE

The smell of something meaty was drifting through the hallway as Jessica opened her front door. For a moment, she was confused, thinking she'd left the oven on, but then Caroline's voice drifted through the house – 'It's only me!'

Jessica kicked off her shoes and took a moment for herself. She'd been looking forward to an evening alone now that Roly was back at his own flat. It wasn't a complete surprise that Caroline had popped over – but it was that she'd let herself in and started cooking.

The crunch of keys being dumped on the window sill was satisfyingly violent and then Jessica padded through to the kitchen, fighting back a yawn and managing a decent fake smile. A good seven out of ten.

Caroline was sweating like a British tourist on a beach in midsummer Cyprus. Her hair was tied high, straggly dangling threads tickling her cheeks. An apron that definitely didn't belong to Jessica was tied tightly around her waist. The window was open, but the kitchen still felt like a sauna where some idiot at the gym had overdone it with the steam.

'I thought I'd cook,' Caroline said as she wiped the sweat from her brow. 'It's nearly ready.'

Boiling water spilled over the top of a saucepan, sizzling on the stove as Caroline spun back to the cooker and swore under her breath.

She continued speaking as she emptied a pan of vegetables into a colander. Jessica had no idea from where either the veggies or the colander had appeared. Definitely not her kitchen.

'Want to talk about it?' Caroline asked.

'Sorry?'

Caroline half turned from the sink. 'You look like you've had a bad day.'

Jessica blinked. Maybe the fake smile had only been a three or four out of ten. 'Do I?'

'You've got that sort of... *look*... about you.'

'What does that mean?'

Caroline shrugged innocently enough. She wasn't trying to be annoying – though she was managing it. 'I don't know. It's like the old days. Bad guys being bad. That sort of thing.'

The vegetables were dumped into a large bowl and then Caroline delved into the oven, sending wafts of steam into the air and the smoke alarm near the door into meltdown. It was like a paranoid conspiracy theorist, seeing treachery every-where. Jessica would turn the dial on the toaster up a notch and the smoke alarm would *wah-wah-wah* in protest. Someone might light a candle in the house across the road and it would throw an ear-splitting paddy.

Jessica wafted her hand frantically underneath as Caroline continued to serve up dinner. She'd only been home for a couple of minutes and already Jessica wanted to leave again. That or go to bed.

Once the smoke alarm had been soothed, Caroline turned. 'Wait in the other room,' she said. 'I'll bring dinner through.'

Jessica did as she was told, heading into the living room and then spying the gift on the dining table. It was rectangular, wrapped neatly with a purple bow on top. A cartoon cow was attached to the side, with Jessica's name scrawled on the opposite side. A heart had been drawn instead of the letter 'A'. Jessica ran her fingers across the writing, feeling too old for it all. It felt like being back at school, doodling boys' names, gossiping about who was snogging whom and trying to figure out what they might get up to when the weekend came.

Caroline soon bumbled into the room, a plate in either hand. She returned twice more, bringing in the vegetables, gravy, leftover chicken, roast potatoes.

'I think I made too much food,' she said when she finally sat.

'If we were a family of six, it'd still be too much food.' She paused and then added: 'Thank you, though.'

Caroline jabbed her fork towards the present. 'You didn't open it.'

'I thought I'd wait for you.'

It didn't take Jessica long to obliterate the wrapping, unveiling a Freddo Easter egg in a slightly crumpled purple box.

'You're always going on about the price of Freddos,' Caroline said. 'If it's not that, then it's the size of Wagon Wheels.'

Jessica eyed the box and then her friend. This time the smile was genuine. 'I don't even remember the last time I had an *actual* Easter egg,' she said.

'Like the old days, isn't it? You get home and I'm cooking.'

Jessica nodded, thinking it was too much like the old days. She liked her own space now.

Caroline continued speaking, oblivious that Jessica had been thinking any differently. 'Do you ever wonder what might have happened?'

'With what?'

'The only reason we stopped living together was because of Randall and what happened. Do you think we'd have still been in that flat if I'd never met him...?'

Jessica had a roast potato halfway towards her mouth when she stopped. Could it be a coincidence that Caroline had brought up Randall? Did she know they'd been meeting?

How could she know?

They looked at each other, but Jessica couldn't see anything in her friend's expression that might indicate this was all some ruse.

'Do you ever think about him?' Caroline added.

'Randall?'

'I do. I wonder what might have happened if we'd stayed together. If you'd not found out who he was.'

Jessica put down her fork. She hadn't meant to but, from nowhere, the words were on the tip of her tongue. The stars had aligned to screw her over.

'I think I have to tell you something.'

'You *think*?' Caroline finished swallowing whatever she'd been eating and then put her fork down. She spoke so quickly that the words became one: 'Oh my god, you're pregnant!'

Jessica looked down at her stomach, fingered her belly button through the material of her top. 'Pregnant?'

'Oh, I thought...'

'Who'd be the father?'

Caroline's features slumped. She was disappointed. 'I don't know... I guess I just thought...'

'I've been to see him,' Jessica said quietly.

Caroline looked up, blinking and wide-eyed. 'Who?'

'Randall. I've been visiting him for six months.'

Time stood still and Jessica suddenly felt the weight of having known a person for so many years. Neither of them spoke for a while, but Caroline's mouth hung open.

'Why?' The word creaked from Caroline's lips.

Jessica blinked. Not quite sure what to say, let alone why she'd mentioned it in the first place. 'I'm not sure. First it was for a case. We were looking for someone who'd been housed at the same secure facility. Then I went back the next month, then the one after that.'

Caroline shook her head slowly. 'What do you do?'

'Talk.'

'About what?'

Jessica bit her bottom lip, wondering how to reply. It wasn't that she wanted to shy away from the storm she knew would be coming, simply that she didn't know the answer. What *did* they talk about? Everything and nothing. The doorway to Ashworth was a science-fiction amnesia gate. She walked out having forgotten everything that went on inside.

'Are you friends?' Caroline's stare burned through Jessica, who couldn't return it.

'No.'

'Then what are you?'

'I don't know.'

Caroline's chair slipped backwards. 'Do you talk about me?'

'No.'

'So what *do* you talk about?'

Her voice was calm, yet brimming with rage. Jessica couldn't believe she'd misread the situation so badly. Caroline hadn't known about Jessica's visits to Ashworth at all. The topic of conversation *had* been a coincidence. She'd been remembering one of the biggest things to ever happen in her life. Jessica had been there, too – so it was only natural it would come up intermittently.

'Well?'

Caroline's demand was so forceful that Jessica found the words coming from her mouth without thought.

'I don't know what we talk about. Just... things...'

Caroline picked up her fork – but only so she could slam it back onto the table. She jumped up so quickly that she stumbled into the wall behind, her lips a twisted gnarl. Bile started to spew, but then she stopped mid-word, the fury replaced by bemusement. She clasped her midriff, eyes big and bloated like a Japanese cartoon.

'Are you all right?' Jessica asked.

'I feel sick. I—' Caroline cut herself off, looking downwards as liquid dribbled down her leg and started to pool on the carpet.

Had she pissed herself?

A flicker of bewilderment passed between them, the anger gone as the truth dawned for both of them.

'Are you having a baby?' Jessica asked.

THIRTY

Caroline's hands cupped the area underneath her stomach as she screamed. Not just screamed but *screeeeeeeeeeeeeeeamed*. The banshee wail burned through Jessica, a shiver ripping along her spine. She reached for her friend, who had pressed herself against the wall – and then Jessica realised what she should actually do and hunted around the room looking for her phone. She'd had it when she got home but it had disappeared, as it did so frequently. The house gremlins had always been keen on her possessions, with keys a particular favourite.

Caroline squealed once more as Jessica moved frantically into the hallway, finding her keys on the window sill but no phone. It wasn't in the kitchen either – certainly nowhere obvious. After stealing her things, the house gremlins had a habit of leaving them in unexpected places. Shoes in the sink, keys in the bath, sunglasses in the fridge.

Where was her damned phone?!

Another scream howled through the house and Jessica raced back to the living room. Caroline was sitting on the floor, seemingly unaware of the puddle she'd created. She was sweating heavily, hands still on her midriff, panting like she'd just finished a half-marathon.

She grabbed Jessica's hand and squeezed with the brutality of an MMA fighter. Her face was red, cheeks puffy.

'We need to call an ambulance,' Jessica said.

Caroline squeezed even tighter, making Jessica squeal. 'I'm on the pill, Jess. I thought I was just getting fat. I've been sick once or twice in the morning but thought it was hangovers.'

She grimaced, gulping away another shriek. Jessica wasn't sure what to say. It hadn't crossed her mind that her friend might be pregnant.

Jessica pushed herself onto her heels, finally noticing her phone on the dinner table. She could've sworn it hadn't been there minutes before. Jessica reached for it, but Caroline yanked her back to the floor.

'I've been drinking all this time!'

'You weren't to know.'

'I'm one of those bloody women,' she growled through short breaths.

'What women?'

'Like you read about in those dodgy mags. "I didn't know I was pregnant", and all that.'

Jessica finally managed to pull herself free, fumbling with her phone and dialling 999 as Caroline pawed at her free hand.

The next few minutes were a blur, Caroline moaning in one ear; the phone operator talking into Jessica's other. An ambulance was on its way, but it was ten minutes' away. In the meantime, the woman on the phone continued to soothe. From nowhere, Caroline's contractions were only four minutes or so apart. The screams were becoming louder, hand-squeezing up to knuckle-crunching levels.

Seven words dropped Jessica back into the room like a base jumper without a parachute.

'*You might have to deliver the baby.*'

The ambulance was stuck in traffic. Some sort of accident meant gridlock to the north of the city. Always the traffic.

The contractions were becoming longer, the gap between them shorter. There was still no sign of the ambulance. Caroline had stopped trying to speak, sweat flooding from her brow, her arms, her chest, everywhere. She was no longer red, instead her skin was waxy and white. She barely seemed to have the energy to scream, her head lolling to the side, eyes blinking open and closed.

As the spinning blue lights finally flooded through the front window, Caroline flopped towards Jessica, voice barely there.

'I think I'm dying,' she whispered.

THIRTY-ONE

GOOD FRIDAY

Jessica's shoulder jolted back and forth as she jumped awake. Light burned, pink and green stars spinning and spiralling like fireworks on Guy Fawkes Night. A cough caught in her throat and she gasped for air, keeling over and hacking until she remembered where she was.

A vending machine hummed in the corner of the waiting room, the bright red of the Coca-Cola logo imprinted into her line of vision as if marketing companies had finally taken things to the ultimate extreme and started to advertise via telepathy.

'How are you doing?'

It was a female voice: familiar and friendly.

Izzy.

Jessica curled her legs underneath herself, not bothering to suppress the yawn. 'What time is it?'

'Just after five.' A pause. 'That's in the morning. As in the five o'clock no human being should see.'

Jessica yawned a second time. She stretched high, her back cricking, neck creaking. Again. The waiting room was empty except for them. A bulb droned gently overhead, melding with the vending machine to create a steady, hypnotic buzz.

Izzy swam into view. She was perched on the edge of the table in front of Jessica, a pile of ripped magazines at her side. Her dark hair was clamped back with a clip, her lips in a slim smile.

'I didn't think you'd come,' Jessica said.

'I needed a wee in the night. Checked my phone and saw your message. Mal was snoring, so I figured I'd leave him to it.' She touched Jessica's arm. 'You delivered your friend's baby?'

A nod.

'*You?*'

Jessica wanted to smile, but her body wasn't obeying. 'I know. Little boy. She didn't know she was pregnant – she thought she was putting on weight. You see all these mad stories and wonder how women can go nine months not realising they're pregnant – and then it happens to your mate.' A pause and then: 'Not much of a detective, am I? I didn't notice.'

Izzy yawned and then Jessica copied.

'How is she?' Izzy asked.

'Not good – she has some sort of internal bleeding. The paramedics were delayed, but they rushed her here. Caroline's in intensive care, the baby's in *newborn* intensive care.'

There was a poster on the wall advertising some sort of Easter egg hunt at a local park. The colours were bright, showing a string of stick children chasing a bunny across a field. In a different context, it could be a poster for the RSPCA condemning the harassment of rabbits.

'Are they going to be okay?' Izzy asked.

Jessica gulped away another yawn, but there was a larger lump in her throat that couldn't be swallowed. 'I don't know. Her boyfriend's in Australia. It was tomorrow there when I called.' She scratched her head. 'Or later today... I don't know.

He was awake – said he'd find a way home. I've never heard him so normal.'

Izzy rubbed Jessica's arm once more and then nodded towards the vending machine. 'You want something to eat?'

Jessica shook her head, blinking and yawning, trying to wake up. There was a short silence and then Izzy took a seat next to Jessica and started to speak. It was nice to hear her voice, even if she was only talking about what she'd been doing with her days off. Jessica did nothing except listen. It was comforting to hear about the normality of someone else's life – the housework, the weekly big shop, reality TV. Anything that wasn't work or the hospital.

Izzy tailed off when a weary-looking woman appeared. She introduced herself as a doctor, but Jessica was busy trying to read her face.

'Is Caroline awake?' Jessica asked.

The doctor looked around the room as if to confirm the walls weren't listening. She glanced towards Izzy, but Jessica said they were friends. The doctor then perched on the table, much like Izzy had. She squeezed her elbows between her knees, making herself small. 'Does Caroline have any other family?' she asked.

'No one anywhere near,' Jessica replied. 'Her parents are in Canada. I tried calling but there was no answer. Her boyfriend's in Australia – he's trying to get a flight home. It's just me.'

The doctor started to say something but stopped as a gurney squeaked past at the furthest end of the waiting room.

'Caroline's in a very serious condition,' the doctor said.

She explained that, though they had managed to stem the bleeding, they had induced a coma.

It took Jessica a few moments to take it in. The word 'coma' never meant anything good, induced or not. It was so harsh, so brutally upfront. Never, 'Your friend's having an extended nap'. Just 'coma'.

'Will she be okay?' Jessica asked croakily, unsure what else to say.

The doctor managed 'we're doing all we can'. It wasn't a direct answer to the question, but the sleight of word evasiveness told its own story.

As for the baby, he was more than a month premature and very underweight. Although he was in intensive care, his condition wasn't critical.

'He just needs time,' the doctor concluded, before correcting herself. '*They* just need time.'

THIRTY-TWO

Longsight Police Station was quiet.

Jessica sat alone in her office, staring at a report on her monitor. There had been a pair of burglaries over the past couple of nights in the local area. Nothing particularly sophisticated – someone crowbarred open a back window in the early hours, grabbed an armful or two of electrical goods and then scarpered. Nasty enough, of course. An officer was on the case and the report was more for her information than anything on which she had to act.

She moved on, swishing from report to report until she arrived on the one about the car park fall. There had been no suicide note, though nothing else to suggest Lucy had been pushed.

The image of the man from the car park whom they suspected was the mysterious Ezra was still the only lead they had on him. Jessica stared at his photo on her screen, thinking about how Lucy must have felt when she fell from the top of the car park. Was she pushed? Encouraged to jump? Perhaps it had been an accidental tumble…?

Perhaps.

She zoomed in and out of the image, hoping for inspiration or some sort of clue from his clothes about where he might be. It'd really help if finding him could help them find Francine as well. His image would end up in the news – but that didn't necessarily mean much, especially over a bank holiday weekend when people had better things to do.

Jessica sifted through her emails. There was a leave request to process; some internal memo about overtime budgets to read and respond to; the usual handful of buffoons who didn't understand how 'reply all' worked. The mini barrage of spam. Nothing urgent. Not really. People kept sending emails five minutes before they went off shift, knowing they wouldn't have to deal with the aftermath for a few days. A shit's trick, albeit a good one.

It was Good Friday, a cherished bank holiday – and yet little shites never stopped being little shites and there was no rest for the wicked, let alone those who went after the wicked.

Jessica clicked away from her actual work and started reading stories about women who didn't realise they were pregnant before giving birth. It was nowhere near as rare as she had thought – and not confined to the type of attention-seekers who sold their stories to cheap magazines. Huge swathes of women, young and old, had babies every year without knowing they'd been pregnant in the first place.

She'd been pregnant once, of course – but she'd very much known it. It wasn't only the obvious weight gain, it was feeling the movement within her body until, one day, she didn't. She wondered if Caroline had felt the same things, if she'd put them down to stomach cramps or dodgy cooking.

When she woke up, Jessica would be able to ask her.

If she ever woke up.

As ever, like night following day or dodgy expense claims following a politician, one internet search led to another. Jessica soon found the stat that 300,000 women died every year during childbirth. She stared at the number, unable to look away. It was surely too high, what with it being the twenty-first century and all.

She wondered if Caroline would be an extra one.

Three hundred thousand... and one.

Jessica closed her eyes and...

...the phone was ringing. Jessica blinked around the room, trying to clear the hazy grey from the edge of her vision. She snatched her mobile from the desk but the screen was blank. It took her a moment to realise that it was the desk phone, DCI Topper's voice on the other end. If he realised he'd caught her sleeping, he didn't say anything – his tone was far too stern for that. Instead, he invited her up to his office.

Topper wasn't dressed for the office. It didn't exactly surprise Jessica that he was wearing a dad jumper. It was some sort of criss-cross, cream and maroon monstrosity. A proper puffing-on-a-pipe-at-Christmas-in-a-rocking-chair horror show.

He was pushing the wrong half of his forties, perhaps eyeing an early retirement or a cushy job somewhere at HQ where he could wile away his days glad-handing supposed dignitaries at civic functions. Jessica was never quite sure which way he would fall if things ever got really tough. Would he be with the comrades in the trenches, or standing at the back wafting a limp-handed cheerio as his colleagues went over the top? Sometimes – perhaps most times – it felt like he was with her and the rest of the gang, that he had their backs when it came to saying the right things to upper management. Other times, she wasn't sure. There would be a hesitation to his voice, a sideways glance, and she wondered if – perhaps – she would one day regret putting her trust in him.

Topper cleared his throat as Jessica entered the office,

offering a weary, 'yes, I know it's Good Friday' look. He smiled thinly, nodding at the free chair across from his desk.

'Busy morning?' he asked.

Jessica wondered if she should mention the whole 'delivered-a-baby' thing. The 'my-friend's-in-a-coma-and-might-not-wake-up' malarkey. The near all-nighter she'd pulled.

'Not really,' she replied.

It was almost funny.

'I'm off for the weekend,' Topper replied.

'Looks like it.'

He glanced down at his jumper and then up at her. 'Shocker, isn't it? Christmas present from the wife. I have to drag it out every now and then because one of her friends made it. We're having afternoon tea with them later, so I had to find it in the wardrobe.'

'Suits you.'

Jessica smiled and so did Topper. Then she found herself telling him about Caroline being in the coma, about the time she'd spent in the hospital waiting room and how her best friend might not wake up. Once she finished, they both sat in silence for a moment. Topper drummed his fingers across the desk, peering at her like a headmaster with a favourite pupil.

'You really know how to pick your moments, don't you?'

'I think I must've walked under a bunch of ladders recently.'

He puffed out a breath. 'Do you need time?' he asked.

A shake of the head.

'You sure? I can make arrangements. There's always someone to cover.'

Another shake.

Topper's eyes narrowed and then he started to nod, mind made up. 'I had a call this morning. Something... unexpected.'

'About me?'

He gave her the old head tilt. Nothing good ever came from that. 'Jefferson Cass,' he said.

'What about him?'

'We have to leave him alone.'

'Says who?'

'Says me.'

They stared at each other, but Jessica had to look away first. It was rare that Topper put his foot down, but his tone of voice made it clear he was doing just that. They rarely used the word 'order'. No one banged a fist on the desk and said, 'that's an order'. The language officers used between themselves was subtler.

'What do you mean by "leave him alone"?' Jessica asked.

'What do you think I mean?'

'If I see him nicking a Mars bar from the local Tesco, do I leave him to it?'

The sideways head tilt was back. 'You know precisely what I'm talking about.'

Unfortunately, Jessica did. 'He's up to something,' she said.

'That may be the case – but you're still going to leave him be.'

'But—'

'Not this time, *Inspector*. No buts. You *will* back off Jefferson Cass. Is that clear?'

He'd made her title sound like an insult: a reminder that, regardless of the dad jumper and previous friendly tone, he still outranked her. For once, this *was* an order.

'Who called you?' Jessica asked.

'You wouldn't know the name.'

'Why have we got to back off him?'

Topper bit his lip. Thought about it. 'I can't say.'

His eyes told a different story, willing her to read between the lines. To think about what he wasn't saying, not what he was.

And then Jessica got it.

So much of it made sense – his sudden appearance, the way he knew how to talk to others, the reason why he was on the Lees Estate.

'He's a ghost?' she said.

Topper couldn't meet her gaze. 'You said that, not me.'

THIRTY-THREE

With the idea now planted in Jessica's mind, she couldn't shut up. She wondered why it had taken so long for her to get it.

'Pete said it himself,' she said, more talking to herself than to the DCI, 'the coverage was dreadful. They said it was the most dangerous estate in the city or the knife crime capital of the north – no wonder they sent someone in.'

Topper said nothing.

'Jefferson's criminal record is made up. No wonder he said "no comment" to everything. There was no point in pushing the lie further. I wonder what his real name is...'

Still no reply.

Jessica pressed back into her chair, thinking it over. A ghost was what they called officers working undercover. It had largely gone out of fashion due to numerous collapsed court cases. It was hard to get a conviction when the officer posing as a member of an animal rights protest group got someone pregnant. Harder still when the officer pretending to be a football hooligan ended up kicking someone's head in so as not to blow cover.

'I've probably done him a favour,' Jessica added.

'How?'

'By nicking him, it gives an even better front for those kids he's got working for him.'

'Leave him alone, Jess.'

'I still don't understand what he's got going on. Why all the comings and goings at the flat? We found a kid with thousands of pounds stashed in a bike frame about to go into his flat. There's no way he's working as a ghost to stitch up a bunch of kids.'

'I don't have any answers for you.' Topper pushed himself to his feet and straightened his jumper. 'I didn't tell you anything and it's time for me to get back to the family. I figured I'd pass the message on in person rather than on the phone.'

'Right...'

He stepped past, opening the door of his office and holding it for her. He didn't say 'clear off', but he might as well have done.

Jessica paused in the doorway. 'I want to talk to his handler,' she said.

'What part of "leave him alone" are you not understanding?'

'There's too much that doesn't make sense. He's—'

'He's nothing to you. He's a man living on an estate. End of story.' Topper shuffled closer, practically pushing Jessica into the corridor. 'Now, if it's all right with you, I'm going to go and enjoy the bank holiday. If you could go three days without causing a riot, it would be really appreciated.'

DC Rowlands was at his desk when Jessica ambled onto the station's main floor. It was emptier than usual, with the lucky few seemingly getting their leave requests approved and those unlucky stuck behind desks. Those with kids often tried to work their rotas and days off around the school holidays.

A red-top was splayed in front of Rowlands at the sports pages and he noticed her too late to cover it up.

'I didn't think you ever read past page three,' Jessica said, perching herself on the corner of his desk. 'Where's the chocolate?' she added before he could reply.

'What chocolate?'

Jessica raised her eyebrows and Rowlands reached for his bottom drawer, pulling out a ball of crinkled purple foil. 'All gone,' he replied.

She poked the corner of her mouth and Rowlands got the message, wiping his face clean.

'I don't suppose you've found Francine, have you?' Jessica asked.

'No sign of her.'

'Ezra?'

'Not a peep. We've had more Easter Bunny sightings. Someone from the press office was supposed to be emailing me, but I think they're off for the weekend. Do we know if his real name is Ezra?'

'There's no one called Ezra in the files, plus the images we have are too vague to match to any other ID. For now, "Ezra" is all we have.'

Rowlands gave a 'suit yourself' shrug. 'We've been going round the churches, plus checking the usual haunts where Francine hands out her flyers. Lots of people vaguely remember some crazy lady giving them leaflets – no one's seen her recently.'

'No luck at the hostel?'

'No – and we've tried other hostels and homeless shelters. A couple of food banks, soup kitchens. The lot. She's disappeared.' He paused. 'Perhaps she's left the area?'

Jessica shook her head. She'd thought the same, but it didn't feel right. If Francine was determined to spread her warped ideas, why leave now? If it was something to do with her, why stop after the deaths of Henry, Mark, Lucy and Tiffany? She would have targeted them for a reason. There'd be others.

'I don't suppose anyone's come up with a link between the victims that doesn't involve Francine?' Jessica asked.

'Nothing.'

'If she's not returned to the hostel, she has to be staying somewhere. She doesn't seem the homeless sort – plus, people have been looking for her on the street. We'd have found her. It's Easter – Jesus was getting crucified two thousand years ago today. This has got to be the highlight of her year. There's no way she's gone to ground – not today.'

Rowlands's frown didn't hide his scepticism. 'What are you thinking?'

Jessica clucked her tongue into the top of her mouth: 'Have you got the overnights?' she asked.

Rowlands clicked through some screens on his computer, then shuffled sideways so that Jessica could fit alongside him. The overnights were a list of phone numbers that had dialled either 999 or 101, along with the details the caller had provided. Any definite emergencies were passed onto ambulance, fire or police. Non-emergencies were filed through the system, ready for an officer to act. Everything else was logged.

Weekends were particularly bad for people wasting the time of call handlers. Very little of it was deliberate crank calling, much was down to people feeling lonely and wanting someone to talk to, or those with mental illnesses not having a proper outlet through which to have their problems dealt.

Filtering out the repeat callers was easy enough, as was removing the names and numbers of callers with genuine emergencies. That left Jessica and Rowlands with a few dozen numbers to check. The method wasn't exactly high-tech: they cut and pasted each one into Google and waited to see what it threw up. There was a long list of nothings until one number produced a hit.

Jessica and Rowlands saw it at the same time – the phone number wasn't a random residential listing.

It belonged to St Benedict's Church.

THIRTY-FOUR

The call handler's voice was soft but authoritative: 'Emergency. Which service, please?'

There was a definite stammer in the man's voice as he replied: 'Police, I think.'

A moment of silence and then a different woman asked the reason for the call. There was a gulp, another stammer and then the man apologised.

'Actually, I made a mistake,' he said. 'I thought there was a problem, but it's fine now. Sorry for wasting your time.'

Before the handler could reply, the voice was gone.

Jessica and Rowlands listened to the call twice. It had been passed through to the police as something that might have to be followed up – but no one had got to it. There was nothing unusual in any of that. People did sometimes call 999 by accident, or change their minds about what counted as an emergency. It was occasionally something more serious. A domestic abuse victim whose partner had them cornered and dropped the phone; someone whose home was being broken into who didn't want to speak too loudly. There were all sorts of reasons for abandoned calls – and the numbers were always passed through to the local force. If things sounded particularly serious – shouting in the background, bangs, crashes – a handler would elevate it as a possible emergency. That hadn't happened with the call from St Benedict's Church, it had simply been flagged for someone to follow up. That meant a phone call or a visit.

And who better to visit...?

Jessica parked the car a couple of streets away from St Benedict's. It was late morning but the area was quiet, with people sleeping in on the bank holiday and students disappearing home for the long weekend. She and Rowlands hurried through the streets, pausing at the gateway to the church. The large doors at the front that had been so welcoming on their first visit were closed. The times of service board at the front said there was supposed to be a service at six o'clock that evening – except the word 'cancelled' was now written at the side.

Instead of heading to the main doors of the church, Jessica led Rowlands to the side were there was a large car park. A battered Nissan was in the corner alongside a row of recycling bins. Moss poked through the cracked tarmac, with the spire of the church casting a seemingly permanent shadow. The car park was a dead end.

'What now?' Rowlands asked.

Jessica pressed herself onto tiptoes and turned towards the church, then looked back to the recycling bins. Trails of ivy or something else green and bushy were spiralling over the wall, intermingled with the branches of an overhanging tree.

'Over there.'

'It looks like someone's back garden.'

Jessica stepped towards the wall. 'Exactly.'

Before he could protest, Jessica had hauled herself on top

of the large metal bin that was meant for recycling clothes and shoes. She tugged the tree branches to the side and peered beyond.

'It's the back of the church,' she said. 'There's some sort of house over here.'

'Surely that means there's a proper gate?'

It was hard to see anything other than the thick foliage of the tree. 'It might have a second entrance on a different road.'

'Shall I go look for it?'

Jessica turned back to Rowlands. 'We *could* do that, or...'

'—Jess.'

Too late.

Jessica dropped over the wall, landing with a plop in a shadowed patch of mud. There was some sort of green underfoot, but it didn't provide much of a blanket as her foot glooped through the surface. She fought her way through the branches, the sharp claws scraping through her clothes until she emerged next to a water butt sitting in a puddle at the edge of a patch of lawn.

There was a house – more precisely a cottage – its redbrick mix of modern and dated matching that of the church. There was a blocked drain next to the butt, with a stench of sewers that took Jessica's breath. She gulped, moving towards the centre of the lawn. There was a separate gate off to the side, which must lead onto a different side street. With the church and the wall of the car park separating the cottage from the main road, it was a nice, private residence. The only way in was through the gate – or over the wall.

There was a splosh and then Rowlands emerged from the tree. The lower parts of his trousers were caked with mud, his shoes covered with sludge.

He tugged them upwards, grimacing. 'Landed in a puddle,' he said. 'My feet are drenched.'

'Something round here's definitely wet.'

Rowlands looked towards the cottage and then realised what she'd meant. 'Oh, ha ha,' he mocked. 'We could've just headed round the back to find the gate – but, oh no, you had to go over the wall.'

'No one told you to jump in a puddle.'

'I didn't *jump* in a puddle. I landed in one.'

'Same difference.'

Rowlands frowned and tugged at his trousers once more. Jessica was pretty sure she heard a squelch.

'I'm going to have to go home and change,' he added.

Jessica nodded at the door. 'Let's go and say hello,' she said.

She crossed the lawn to the path, Rowlands in tow, his soggy feet splish-splashing with every step. Jessica rang the doorbell and waited.

'No one's in,' Rowlands said after barely a few seconds.

'Shush.'

Jessica pressed her ear to the window next to the door, straining to hear anything from inside. She pushed the doorbell again and then knocked.

'Matthew?' she called.

When nothing happened, she tried knocking again – then pushed open the letter box. She crouched but was unable to see anything except dark bristles.

'Matthew?' Louder this time.

She tried the doorbell once more.

There was a scrabbling from inside the cottage, followed by the clunk of one bolt, two – and then the door swung inwards.

The vicar didn't appear as either man of God or wannabe hippy this time. He was wearing striped M&S pyjamas, his beard unkempt, hair uncombed.

He blinked at Jessica, groggy and heavy-eyed, in need of a good kip.

'Oh,' he said, taking half a step backwards.

'Can we come in?' Jessica asked. 'My colleague might have to take off his shoes but...' She strode forward and Matthew took one more step backwards.

'Right, I er—'

'Nice place,' Jessica said, wiping her feet on the welcome mat and stepping onto the tiled floor of a large hallway. There was a door to her right, almost concealed by a hat stand mounded with coats. Dirty boots were lined up neatly nearby and an umbrella was in the corner. Three more doors led out of the hallway.

Rowlands waited outside, grumbling under his breath as he untied his filthy shoes.

'Can my colleague use your bathroom?' Jessica asked cheerily. 'He needs to clean himself up. Jumped in a puddle like an excited three-year-old.'

Matthew looked from Jessica to Rowlands. He'd backed further away and was standing next to a large grandfather clock.

'I, um... it's through there.' He pointed at the door next to the hat stand.

Rowlands scuttled in behind Jessica, leaving his shoes outside. Jessica closed the door behind him.

'Is everything all right?' the vicar asked.

'You called last night,' Jessica replied. 'Just after ten. You dialled 999 and then said everything was fine.'

Matthew stared back at her. He fiddled with the sleeve of his pyjama top. 'It was a misunderstanding,' he said eventually. 'I thought there was an intruder in the church.'

'Was there?'

He shook his head. 'No – I jumped the gun, I'm afraid. Silly me. I went out to check, but it was a squirrel or something like that.' He laughed but Jessica didn't and he tailed off.

'Are you sure everything's all right?' she added.

'Of course – no need for you to visit. I didn't realise you did that...' Matthew motioned towards the door. 'Thank you for checking – but it's a really busy time at the moment. I'm sure you understand.'

'Why did you call off today's service?'

'Sorry?'

'The board outside says today's service is cancelled. Isn't Easter kind of crucial for you...?'

The vicar glanced towards the door again and then coughed. 'I've been feeling a little off colour. Should probably go to the doctor – but you know what it's like with waiting rooms and the like... They've never been my thing.' He smiled again, forced it so hard that he looked like a maniacal clown.

There was a low clatter from behind and they both turned towards the bathroom. The door remained firmly closed and Jessica didn't want to think about what Rowlands was getting up to in there.

'I did have a couple of other questions for you,' Jessica said.

Matthew had one hand on the door. 'Oh...?'

'I was wondering if you'd seen or heard anything of Francine since we were last here.'

He poked out his bottom lip, shaking his head. 'Nothing, I'm afraid. I don't know what to tell you.' He suddenly sounded assertive, trying to take control of the conversation. 'If that's all—'

'What about Victoria?'

The name of his wife seemed to take Matthew by surprise. He straightened his back, standing taller. 'What about her?'

'Has she seen anything of Francine?'

'I wouldn't have thought so.'

'Can I ask her?'

His eyes darted to the door at the rear of the hallway and then quickly back to Jessica. 'She's gone shopping.'

'On Good Friday? She's brave. There are all sorts of bank holiday sales going on. The Arndale will be heaving.'

He shrugged. 'I really *do* need to be getting on with my work. Is your friend—'

'What happened last night?'

'Sorry?'

'With the phone call. People don't usually call 999 because they've heard a squirrel.'

'I told you – I heard noises around the church. When I went out there, a slate had fallen off the roof. It happens now and then. The building is falling into a bit of disrepair. Just one of those things.'

'So it wasn't a squirrel?'

'Sorry?'

'You didn't mention a slate before.'

Before Jessica could ask anything else, the toilet flushed and Rowlands emerged from the bathroom, wringing his hands. He looked between Jessica and the vicar, his lips tight. He may as well have said, 'I'd leave it a few minutes', because his face was screaming it.

The dirty sod.

'Everything all right?' he asked instead.

'We're leaving,' Jessica replied.

Matthew let out a large sigh of relief, prising the front door open wide for them. Jessica held out her hand for the vicar to shake and he did – but before he could pull away, she pressed a finger from her other hand to her lips. She nudged Matthew towards the grandfather clock, pointed Rowlands back into the bathroom – and then closed the front door with a deliberately loud click.

The vicar's eyes were wide, but Jessica kept the finger to her lips and backed into the bathroom. She waited, holding her breath, hoping Rowlands would follow her lead.

Silence.

Matthew was a statue by the door, arms rigid at his side, eyes locked to Jessica's.

They waited. Five seconds. Ten. None of them moved.

Then a woman's voice echoed through from the other side of the hallway. There was steel despite the elderly tremble.

'They've gone then?'

THIRTY-FIVE

Matthew's bottom lip bobbed as he turned away from Jessica to face the other side of the hallway. 'Yes, they er...'

'I heard.'

There was a scrape on the hard floor as the owner of the voice moved into the hallway. The angle meant that Jessica couldn't see who it was – but neither could she be seen.

The woman continued speaking. 'So, you *did* call them...?'

Matthew remained in Jessica's full view. He stepped backwards towards a musty bookcase. 'I didn't realise what was happening. I hung up straight away.'

'So why are they here?'

'I don't know. I think they're following something up.'

'They asked about me.'

Jessica exchanged a quick glance with Rowlands – but he looked down to where his sodden socks were still dripping on the floor. One quick stamp on the foot and he'd be out of the game.

'They visited before,' Matthew said. 'They wanted to know if you'd been to church services.'

'What did you say?'

'That you'd been here at Christmas.'

Jessica edged closer towards the entrance of the bathroom, careful to stay out of the sight line of the other door.

There was another scuff of shoe on floor and then Francine's haggard shape shuffled into view. She was wearing the same outfit as when Jessica first met her. The blue jumper looked dirtier than before and there was a large snag of wool hanging from the back. Jessica was about to tiptoe forward when she realised Francine wasn't alone. Matthew's wife, Victoria, was in front of her, almost hidden by the other woman's shape. Somehow Jessica had missed that there were four legs moving across the floor, not two. It was only Victoria's long reddy-blonde hair that caught her attention.

Francine's arm was angled forward, her wrist across the other's woman's throat. It only took a small sidestep for Jessica to spot the knife.

She felt Rowlands pressed in behind her. They could both see what was happening.

'Why did you call them?' Francine asked. If she turned, she'd see Jessica and Rowlands through the open doorway.

Matthew remained fixed on Francine, seemingly forcing himself not to glance past her towards the bathroom. 'When you came here last night, I didn't realise it was you who wanted my help...'

There was a slight squeal from Victoria, but Francine's shoulder relaxed a little.

Jessica edged forward, pressing onto the tips of her toes and straining to step across the hard floor so that she was standing on a large rug. For a moment, she thought Matthew's gaze had slipped, that he'd actually looked at her. If he had, then Francine hadn't spotted it. She remained standing with her back to Jessica, an arm across Victoria's neck.

'Would you like to pray?' Matthew asked.

'Pray?'

'You came here asking for sanctuary. Perhaps we should ask for His guidance...?'

Francine's shoulders dipped a little further, her arm slackening. Jessica took another step forward.

'I know what I must do,' Francine replied.

'But it can't do any harm to ask for direction...?'

There was a moment in which it felt like everyone had frozen. Jessica was a little over a metre from Francine, not daring to move. Matthew was eyeing Francine, forcing himself not to look at Jessica. Meanwhile, Francine's arm remained around Victoria's neck.

Stalemate.

Then Francine dropped her arm to her side, the knife still in her grasp. It was from a kitchen block, the type an expert chef would skim with a flick of the wrist to create perfect julienne vegetables. Short but brutally sharp.

'You are right,' Francine said.

Jessica didn't wait for a second chance. She sprang forward, head down, shoulder poised, slamming herself into Francine's lower back while grabbing the woman's wrist. They cannoned forward into the bookshelf, a booming thud of skull on wood echoing around the hall.

Jessica's skull.

Francine was slight and Jessica had misjudged the distance between them. She barrelled over the top of the other woman, bouncing off the shelf and landing on the back of her neck. Something cracked – and then there were only stars.

Shapes swirled and swarmed among the haze, voices shouted over the top of each other but Jessica couldn't figure out to whom they belonged. It felt like being in a kaleidoscope, lines and sounds spiralling around her.

Something slammed into Jessica's ribs, an arm or an elbow, then there was a hand pressing at her face, the palm across her mouth, a thumb squeezing into her eye socket.

She screamed – but it was as if the pressure in one eye sparked her other to life. Suddenly Jessica could see again. Francine was straddled across her, a nest of grey hair flapping as if there was a wind machine nearby and she was making a conceptual pop video. She was screaming something Jessica couldn't make out, top lip snarled with fury.

Jessica pushed upwards, thrusting with her hips – but her arms were locked at her side by the other woman's knees. She wriggled, but Francine was stronger than she looked. One hand remained on Jessica's face, the other reaching high with the knife, the tip of the blade glinting in the light, ready to plunge downwards.

THIRTY-SIX

A blur flashed from the side of Jessica's vision and then she realised she could move her arms. Her head swirled as she grunted her way into a sitting position, her stomach knotting as the thought occurred that she should probably get into the Pilates classes that some of the women at the station were always banging on about. 'Good for the core,' they parroted. As it was, Jessica's core bloody hurt as she tried – and failed – to stand.

'You all right?'

Jessica managed to twist to where Rowlands was kneeling on Francine's lower back, cuffing her hands together as she writhed underneath him. There was a trail of sodden sock prints on the floor between them.

'You took your time,' she said.

'I thought you had her. I didn't realise you were trying to headbutt the wall.'

'I wasn't trying to headbutt the wall!'

It might have been her ropy vision, but Jessica was certain she saw Rowlands wink.

'Same difference,' he replied.

. . .

Jessica rubbed her hip, using the interview room table as a shield so that neither the cameras nor Francine would see. Rowlands said she should go to the hospital but she'd had enough of that place for one day. Given the close-knit relationship her head had enjoyed with the bookcase, she had come off pretty well. There was a hint of purple under her eye from where Francine had gouged; her neck was stiff, her hip bruised, knee a bit clicky – which wasn't a medical diagnosis in the strictest sense but was accurate enough. A couple – well, four – paracetamol tablets and she was good to go.

She'd had hangovers that were worse.

'You'll be pleased to know that Matthew and Victoria Wells are both safe and well,' Jessica said.

Francine had refused everything on offer, be it water, food or legal representation. Her hands were cuffed to the table and, for once, she wasn't struggling. She didn't reply.

'I'll move past the whole, "assaulting an officer" thing for now – so let's start with last night.'

No reply. It was like Jessica's weekly phone calls with her mother – all the talking coming from one direction. This time, Jessica was on the opposing side.

'What happened last night?' Jessica asked.

Nothing.

'Why did you go to the church?'

'It is God's church.'

'Why did you go to *God's* church?'

Jessica had hoped Francine's moment of engagement might lead to the odd question being answered, but the other woman was apparently more interested in using her thumb to pick at her fingernail.

'You knocked on the window of the cottage at ten o'clock. You then threatened Matthew Wells with a knife, telling him to let you inside. Once you did that, you kept them hostage overnight.'

Jessica waited in case Francine wanted to add anything. She didn't.

'What were you hoping to achieve?'

The woman continued to pick at her fingernail, managing to loosen a few flecks of dirt that dropped onto the table.

'Francine?'

'It is *God's* house. It is His will.'

Jessica figured she wasn't going to get much sense by pushing the issue of what Francine had been hoping to achieve by barging into the cottage. She had statements from both Matthew and Victoria, which would do for now. At least they wouldn't have to let her go again.

She pushed a photo across the desk, watching as Francine's gaze flickered towards it and then away again.

'When did you last see this man?' she asked.

'God's will be done.'

'He's known as "Ezra". How do you know him?'

'God's will be done.'

A picture of Lucy, the one Emily had given them. It showed a young woman smiling and happy. Not the domestic-abuse victim. Not the person who'd fallen from the top of car park. 'Do you know this woman?'

'God's will be done.'

'Her name is Lucy. You argued with her at the hostel.'

'God's will—'

'I get it. Lucy fell from the top of a car park and Ezra was spotted disappearing through a fire escape moments after-wards. He was doing your bidding, wasn't he?'

Francine had stopped picking at her nails and was instead staring at the table. She seemed unconcerned by her predicament.

'God's will be done.'

'Is people dying *really* God's will?'

There was the slightest flicker of recognition as Francine's brow rippled. 'It is not for man to interfere with His plan.'

'What do you mean by that?'

'I do not have to explain myself to you. I am at peace.'

Jessica pressed back into her seat and suppressed the urge to sigh. Having any sort of conversation with Francine felt like it should come with a public health advisory. Warning: might cause excessive sighing.

'You won't be bailed,' Jessica said, her last gambit. 'Not this time. There are too many connections between you and people who have died. Witnesses who know you and Ezra are associates. At the absolute least, you'll be charged with breaking and entering, kidnapping, threats to kill, possession of a deadly weapon, assaulting a police officer. You won't be able to hand out leaflets any more. There's no more picketing. This is it. If you want your message to be heard, the only way you're going to get it out is by talking to me.'

Francine looked up, staring past Jessica towards the back of the interview room. Her eyes narrowed, lips pressed together as she realised Jessica was telling the truth. Everything was ultimately futile unless there was someone around to report it. A tree falling in the woods might as well be silent unless there was some bloke with a camera phone to put the footage on YouTube. It might not have been planned in such a way, but if Francine was guilty of anything close to what they suspected, the end game was that she *needed* to be caught. Perhaps that was why she'd barged into the cottage at the church in the first place.

'He has a plan for us all,' Francine said quietly.

'I understand that.'

'Man should not interfere for His will must not be defied. All these modern ways – medicine, doctors, hospitals – trying to subvert His plan. Someone had to stand up for what's right...' She tailed off. It wasn't quite a confession, certainly nothing that would stand up to scrutiny, but it was more conclusive than anything else she'd said.

'What did you do?' Jessica asked.

'I am but a vessel.'

'For what?'

Francine smiled, showing off a set of decayed, gum-disease-ridden teeth that surely couldn't be part of anyone's plan. 'For doing His work.'

'What sort of work?'

She continued smiling but didn't reply. After a moment of impasse between them, Jessica poked the photograph of Ezra once more.

'Where is he?'

'My son...'

Definitely not a literal relationship.

'Ezra... your son... where is he?'

Francine's grin spread further still. If she could have removed her hands from the cuffs, she surely would have done, splaying them behind her head, leaning back and putting her feet up.

'The only person by my side is the Lord.'

The effort of not sighing was becoming too great for Jessica. She took a breath and counted to five. 'If Ezra is your son, you must know where he is.'

'I will say no more.'

Jessica took her at her word. Someone else could have a crack at her in the coming hours. For now, she'd had quite enough.

'You not talking to me?'

Jessica sat at the side of Caroline's hospital bed, hand resting on top of her friend's. If she hadn't been told differently, she would have sworn that Caroline was sleeping. They'd seen one another doze many times before: top to tail while backpacking, side by side at a festival one time when Jessica was too young to know any better. Caroline's chest rose slowly and then dropped back into place. Her eyes were closed but there was the odd flutter of lashes whenever she breathed out. She was in a ward on her own – if it could be called that. It was more of a large cupboard. She was breathing by herself, no better than the night before but no worse either.

'I know I told you this,' Jessica said, 'but it's a little boy. He's doing okay. If you can wake your lazy arse up, you can go and see him. He's just down the hall.'

Jessica squeezed Caroline's hand gently but there was no reply. No movement except the gentle breaths in and out.

What was it with people she knew, comas and this bloody hospital?

If this was some sort of investigation, she'd be the connection. Some rampaging off-the-leash officer would be putting pieces together, seeing how many of Jessica's friends had ended up in this place and deciding it had to be her fault.

Jefferson Cass with his stupid pirate talk and the correlation theory. Fewer pirates meant global warming; knowing Jessica meant a greater likelihood of ending up in a coma.

Was it true?

Not the pirate thing.

She reached into her bag: 'I've got a fruit and nut bar here,' Jessica said. 'Cost a sodding fortune. Chocolate's more expensive then crude oil nowadays.'

She unwrapped the paper and wafted the bar across the front of Caroline's face.

'For every minute you continue dozing, I'm eating a square. If you want some, now's a good time to wake up.'

Jessica cracked the first strip of chocolate loose and then broke off a single piece, holding it up.

'C'mon, Caz. You're missing out. Remember when we used to buy a huge bar and then sit under the tree at the back of my mum and dad's house? Then boys came along and we stopped eating for fifteen years.'

There was no reaction, so Jessica popped the chocolate in her mouth and sucked it down.

'You're really going to make me eat the whole thing, aren't you? You're trying to make me fat.'

A second square was inhaled and then Jessica put the bar down on the side.

'Hugo's somewhere around Hong Kong – well, he was. I'm not sure which time zone he's in, or when he's due here. He said he had to swap planes, but they'd lost his bags. Then there was some sort of delay. Sounds typical, really. At least he's not on Ryanair – they'd fly him into Dublin and call it Manchester West.'

She tugged a magazine out from her bag and laid it flat on the edge of the bed.

'Bought you a second present,' she said. 'It's the type of trashy women's mag you used to leave lying around when you were done, then I'd read it, pretend I hadn't and throw it out.'

Jessica flipped through the pages of real-life stories, diet tips and crosswords, looking for something vaguely interesting.

'Right, quiz time – are you a sizzling siren between the sheets? Question one: What is your favourite position in bed?'

She paused, fishing a pen from her bag and waiting for the reply that didn't come.

'Right, I'm putting you down as "who needs a bed?" – that's five slut points. That's an easy one for me – "wherever's closest to the plug socket with the phone charger" – that's one slut point. Question two: What do you do if you spot a guy you fancy across a bar?'

Jessica looked up at Caroline, who hadn't moved.

'I'm "keep drinking and hope my sexy drunk talk does it

for him", but I'm putting you down for "stick my tongue down his throat". That's five points for you, two for me. Question three...'

Jessica continued her way through the quiz, ticking off Caroline's answers and making up her own. By the time she reached the end, the conclusion was clear.

She put the magazine down on the table next to the bed. 'Sorry,' she announced. 'The test doesn't lie. You're a total hoebag.' She stood over her friend, desperately wanting to see a crease of the lips. A twitch of the eyes. Anything.

Then she bent over and gently kissed Caroline's forehead.

'See you tomorrow, hoebag.'

THIRTY-SEVEN

The television was on mute as Jessica sat in her silent home. She constantly told her colleagues she wanted a bit of peace and quiet – lots of people did – but there was little fun to be had from the actual silence.

She could turn the volume up, but that would be admitting she needed the white noise. Needed the inane background chatter, or the voices to tell her what she should be buying.

It would be admitting that she was otherwise alone.

She noticed the digital clock of the TV box blink across to exactly ten o'clock. It had been a day ago that Francine had gone to the church with a knife. She'd not interviewed Matthew and Victoria herself, but she knew they'd been terrorised throughout the night by Francine with her knife, making threats to hurt one or both of them.

'That was a good Friday,' Jessica said quietly.

Her voice seeped into the corners of the room, disappearing into the dark.

There was nobody to reply, so she repeated herself.

What *did* people who lived alone actually do with themselves? She'd lived by herself before and yet she couldn't remember. Some of the lads at the station kept banging on about Tinder, but, bloody hell, she'd wear her thumb down to the bone with all the swiping left. Or was it right? Either way, there was swiping involved. She'd rather cut off her own arm than get into one of those stupid Facebook games that people kept sending her invites for – and then there were all those movies and TV shows on Netflix she'd hated first time around. She could go out, but what would she do then? Talk to people? To strangers? She had enough of that from the day job.

One minute she'd been up with technology and all the spangly, sparkly new things, the next her colleagues were talking about some app that let people rate pictures of genitalia and she wondered what had happened.

Jessica jumped as someone rapped loudly on the front door. Nobody *ever* knocked on her door, partly because no one except Caroline – who had a key – ever came to see her, but mainly because there was a doorbell. She was on her feet before she knew it, levering the front blind apart and peering onto her darkened path. There used to be a security light that came on when someone opened her gate or, if she was honest, walked within half a mile of the house. She was never quite sure how the sensor operated. It had stopped working a few months before and she'd never got round to figuring out what was wrong with it. Either way, she couldn't see anyone at her front door.

'Bloody kids,' she muttered.

She was back on the sofa when a second knock rattled through the house. This time she didn't bother with the blind, racing to the front door instead. She grabbed the key and unlocked it in one fluid movement, then yanked it open, expecting to see a retreating hoody haring along her path.

Instead, there was a woman who didn't flinch at Jessica's sudden appearance. She was wearing a woollen jacket that stretched to her thighs and was belted tight across her midriff. She had short, spiky dark hair.

'Jessica?' she said.

'Um...?'

'Are you Detective Inspector Jessica Daniel?'

'Sorry, I have no idea who you are.'

The woman reached wearily into her pocket with a slight roll of the eyes and then flashed a warrant card. Jessica was busy checking it over as the newcomer continued speaking.

'We can do the whole comparing rank thing if you want – you're an inspector, I'm an inspector, let's go give some constable a good kicking – or you can just call me Nina and invite me in.'

Jessica was more than a little taken aback by the fact there was not only a police officer on her doorstep so late in the evening but also that the other woman apparently knew a reasonable amount about her. She held the door wider and stepped away, allowing Nina to enter.

Without the explicit invitation, Nina found her way into the living room and took a spot on the sofa. Jessica perched on the lounge chair, wondering what had just happened.

'You asked and here I am,' Nina said. She was looking around the room, being nosy as if she was interested in buying the place.

'Sorry... I asked for what?'

Nina turned to face her, unbelting her jacket at the same time. She had the sharp cheekbones of someone who didn't do an awful lot of eating, the veiny hands of a person who saw the gym as a second home.

'We have a mutual acquaintance,' she said.

It took Jessica a few seconds to get it. With Caroline, the hospital, Francine and the whole headbutting a wall palaver, she'd almost forgotten about Jefferson Cass.

'You're his handler...?'

Nina shrugged non-committedly, unwilling to say the words.

'What are you doing here on Good Friday?' Jessica added.

'Nothing better to do. I did pop round earlier, but you were out and about.' She glanced towards the photograph of Jessica and Adam that was underneath the television. 'Got a lad on the go, have you...?'

'I, um...'

Nina turned back, fixing her stare on Jessica, now serious. 'Well... you wanted to see me, here I am.'

'Do you want a tea, or something?'

Jessica was stalling for time, trying to get her thoughts together, and Nina knew it. Jessica wondered if that was why she'd visited so late – and at her home. It would throw anyone off their game.

'Can we get on with it?' Nina replied.

'It's just... Jefferson Cass...'

'What about him?'

'Is he... one of us?'

Nina rolled her tongue across the top of her teeth, seemingly weighing Jessica up but really emphasising her position of power and knowledge. She was in the know and Jessica wasn't.

'I can't confirm that. Let's just say that you know him and I know him.'

'I don't understand why you're here if we can't have a straight conversation.'

'What do you want to know?'

'If Jefferson Cass is one of us, if he's a ghost, then what's happening on that estate? He has people coming and going from his flat all hours, there's at least one old bloke being terrorised by it all. Every time I'm there, you can sense the tension – and yet nobody will talk.'

'Perhaps there's nothing to talk about – or maybe it's just that they won't talk to you...?'

Jessica wished she had a smart reply, but there wasn't one. It was hard to describe Jefferson's influence on the estate, on the kids, because Jessica herself wasn't sure.

'I gather there was an incident,' Nina said.

'You could call it that.'

'What do you call it?'

'Being cornered by half an estate's worth of people? Terrifying is what I call that.'

'And yet no one was arrested, no charges laid. For all intents and purposes, what you say happened never happened.'

Nina didn't sound as if she was deliberately trying to push Jessica's buttons, she was stating a fact that was true. Stating a fact in a *really* annoying and patronising way – which would have been bad enough even if she wasn't sitting on Jessica's sofa to do it.

'It sounds like many of the problems on that estate have come since you started your new role there...' she added.

Jessica bit the tip of her tongue, forcing the politeness. 'I'm not trying to cause any problems, I'm trying to figure out why an old man has had his windows put through and his flat vandalised simply because he has the misfortune of living directly above *your* man. I'm trying to work out why the kids who live there hold *your* man in such high regard and how he can get away with hitting one of them across the face and have no repercussions from either them or you.'

Nina stared at her, momentarily confused, and Jessica knew she had her.

'Someone told you that he hit them in the face?' Nina asked.

'No – that's what I saw.'

'When?'

Suddenly the power had shifted and they both knew it. Nina was leaning forward, so Jessica slouched back, shaking her head.

'I don't trust you,' she said. 'I don't know who you are.'

'Perhaps you saw something that looked like he was hitting out?'

Jessica laughed. '*Really*? That's your best explanation. I do have eyes. I know what I'm doing. I'm not some conspiracy theorist who thinks she's seen a UFO. Jefferson Cass hit that lad across the face and his mates acted like it was normal.'

Nina took a moment, examining Jessica and then seemingly taking her word. 'Perhaps things are more complex than you think?'

'Complex enough that an undercover police officer is attacking kids?'

Jessica hoped for a reaction but Nina's features remained taut and then she pushed herself to her feet, rebuckling her jacket.

'I'll see what I can find out, but that doesn't mean you're seeing all the sides of this.'

'And you are?'

A shrug, then Nina offered her hand. Jessica shook it as she stood and then guided the other woman back to the front door.

'I came as a matter of courtesy,' Nina said. 'But everything you were told still stands. Our mutual acquaintance is off limits.'

Jessica held the door open. 'He's not what you think,' she said. 'Whoever you think he is, whatever role you think he's playing, you're wrong.'

'You'd know?'

'I've seen a lot of bad guys.'

Nina laughed as she stepped onto the path. 'And that's your argument? You've seen bad guys, so you know one to look at one?' A pause. 'You should get over yourself. It's not all about you.'

She hesitated for a moment and then strode away, chuckling as she moved along the path. She left the gate hanging open, not turning back as she disappeared into the night, mocking laughter still ringing.

The air was cold and Jessica stood in the doorway breathing it in. The dim orange bulbs of the street lights glowed against the cloudy, dark sky.

Jessica was about to head back inside when she realised that the open gate would annoy her all night if she didn't do something about it. It wasn't an OCD thing, more that it felt like Nina had got one over her by coming to her property and then leaving things differently to how they were. She left the door on the latch and then bounded along the path, slamming the gate into its clasp with a loud, satisfying bang that would *definitely* show that cow who was boss.

She paused for a moment, sniffing the air and the rotting whiff of her neighbour's bins. It would have been bin day except for the bank holiday, yet next door had left their rubbish on the kerb anyway.

Jessica turned back to the house and then stopped once more. There was something about the decaying stench that flicked the switch in her brain and allowed her to *finally* put two and two together.

It wasn't the only rotten odour she'd smelled that day...

THIRTY-EIGHT

Beams of white light pierced through the garden at the back of
St Benedict's Church, turning night into day. Jessica was
standing next to Matthew, the vicar, at the front door of the
cottage, both wearing thick coats to protect from the chill, yet
neither willing to head inside. A shield had been set up around
the water butt to the side of the building and two poor sods in
white paper suits were going about their business. A couple of
uniformed officers were meandering close to the gate, but it
was otherwise quiet.

'I didn't know...' Matthew said.

'No reason why you should,' Jessica replied. 'Francine
must have dumped the body before interrupting you with the
knife.'

'And is it... Ezra?'

'It seems so. I don't think there's a lengthy line-up of six-
foot-something black guys who live around here, let alone ones
who follow Francine around.'

'What happened?'

Matthew's voice quivered. If being held at knifepoint

hadn't been bad enough, then being woken up in the middle of the night by a group of officers who subsequently found a dead body in his garden had certainly rocked him.

'It looks like he'd been stabbed in the chest.'

'By who?'

Jessica said nothing, partly because she didn't know the answer but mainly because she didn't want to speculate in front of him.

Underneath his jacket, the vicar was still wearing the furry Kermit the Frog slippers in which he'd opened the door. A long dressing gown was tied around his waist and he had his arms folded tight across his chest. He stared towards the back of the garden, even though he'd not been allowed near the water butt and hadn't seen what was behind the screen.

'If *she*, if Francine, killed him, how did she get him here? I saw him – he was massive. She had a knife, but how would she have picked him up, or dragged him?'

'There'll be a proper team here in the daylight to look for signs.'

They stood together staring towards the screen at the back of the house. Jessica hugged her arms across her front, trying to remember when she'd last slept. Slept properly in her own bed, in any case. It was a while ago. She looked down at her feet, then Matthew's, taking in Kermit's bulbous eyes.

'How's Victoria?' she asked.

'Shocked,' came the reply, as Matthew glanced momentarily towards the cottage. 'I made her take a sleeping tablet.'

They went silent for a moment, each staring towards Ezra's final resting place.

The truth was that Francine could never have dragged Ezra's body around the garden. She was wild and Jessica had felt the other woman's surprising strength when she'd been trapped underneath her – but that was nothing like what it would have needed to take down a man who was more than six feet tall and close to twenty stone. Jessica didn't think he'd stabbed himself in the chest and then folded his body into the great big plastic container. Which left her with the sinking, stonking great problem that if Francine hadn't dumped Ezra's body in the water butt, then who had?

THIRTY-NINE

SATURDAY

Jessica leant against the wall and glanced towards the door to the interview room. 'Why does it have to be me?'

For a man who protested his innocence about choosing to wear dad jumpers, DCI Topper was showing himself to have at least two. The second was even more unforgiveable than the first: some sort of zigzag brown and white mystery eye pattern that made Jessica feel dizzy by being in its general vicinity.

'You just couldn't give it a few days, could you?' he said.

'What?'

'It's a long weekend, Jess. Two bank holidays and Easter Sunday all thrown in together. This is better than Christmas – but you had to go and find a dead body, didn't you?'

Jessica wasn't entirely sure whether he was joking. His hybrid Scottish-Irish-drunken-bloke-in-a-bar accent made it hard to tell. It always sounded like he was chewing on nails.

'It's not my fault,' she protested.

'I'm supposed to be off for a few days, not swanning about here signing off overtime forms and negotiating forensics.'

'I'm not the one who killed him.'

'No, but you bloody found him, didn't you? Couldn't wait

till Tuesday.' He nodded at the door. 'Anyway, you've done the crime, so get in there and do your time.'

Jessica was out of excuses so did as she was told, ignoring the smirk of the onlooking uniformed officer.

Francine was cuffed to the interview room table once more, still wearing the clothes she'd had on every time Jessica had seen her. She was starting to smell but had refused the voluntary shower. If she kept it up, she'd be getting one whether she wanted it or not.

Jessica sat and tugged her hair away from her face. She'd had a few hours' sleep but nowhere near enough to prepare her for another round.

Francine started to laugh before Jessica could say anything. Her hands buckled against the restraints, but not because she was trying to get away. She rocked back, still cackling.

'Care to share the joke?' Jessica said.

'The final pieces are coming into play. Everything's in place.'

'Final pieces of what?'

'His plan.'

Jessica sat, unamused and waiting for Francine to calm herself. It took at least a minute, but the other woman eventually slouched forward, grinning toothily.

'Are you ready to talk?' Jessica asked.

'I will talk about His plan as much as you like.'

'I was thinking more about the present you left for Matthew Wells and his wife.'

The grin widened. 'His will is to be done on the day the Father's son rises again.'

'Is that right?'

'Sinners will face His Reckoning.'

'Reckoning? Sounds like a good name for a movie. Someone should make that.'

Francine didn't react. She was rocking against the restraints, though not fighting them. She eyed Jessica with glee.

'For once,' Jessica said, 'do you think you could talk in something other than riddles?'

The other woman raised her hands as much as she could – which wasn't a lot. 'It's time for sinners to pay.'

'Aren't we all sinners? I've not read a lot of the Bible, but isn't the point supposed to be that everyone's a sinner and we're supposed to ask for God's forgiveness?'

Francine nodded, which was about as much of an acknowledgement as Jessica had received in all the time she'd been in a room with her.

'But those who go out of their way to defy the Lord's wishes will pay first.'

'What does that mean?' Jessica asked.

'His will is to be done on the day the Father's son rises again.'

'You already said that.'

Francine smiled back and then relaxed into her chair. Jessica did the same and the two women stared at each other. Jessica had had conversations with brick walls that spewed more sense.

'What about Ezra?' Jessica asked.

'What about him?'

'I thought you were friends?'

'He defied God's will – and all who do must be punished.'

'How did he defy God's will?'

Francine's only reply was to start reciting the Lord's Prayer. When she finished, she started over again. Jessica watched and then peered up to the watching camera before deciding she'd definitely had enough.

. . .

Jessica found Topper in his office, munching on a Rolo Easter egg. He reached into his drawer and then placed a single Rolo on the table between them.

'Peace offering,' he said.

'I need to get some sleep,' Jessica replied. She took the chocolate anyway.

'I'm not sure much more will be forthcoming today anyway,' he said. 'But there is one thing...'

'What?'

'It's a bit late – but we finally got a useful phone call about Ezra.'

Jessica was confused: 'Somebody telling us where he was?'

'No – a member of the public called in last night, saying they recognised the photo that's been doing the rounds. His name isn't Ezra. Well, it's not his *real* name. Our caller recognised him as Lucas Williams, reckoned they used to work together a few years ago down south. If it checks out, Lucas was attacked with a knife five years ago. He needed a blood transfusion to save his life but then refused to name his attacker. After that, our caller reckoned he disappeared – but I assume he moved up here and didn't tell anyone.'

Topper passed across a few sheets of paper that Jessica skim-read – case files from another force relating to his stabbing. From the photos, it was apparent that Ezra and Lucas were the same person.

'Francine said that Ezra defied God's will,' Jessica replied. 'I guess this is what she meant.'

Topper took the pages back. 'I need to get someone from the mental health team to assess her,' he said. 'It doesn't suit anyone for us to keep her here and there's no way I'm going to the super to ask for more time. She's got a solid alibi for the killings of Lucy at the car park and there's nothing directly to link her to Henry Taylor ending up in front of that car, Mark Stanley's drowning, or your burns victim. We've got circumstantial from her leaflets and general rantings, but that's not going to get you far. We could do her for the home invasion, knife possession and assaulting an officer – but it's better if we hand her over for now.'

Jessica wasn't going to argue – anything that meant she didn't have to spend any more time in an interview room with the woman was fine by her.

'There's something else,' Jessica said.

'Not today there's not.'

'Ezra, Lucas, whatever he's called. There's no way he ended up in that water butt by himself and Francine couldn't have got him there.'

Topper was twiddling his thumbs, mind elsewhere. 'Is there anything to say she has any other associates?'

'No – but she was handing out those flyers over months, so who knows what sort of nutter might've ended up taking one. It's not as if the city's got a shortage.'

'So what's your plan? We arrest all the Greater Manchester nutters? *You're* going to have a long weekend if that's the case.' He pushed himself up from the desk, making it clear the conversation was ending. 'We'll regroup next week. You've done all you can for now. Francine's in custody and her associate is dead. That's the two people we've been searching for. This is what they call a result.'

It didn't feel like one.

'Go and get that sleep you were talking about,' he added. 'There are people in all weekend and all these cases are being looked at individually anyway. We're still waiting for the official report for the food truck fire.'

Jessica thanked him and headed for the door, thinking sleep would be lovely – but there was somewhere she needed to go first.

FORTY

The heater at the back of Roly's kitchen was rattling like a rickety steam train, pouring a plume of air that was as hot as the sun into the room. Jessica was sitting at the dining table, slightly out of the heater's direct blast zone, though still enjoying the warmth. It was like a sauna, with more clothes and fewer creeps. Her fingers were wrapped through a mug of tea, Archie at her side. He was wearing the full suit and shirt, as if he was actually at work.

Archie and Roly had spent the best part of an hour banging on about how wonderful Manchester was. They had each grown up in areas ridden with poverty but overflowing with 'characters'. Roly soon had Archie howling with tales of underage drinking, police raids at the local pub and how the kids would hide in the cellar with a barrel of cider. It turned out that despite the forty-odd years between them, they had a ridiculous amount in common. Roly told stories of the ancient Stretford End at Old Trafford, Archie replied with tales of the glory nights of Sir Alex.

Jessica was a spare wheel, which was fine by her. She yawned her way through the evening...

...And then she jumped awake, realising not only that she'd fallen asleep – but that both Roly and Archie had been watching her. The mug of tea wasn't wrapped through her fingers at all, it was on the draining board, empty and upside down.

'You looked pretty comfy there, love,' Roly said.

Jessica pushed herself up in the chair, feeling the throb in her neck from where she'd cannoned into the bookcase at Matthew's cottage the previous night. It probably didn't help that she'd been dozing with her head resting on her chest.

'I didn't realise you were such a drooler,' Archie said.

Jessica rubbed her chin but there was nothing there and both men started laughing.

'Long night,' Jessica replied. She stretched her arms high and cricked her neck.

Roly looked between the two of them. 'You two together?'

Jessica and Archie both answered 'no' at the same time and Roly held up his hands, backing away to the window and laughing to himself.

'All right, all right. I'll ask no questions, you tell no lies.'

'I've got a girlfriend,' Archie said.

'I'm not judging,' Roly replied, a twinkle in his eye.

Jessica cleared her throat loudly, partly to wake herself up, mainly to stop Roly from talking. She peered around him through the window to where the sun had almost set. A wibbly haze of orange was seeping between the houses beyond, but the sky was dark.

'Are you ready?' she asked.

Roly straightened, suddenly serious. He glanced at the door.

'You don't have to do this if you don't want to,' she added.

He fished into a drawer and pulled out a packet of cigarettes, lighting one and leaning over the sink so that he was closer to the window. 'My choice, innit, love. Just give me a few ticks to finish this off.'

Roly took a long puff of the cigarette and blew the smoke towards the window.

'Can I ask you a question?' Jessica said.

'Go ahead.'

'The window. Why's it always open even though you have a heater in here? It's the same all over the block. Loads of people leave the windows open, even if it's just a bit.'

'It's the heat. There are huge hot water pipes that run below and above all these flats. It's bad enough in the winter, but you should feel it in the summer. Fans make no difference 'cos it's just blowing the hot air about. Everyone leaves their windows open a bit – usually at the back.'

She nodded towards the heater: 'So why that? Must cost a fortune in bills?'

Roly smiled, gave a slight head tilt. 'You'll understand when you get to my age, love. One minute I'm too hot, then I'm too cold.'

He sucked on the cigarette once more and then, in the absence of any other questions, gulped the rest of it down. When he was done, he sprayed a gust of air freshener into the room before straightening his clothes.

'I'm ready,' he said.

'Arch will whistle when we're in place,' Jessica replied.

'Are *you* sure about all this?' Roly replied.

Jessica was already on her feet but stopped dead. 'Why wouldn't we be?'

He shrugged. 'I don't want you getting in trouble for me.'

She glanced towards Archie, who met her stare. He was up for anything. The week of suspension had him itching for action. In that instant, she knew they were a brother and sister in arms. There were plenty of things she disliked about him – *hated* about him, perhaps. The bragging, the lad-about-town, the banter with his mates, the football talk, the misogyny when he talked to his friends, even though she knew it wasn't the *real* him. That was the opposite of everything she was, and yet, despite that, they both needed the buzz that only this job could bring.

Archie smiled and Jessica nodded back. He knew the same thing about her that she knew about him.

'If we get in any sort of trouble, it's entirely on us,' Jessica replied.

Roly nodded towards the floor. Towards Jefferson Cass. 'You say he's some sort of undercover dib...?'

'I don't know.'

'He ain't like any I've ever seen. If he's dib – one of you – he has a funny way of showing it.'

Jessica didn't reply. If Jefferson was playing a role, he *shouldn't* be acting like a police officer. At the same time, there was hitting the kids and the control he wielded. Things didn't add up – and she'd seen in Nina's face that she didn't think it was right either.

Archie led the way out of the flat, heading down the stairs at the furthest end and then slinking into the shadows at the back of the block. There was a row of terraced houses on the next street over, but the space between was a crumbling strip of tarmac and an area of wasteland peppered with patchy grass. Fly-tipped junk and a pair of skips that had long since been abandoned were speckled intermittently.

It was quite the view.

Archie slotted in next to one of the skips, Jessica at his side, both of them swallowed by the darkness. They were only a few metres from the flats and it was a strain to stare upwards – but Roly was silhouetted in his kitchen window as he peered out to the night beyond. Jefferson's flat was directly ahead of them: close enough that it was no more than a stone's throw for Jessica – and she was *terrible* at throwing. The back window was open a sliver, with one of the blinds rippling through to the outside.

'You sure about this?' Archie whispered.

'No. You?'

'No.'

He said nothing for a moment before sticking a pair of fingers in his mouth and hissing a shrill, sharp whistle.

Roly's shadow disappeared.

Jessica leaned gently on Archie's shoulder, wanting to grip his hand but making herself hold back. The reassurance would have been nice, but he was pumped and ready to go, bobbing on his heels like an athlete waiting for a starting gun.

The scream was a lot louder than she thought.

It was possibly because Roly's back window was still open, but the terror in his voice still made her jump. She heard a door bang open – Roly's – and then the word 'snake' was shouted.

If she heard it that clearly then other people definitely would have.

She counted silently in her head – not seconds, but the number of times Archie was rocking forward and back. She got to five when she heard another door opening. Five more – and then there was another whistle.

It was as if Archie had heard it a second before she had. By the time Jessica had clocked Roly's signal, Archie was already striding towards Jefferson's window. He dug inside his top and pulled out a flattened metal coat hanger that he'd appropriated from Roly's wardrobe. He thrust it into the gap between the window and the frame and started to wiggle. Jessica had left the planning to him and he was uncannily too well prepared.

It only took a second or two before he pushed the hanger upwards with a click and then the window was loose. He pulled a pair of nitrile gloves from his pocket, stretched them onto his hands with precise, quick movements and then reached in carefully, lifting the latch and levering the window open.

Jessica breathed.

Archie didn't wait, lifting himself up on the window frame and then dropping through between the blinds. Jessica pulled on her own gloves and followed, plunging soundlessly onto the pristine coffee-coloured carpet of Jefferson's apartment. She couldn't resist looking towards the snake tank. The bulb at the top was darkened and, from what she could see, the reptile inhabitants were either sleeping or dead. She certainly wasn't getting any closer to find out.

'I can't stand tidiness,' Archie said quietly. He was hunched over the sofa, lifting up the cushions and looking underneath. 'You can only be this tidy if you're hiding something.'

Jessica didn't disagree. She crossed the room and picked up the cushions from the armchair, unzipping the cover and peeping inside, before replacing it. The chair itself was bare but meticulously clean. She pressed on the sides and then lifted it to look underneath. There were no slits in the lining, nothing that made it look like it hadn't come directly from IKEA.

'Anything?' she asked.

'Not even a bitten-off fingernail down the back of the sofa.' He replaced the cushions and flattened them into place. 'Now I know he's hiding something. There's *always* a fingernail down the back of the sofa.'

There was a thump from Roly's apartment above.

'Hurry up,' Jessica said. 'You take the bedroom, I'll do the kitchen.'

The layout was identical to Roly's flat and, as Archie disappeared through the door that led off the hallway, Jessica crouched and started to look under the sink. There were rows of cleaning products – two full bottles of washing-up liquid, bleach, various different colour sprays for countertops and floors, two dustpans and brushes, a spare mop head, bin liners too numerous to count. It was like the aisle of the supermarket that nobody entered had been transported and dumped in the cupboard.

Jessica checked underneath the products and rattled the pipes that led from the sink – but nothing seemed amiss. There was nothing taped to the underside of the sink itself, nor any of the kitchen cabinets. She looked in the fridge and the freezer – which were both sparse – and then checked the oven and the microwave.

Nothing.

She looked inside cereal packets, tinkered with the light fitting, went through the cutlery drawer.

Jessica pulled out the metal rack into which knives, forks and spoons had been sorted, stopping when she saw what was at the back of the drawer.

It wasn't what she expected.

'You got something?'

Jessica muffled a shriek as she just about managed to keep hold of the drawer organiser. Archie was in the doorway, hands on hips.

'Jesus, Arch...'

'Sorry.'

She pulled out a knuckleduster and held it up for Archie to see. She didn't know for sure but thought it was probably made of brass. It was ludicrously heavy.

'That it?' he replied.

Jessica returned the weapon to the back of the drawer and replaced the organiser. It was a weapon that Jefferson shouldn't have – but she was hardly going to be able to get a warrant based on that, especially as she'd have no way of explaining how she knew it was in the drawer.

'Did you find anything?' she asked.

'Nothing. He hangs up his pants, Jess. His pants! What's wrong with this guy?'

There was another bump on the ceiling from above and they both stopped to listen. It had been five minutes since Roly's distraction.

Archie and Jessica headed back into the living room, but there was only one place they hadn't searched. Jessica looked to the snake tank and then turned to Archie.

'Go on.'

'Bollocks to that.'

They took a step closer and Jessica could see the beasts at the bottom of the tank. She counted three snakes, none of which were sleeping or dead on closer inspection. The trio seemed to be watching her and the one with red and black strips in particular seemed like a right nasty bastard. It had its belly pressed to the front of the glass, its head high, eyes fixed on Jessica. Meanwhile, the albino one was coiled at the back of the tank, probably trying to lure them in. The thick browny-grey monstrosity was just there. Do you feel lucky, punk?

Jessica peered closer, looking to where the bottom of the tank was covered with a layer of paper towels.

'He could be hiding something underneath that,' she said.

Archie pressed onto tiptoes and then sank back down again. 'Could be.'

'After you,' Jessica whispered.

'Ladies first.'

'Men just before.'

Another creak from above.

'What are you so afraid of?' Jessica said.

'That red and black one. He's looking at me funny.'

Jessica had been sure the red and black snake had been looking at her, but she wasn't about to argue. Not about that in any case.

'C'mon, Arch. I'll owe you one.'

'Owe me one what?'

'Whatever. Just get on with it.'

For a moment, Jessica thought Archie was going to step towards the tank – but then he reached into his pocket and emerged with a fifty-pence piece.

'Heads or tails,' he said.

'What?'

'I'll flip you for it.'

'We haven't got time for—'

The coin sailed into the air.

'—heads,' Jessica called.

Archie caught the coin and pressed it onto the back of his hand.

'Shite,' he said.

Jessica had never been more relieved to see a coin come down heads in her life.

Archie wasted no more time, rolling up his sleeves and taking a big gulp. Jessica did her bit by standing at his side and lifting the lid. She expected a barrage of hissing, snarling nightmares, but it was quiet... which, in many ways, was worse.

'Tell my mum I love her,' Archie said.

'I'll tell her she's got a great big chicken for a son.'

Archie spun to look at her and Jessica grinned.

'Get a shift on,' she said.

After another deep breath, Archie motioned to reach into the tank. There was a glistening line of sweat along his hairline. Jessica held her breath as he stretched... and stretched... and then stopped. He removed his hand from the tank in a flash and then reached behind it to pull out a half-metre-long plastic ruler that had been wedged between the tank and the glass.

'Thank god for that,' he said.

'I don't think snakes like to be poked with sticks.'

Archie ignored her, dangling the ruler into the tank and

scratching at the paper towards the back. Jessica eyed the snakes suspiciously, expecting them to leap up at any point, but none of them bothered to move. The red and black one at the front continued to press itself against the glass, while the albino one remained coiled and the browny-grey thick acted docile.

'There's something under here,' Archie said.

Jessica kept holding the lid, twisting so that she could peer towards the back of the tank. 'What?'

Archie continued scratching until he managed to flip the paper completely backwards. The albino snake hissed softly, its eyes fixed on the ruler.

Jessica didn't need to ask a second time as she could see for herself. There was money.

Lots of money.

Ten- and twenty-pound notes had been flattened and stacked, before being covered with the paper towels.

'There's loads here,' Archie said, as he continued to prod with the ruler. 'Tens of thousands. More.'

He had to be guessing – but the tank was a good metre and a half long. If the entire thing was concealing money, then Archie would be right. The amount would definitely be in the six figures. It still wasn't enough – not by itself. Jefferson could be one of those people who didn't trust banks and hoarded cash. Nothing had been proved.

'Anything else?' Jessica asked.

'Nope.'

There was another scraping from above and then a bump. Jessica froze as two more bumps came in quick succession. That was their signal.

Archie quickly flattened the paper at the back of the tank and then Jessica dropped the lid on top.

'Quick!' she hissed.

'What do you think I'm doing?'

Jessica lunged for the window, pressing down on the window frame and heaving herself upwards. She hadn't asked, but Archie's hands were on her backside, pushing her through the window far quicker than she'd expected. Before she knew what was happening, she was toppling forward, arms outstretched in an effort to stop herself from landing on her head.

She crumpled onto her already painful shoulder, groaning quietly as she rolled onto her back, winded.

Archie pushed the window closed and then he was at her side.

'C'mon,' he said.

'I really hate you sometimes,' she replied.

Archie offered his hand and pulled her to her feet. Her shoulder throbbed but his smile was infectious. 'You keep telling yourself that,' he said.

FORTY-ONE

The kettle was bubbling by the time Jessica and Archie were back in Roly's kitchen. He was grinning from ear to ear, a kid who'd been caught up to no good but didn't care.

'He wasn't happy,' Roly said.

'Jefferson?' Jessica replied.

'Said all his snakes were in the tank. I just kept pointing under the sink and saying I'd seen one slithering around the back of the cupboards. He was down on his hands and knees, shaking his head, swearing; saying it was nothing to do with him. I told him I never said it was – just that I'd seen a snake. He stomped around the flat saying he couldn't see anything. I asked if I should call the dibs if the snake came back.'

'What did he say?'

Roly shrugged. 'Asked if I was threatening him. I said I didn't know what he was on about – I just didn't like snakes. After that, he said I should be careful who I talked to. Then he left and I knocked on the floor.'

The kettle switched itself off with a click and Roly nodded at the mugs on the draining board. 'You want another?' he asked.

Jessica turned to Archie. 'We've got to head off.'

Archie took a step towards the hallway, but Roly continued speaking. 'Did you find what you were after?' he asked.

'To a degree,' Jessica replied.

She carried on moving after Archie, but Roly took a small sidestep so that he was between her and the door. 'Sorry,' he said.

Archie was already in the hall but stopped to look back, wondering what was going on. Roly was in the middle of them, turning from one to the other.

'It's just...' he focused on Archie, 'in my day, you'd get in a ruck and it was fists. You never know now. You didn't find... guns, did you?'

Archie glanced to Jessica, who nodded with her eyes.

'Not guns,' Archie said.

'Drugs?'

'No.'

'What then? You get to go off home, but I have to live here.'

This time, Archie didn't look to Jessica for permission. 'Money,' he replied. 'We found money.'

'What, like a few quid?'

'A lot of money.'

'Where'd that come from?'

Jessica was boring holes into Archie, wanting him to shut up, but it was already too late. For some reason – the Manc connection or his own damned stupidity – he kept speaking.

'I don't know, mate. He's obviously into something he shouldn't be.'

Roly stepped to the side. 'What are you going to do?'

Jessica answered before Archie could continue blabbing. 'We don't know, Roly. You've got my number, though. If anything else happens, then call. If not me, then 999.'

'Right.'

She continued into the hallway, nudging Archie in the back until he got the message. They were out of the front door, along the balcony, down the stairs and halfway back to the car when she next spoke.

'What is wrong with you?' Jessica hissed.

'What?'

'What do you think? It's bad enough we involved Roly in the first place, then you had to tell him what we found.'

'So what? He's an old bloke. He's scared. What if it was your old man? I'm only trying to help him sleep at night so he's not worrying there's an armoury in the flat below him.'

'And what if he goes to the papers? Tells them about the problems he's had and that the bloke in the flat below him has a load of cash? What if he lets it slip to another neighbour? Or Jefferson himself? How are we going to answer that one?'

'He won't tell anyone.'

'How'd you know that?'

'Because he won't.'

Archie spoke as firmly as Jessica had known him. It was the end of the conversation, regardless of who outranked whom.

From nowhere, she could picture her father in the hospital the final time she'd seen him...

When he'd said what he said.

At the time, before he said goodbye, she thought that she'd think about him every day. It wasn't quite like that now. Every now and then he would pop into her head, perhaps because of a song on the radio, a smell, or the way somebody might phrase a word. He wasn't the constant presence she thought he'd be.

Jessica realised that she'd stopped walking as Archie had continued onwards. He turned to look at her, illuminated by the dim orange of a street light. They were in an alley, deserted and silent.

'You all right?' he asked.

'Yeah.'

He shuffled from one foot to the other, wanting to ask something. He'd never been great at hiding what he was thinking or feeling. 'I was just wondering if—'

Archie was cut off by the buzzing of Jessica's phone in her pocket. She held up a hand to stop him speaking and then dug it out, surprised to see the name on the front.

'Hugo?' she said.

The voice on the other end sounded tired, only just comprehensible – though that was Hugo all over. He was like that with or without the jet lag.

'Jess?'

'It's me.'

'Are you still up?'

'Obviously, otherwise I wouldn't have answered my phone.'

'Can you pick me up? At the immigration queue at the airport.'

Jessica reached into her other pocket for the car keys: 'I'll be there as soon as I can.'

FORTY-TWO

Hugo turned heads wherever he went. He always had. It didn't help that he was now a semi-famous magician – not in a way that many people knew his name, more that he had a look that people remembered. He had shaggy dark hair, more dog-rolling-in-the-park than anything he styled himself. Jessica didn't know when he'd last changed his clothes, but he was wearing green cord trousers and a T-shirt patterned as if it was the top half of a tuxedo. Buttons were printed up the centre, with the white collar of a shirt and a green handkerchief in the pocket that wasn't a pocket. He moved in such a lackadaisical way that it was like he was trying to walk backwards. Jessica still found it hard to keep up with him as he strode across the hospital car park.

She was used to him being laid-back and saying very little unless asked a direct question – but this was a new Hugo.

Hugo the father.

The receptionist was somebody new, not Melissa, and nobody that Jessica recognised. She had grey hair and the world-weary look of someone who'd seen and heard most things across far too many late shifts.

She told Hugo that it was no longer visiting hours and he nodded calmly, acceptingly. Then he looked to Jessica before flashing a smile towards the woman.

'No worries,' he replied. 'It's just... I left Australia what I think might have been two days ago. I got stuck in Hong Kong, lost my luggage, had a flight cancelled and then rescheduled, got on another plane somewhere in the Middle East, then got caught up at immigration in Manchester. The last time I slept properly was about fifty hours ago. I don't really know what day it is, let alone what time. I know it's probably too late for visitors – but I'd *really* like to see my girlfriend. She kind of had a baby while I was away – even though neither of us knew she was pregnant.'

He blinked and, for a moment, Jessica didn't know if he was going to open his eyes. The confidence had gone and he was a zombie.

Then his eyes opened again and he smiled once more. 'I'm just *really* tired,' he said.

The receptionist was looking at Hugo as if trying to place him. Wondering if he was someone she *actually* knew. She was probably thinking that she really had heard everything now.

She cracked into a slim smile. 'Let me get someone,' she said.

A nurse led Hugo and Jessica through the corridors that boomed with silence. Nobody spoke and their echoing footsteps were the only accompaniment. Jessica was beginning to know the corridors better than she knew any building and was on such autopilot that she almost veered off towards the ward towards the very back of the hospital. Caroline wasn't there, of course – neither was anybody else she knew.

Not any longer.

Neither Hugo nor the nurse noticed her wavering moment of confusion, though it left Jessica a few steps behind and she hurried to catch up. She entered Caroline's ward a moment after Hugo, but they both stopped in the doorway.

Caroline was sitting up.

She was drowsy but awake. When she saw them, she tried to smile, but it seemed to be too much effort and she rested her head against the metal headboard.

'Aren't you in Australia?' she croaked.

'Me?' Jessica asked.

Caroline tried to smile once more but couldn't manage a reply. Hugo crossed the room and perched on the chair next to her bed. He pecked her on the forehead and then took her hand.

'Caroline came around this afternoon, didn't you, hun?' the nurse said.

'Is she okay?' Hugo asked.

'She will be. She just needs some sleep and the painkillers have her a bit out of it.'

'I am here, you know,' Caroline said – although her final word drifted away. She didn't particularly *sound* as if she was there.

'She needs to take it easy,' the nurse added, turning to Caroline. '*You* need to take it easy.' She checked her watch and told them they had ten minutes before Caroline had to be allowed back to sleep. After that, she left them to it, though there was barely room in the cupboardy ward for two, let alone four.

As soon as the nurse had gone, Caroline rested her head on Hugo's hand and started to blub. He stroked her hair with his other hand as she tried to speak, but her words were barely coherent, more gasps and sobs than actual words.

Caroline's dark hair was greasy and limp, her normally

tanned skin was pale. Whenever she spoke, she squinted as if she had to concentrate on what she was saying.

Jessica had never seen Hugo so attentive. It wasn't that he was deliberately mean to Caroline, more that Jessica had never been entirely sure that he knew they were in a relationship. He was so aloof, with no ego and no self-awareness that whenever Caroline broke into anything remotely lovey-dovey, Hugo seemed to be lost in his own world of making coins disappear or shuffling a pack of cards in either hand. His act meant that he spent a lot of time away from the city and, in recent times, that meant lots of time overseas. Despite that, Jessica was sure that if it was entirely down to him, he'd spend his days on park benches showing tricks to the retired couples and kids who passed his way.

'I promise it's yours,' Caroline said.

Hugo squeezed her hand. His brow furrowed with confusion and, not for the first time that day, Jessica felt like a spare part. She hovered close to the door, ready to leave.

'I never doubted it was,' he replied.

Jessica had one hand on the door handle, but Caroline spotted and groaned. 'Don't go,' she said.

Hugo nodded Jessica closer to the bed and she took a step back into the room.

'They won't let me see our baby,' Caroline said. She tried to push herself up higher in the bed, as if about to march down the hallway and demand a visit. Her body was having none of it and she'd not even got a leg out of the side before she slumped back against the pillow. 'It's a boy,' she added quietly.

Jessica didn't say that she already knew, that *she'd* been the one to deliver it.

'You've got to look after yourself before you can think about looking after a baby,' Hugo replied. It was probably the most grown-up thing he'd ever come out with. Jessica wasn't sure if she liked the new Hugo – she sort of preferred the flaky, mysterious outsider who dipped in and out of her life. If even he was now acting like an adult, then it was all over. She wasn't just *over* the hill, she was partway down the other side, slipping and sliding her way to oblivion.

'I just want to hold him,' Caroline cooed.

Hugo continued to grip her hand. 'I'm sure you'll be able to.'

'Will you get someone? Can you ask?'

He stood and turned towards the door, staring through Jessica before forcing a smile. He wasn't only a man who'd not slept in two days, he really *looked* like a man who'd not slept in two days. Either that, or he was fresh from an audition to be an extra in a zombie movie.

Hugo disappeared through the door, closing it behind him and leaving Jessica alone with her friend.

'Hey,' Jessica said.

'Hey yourself.'

'Do you remember what—?'

Caroline nodded and they stared at each other for a few moments before Jessica couldn't take it any longer. They'd known each other for so long that she couldn't stand to see her friend so debilitated. She also didn't know how she could justify what she'd done.

'It's fine,' Caroline said, her voice so quiet that Jessica barely heard what she said.

'What's fine?'

'Randall. If you're visiting him, I guess there's a reason. Some things are more important.'

'I'm so sorry, Caz...'

Caroline snaked an arm out of the covers. 'There's nothing to be sorry for.'

Jessica took her hand and held it, still not able to look squarely at her friend.

'He doesn't even have a name,' Caroline said softly.

'Hugo?'

They turned to each other and Caroline started to laugh. It quickly became a cough, but a small amount of gentle back-patting helped it morph back into a smile.

'The baby,' she said.

There was a gentle knock on the door and then Hugo re-entered with the nurse. This time, he was pushing a wheelchair.

'Is that for me?' Caroline asked.

'It's for me,' Jessica replied. 'I could really do with a sit-down.'

Caroline was in the wheelchair, Jessica on one side, Hugo the other as they stared towards the small line of incubators. The newborn intensive care ward was tiny – perhaps mercifully so – and only two of the incubators contained children. The nurse hovered behind but pointed to the final crib on the row.

'That's him?' Caroline asked softly. She had to strain up from the chair to get a clear view.

'He's gorgeous,' the nurse replied – although Jessica suspected she probably said that about all babies. Not many medical staff delivered a child and then went on about how ugly he or she was.

'Can I hold him?' Caroline asked.

'I'm afraid not.'

The incubator was connected to a large machine via a series of tubes, which was making sure he got the oxygen he needed. He was even smaller than Jessica remembered, a rounded dome head on top of a minuscule collection of limbs. His eyes were closed, but it was hard to tell if he was actually sleeping. Either way, he wasn't stirring.

Caroline reached for Hugo, who rested an arm around her shoulder. Jessica did the same on the other side and the three of them stood watching the tiny little man's chest rise and fall rhythmically.

In the near-perfect stillness, it took everything Jessica could muster for her not to crack. There was a time when she'd thought she'd have her own moment like this.

Now?

Now, it was further away than ever.

FORTY-THREE

EASTER SUNDAY

It took Jessica a few moments to figure out where she was when she woke up. Her first thought was the hospital – except she wasn't there. A memory of Roly's flat flitted through her mind, as if she'd been dreaming about it very recently. Then she realised that she was in her own house, her own bed. It felt both alien yet comforting with its untucked sheets and pillow that was hanging half off.

Considering how little she'd slept in the past few days, she felt surprisingly fresh. Then Jessica remembered there was somebody else here who'd slept far fewer hours than she had.

Hugo was sitting on the sofa when Jessica found him. He was watching kids' TV – some sort of show where the presenter was talking to a cartoon as if they were side by side.

She plopped down next to him. 'It was Edd the Duck in my day,' she said.

'Mine too – and Gordon the Gopher.'

His hair was messy – but that was normal. He was wearing a shirt and pyjama bottoms that used to belong to someone Jessica didn't want to think about. They'd been at the back of the cupboard in the spare room.

'Have you heard anything?' Jessica asked.

Hugo shook his head. She thought he was going to yawn, but he simply rolled his lips in a weird circle and then went back to watching the television. Even that was odd.

'Visiting is between ten and twelve,' he said.

His lack of yawn made Jessica actually yawn.

She thought about making breakfast for them – something fancy, like pancakes with all the trimmings. Except that would require far too much effort and even more washing-up. Jessica nodded towards the table at the other side of the room, where the Freddo Easter egg that Caroline had bought sat.

'Breakfast?' she asked, nodding towards the egg. 'It is Easter, after all. Jesus would want us to.'

Hugo nodded approvingly. 'According to the Aztecs, Quetzalcoatl stole the cocoa plant from the realm of the gods and brought it to earth. He planted it at the spot where a young princess was murdered to honour the loyalty she showed her husband.'

Jessica stared at the crumpled purple box across the room. 'Was she called Princess Cadbury?'

He blinked at her, wide-eyed, not getting it. 'I don't think so.'

Jessica headed for the Easter egg. She split the chocolate in half and handed one part to Hugo, who nibbled at it like a nervous bunny. With his other hand, he was removing and replacing the handle to one of Jessica's coffee mugs.

'Is that broken?' she asked.

He'd been doing it absent-mindedly, not even looking, but he held the mug up so she could see. 'No.'

'Then how are you removing the handle?'

'Practice.'

She watched him do it once more and for the life of her, couldn't see how he was doing anything other than pulling off the mug's handle, holding it a few centimetres away from the cup and then replacing it with perfect precision.

'Can you stop doing that?' Jessica said.

He smiled. 'Sure.'

Hugo picked off a piece of the chocolate egg and started to suck on it.

'What's it like being a father?' Jessica asked.

He stared at her, unaware there was a smear of chocolate above his lip. He swallowed and then tugged on his hair. 'Life's changed, hasn't it?'

A nod.

'I guess it's a weekend for it,' Hugo added.

'Huh?'

'Rising again... back from the dead.'

It felt like they were communicating on slightly different wavelengths: her not getting his jokes, him not getting hers. Except... there was something he'd said.

'How do you know what to do?' Hugo asked, sounding so vulnerable that Jessica wanted to hug him. Everything about his act was confidence in his ability, even when dressed up with his natural lack of interest.

'I think you just figure it out,' Jessica said. 'Try not to drop the baby and everything else will be fine.'

'I can juggle knives.'

'You probably shouldn't do that around your son – but I don't think that's the same as holding an infant anyway.'

He nodded and then blinked, looking at Jessica properly. 'What's wrong?' he asked.

'Something you said... something I heard on a case. I was interviewing this woman and she was talking nonsense at me. At least I thought she was...'

'What did she say?'

Jessica tried to think of the exact words, but the memory wasn't there. She could check the recording, but that might take too long. 'Something like, "Those who defy the Lord will pay on the day the Father's son rises again".'

Hugo didn't need to say anything because Jessica suddenly got it. She'd been so busy getting annoyed at Francine that she'd not bothered to actually listen.

'The Father's son is Jesus,' Jessica said. 'And he rises again today.'

'So everyone who defies the Lord pays today...?'

Jessica couldn't manage a reply. She'd cursed Francine for wasting everyone's time – and yet she'd given up the information Jessica was after. She apologised to Hugo and then headed into the kitchen, closing the door and taking out her phone. Rowlands answered on the fourth ring. He sounded half-asleep.

'What time is it?' he slurred.

'Do you remember the hospital porter?' Jessica asked.

'What?'

'We spoke to the receptionist, Melissa, and she told us to talk to the porter. He told us about Francine giving out the flyers outside the hospital, but how did he describe her?'

There was a moan from the other end of the line. 'She looked like his mum or something like that.'

'Is that what he said though?'

Another groan. 'I don't remember, Jess.'

'Didn't he say she was "sort of" like his mum? He never said she *looked* like his mum. We assumed that's what he meant, but he never actually said it.'

'Something like that.'

'Why would he say that?'

There was a grunt and a snort, leaving Jessica to wonder if Rowlands was sleeping in a farmyard. 'I guess Francine looks like the porter's mum. He seemed like a bit of a nutter, to be honest. A proper basement-dweller.'

'It's just... Francine called Ezra her son. Emily told me that

Ezra followed her around like she was his mother. Everyone who saw them said they had a weird mother–son relationship. But Ezra didn't dump himself in that water butt. What if the porter wasn't saying Francine *looked* like his mum, what if it was a slip of the tongue and he was another of her "sons"?'

FORTY-FOUR

Melissa was sitting behind the reception desk at the hospital when Jessica arrived. She gave a rolling-eyed 'You're working over Easter as well?' smirk.

They exchanged the usual pleasantries before Hugo headed off to the ward to be with Caroline. When it was just them, Jessica asked about the porter. 'I think he was called Guy,' she added.

'I've not seen him,' Melissa replied. 'Sometimes they swap our shifts around – plus, the porters and maintenance can end up spending whole shifts in other parts of the hospital.'

'When was the last time you saw him?'

A shake of the head. 'Early in the week, perhaps?'

'I really need to talk to him.'

She frowned but didn't ask the obvious question. 'I'll call maintenance for you. Dean manages the porters.'

Melissa rolled her chair away from the desk and pressed a button on the phone. She spun so she was facing the other way and spoke quietly into the receiver. When she turned back, her frown was deeper

'Dean says Guy hasn't turned up for work today,' she said.

A gurgling started to bubble at the bottom of Jessica's stomach. She turned back to the waiting room, where there were a couple of dozen people hoping their name would be called next.

Francine and her metaphorical sons had been targeting those who'd been given a second chance – but why bother with individuals when she could go to the source...

'Where is Dean?' Jessica asked. She must've been more forceful than she meant because Mellissa reeled back in her chair.

'Maintenance. I can call him back to meet you if you want?'

'I'll follow the signs.'

Jessica took off, not quite running but close enough. 'MAINTENANCE' was at the bottom of the directions board and she skirted around a corner, following a path that led towards the wards at the furthest end of the hospital. The area she knew all too well.

Much like the ropy yellow road diversion signs, the directions to the maintenance office disappeared at regular intervals, before reappearing just as Jessica thought she might have to turn back. Almost five minutes had gone when she found herself in a corridor lined with dark edges and gloomy strip bulbs. There was some sort of trolley abandoned further along the hall, half-hidden by the shadows. The type of place where heroines would end up cornered in cheesy horror movies.

Jessica knocked on the door marked 'office' and waited. She thought she heard a radio or television being muted and then the door swung open to reveal a man in a light blue shirt and a name tag that read 'Dean'. He looked like someone who would be in charge of maintenance – big shoulders and thick forearms. Someone who'd done a lot of carrying over the years. There was the faintest whiff of cigarettes.

He blinked at her. 'Hello?'

Jessica introduced herself quickly, flashing her warrant card and not waiting for it to be fully inspected. 'I need to find Guy,' she added. 'I don't know his last name.'

'He's not turned in,' Dean replied.

'Have you called him?'

'No answer. Doesn't even ring.' He stepped back towards his office, sizing her up. 'What d'you want him for?'

Jessica nodded towards the office, asking for permission that was granted as Dean moved to the side. His office was bigger than the one in which she'd met Guy, more the size of a living room than a cubbyhole. A workbench stretched along one wall and was full of various tools and trinkets. There were a couple of filing cabinets and a desk with a computer that had a Yoda bobblehead figure wobbling away next to the keyboard. A portable television was mounted on the wall.

Jessica scanned the wall, looking for anything approaching a calendar, but there was nothing except for a few informational posters about hand-washing and the like.

'Does Guy often miss shifts?' she asked.

'Never. I don't think he's ever been late. I was getting a bit worried about him.'

'How long's he worked here?'

'Before me, so four or five years. I'm not the best person to ask.'

'But you're his boss?'

Dean shrugged. 'On paper, I suppose. Not like I get any more money for it. They sort of manage themselves.'

'Do you sort out the porter rotas?'

His eyes narrowed, wondering what he was being accused of. 'Yeah...'

'I need to check Guy's shift pattern.'

'Why?'

'Because I do.'

'Private information, innit? I'd need to check with—'

'Can we skip all this?' Jessica said, irritated. 'You'll talk to your boss, who'll then talk to my boss. Both of our bosses will get pissed off because it's Easter Sunday and they're busy scoffing chocolate. At the end of all that, probably in a couple of hours' time, someone will tell you it's fine to share the rota. The difference is that I could *really* do with looking at it now.'

Dean stared at her for a few moments and then nodded. 'Fine,' he said, reaching into one of the drawers and taking out an impeccably neat printout. There were different colours and multiple fonts to signify each staff member and which job they would be doing. What it told Jessica was that Dean was a man who had too much time on his hands.

Fortunately, it also made it easy for Jessica to find out what she needed.

Guy had been off work the previous Saturday – which was the day Henry had been shoved in front of Archie's car. He was free on Tuesday, the day Lucy was pushed off the car park. He'd been working the early shift on Good Friday – the day Ezra had been dumped in the water butt at some point during the evening. There was Tiffany and the food truck fire, too – but the timing of that wasn't known for certain.

Dean must've seen it in Jessica's face. 'What?' he said.

'Can you take me to Guy's office?'

'He doesn't have an office.'

'When I was here last, he took me to this, well... cupboard.'

'Oh, right – that *is* a cupboard.'

Dean jangled a set of keys on his belt and then ushered Jessica out. She followed him through a bewildering labyrinth of passages until she found herself outside the door that she thought was Guy's office. Dean unlocked the door and stood aside to let her in. She expected... well, Jessica didn't know what she expected – but it wasn't normality.

She tried the filing cabinet in the corner and it opened – but it contained nothing except files. Foam was still spilling out of the seats and cleaning supplies took up the rest of the space.

'You looking for something?' Dean asked.

'I... um...' Jessica turned in a circle. 'Do you have a changing room, or something like that?'

'Not really – not for us. There are some showers in the toilets.'

Jessica shook her head. It wouldn't be that – then she realised it might be. 'If there are showers, do you have lockers?'

Dean nodded and Jessica could feel her heart thumping.

'Do you have your *own* lockers?' she asked.

Another nod.

'I need to see Guy's,' Jessica said.

Dean didn't say much, but it was only another minute or so until he led her into a locker room. It was classic 1980s swimming baths, with a slightly soggy floor and a faint whiff of bleach. The lockers were tall, in a pair of long rows, with scratched red and blue paint alternating across the metal doors.

Dean pointed to one on the top row. 'That's his,' he said. 'Next to mine.'

There were no names on any of the lockers, which were only differentiated by coin-shaped numbered discs imprinted into the metal.

'I need to look inside.'

Dean shook his head. 'No can do.'

'I *really* need to look inside.'

'Don't matter. The rota's one thing – but I'm not one to go snooping.'

'You have a key though...?'

Dean took a step towards the door, but the inadvertent reach for his hip gave Jessica her answer.

'You've got to open that locker,' Jessica said.

'Why?'

'Because of the whole "your boss, my boss" thing. Sooner or later, someone will ask you to open the locker and I really need it to be sooner.'

Another shake of the head. Dean's last name had to be Jobsworth. 'Can't do it,' he said.

'Fair enough,' Jessica said, reaching into her pocket and then removing the bobblehead she'd pilfered from his desk. She'd had a feeling it might come down to this. 'Do it or Yoda gets it.'

Dean boggled at her. 'What?'

She gripped the figurine's head tightly. 'Seriously, Dean. I'm sure you're a really nice bloke and all that – but open the damned locker before you make me do something we'll both regret. You more than me.'

He took a step towards her, but Jessica held the figure further away from him, gripping the head even tighter and motioning to pull it off.

'Open the locker,' she said.

'That was a Christmas present from my wife.'

Jessica sighed. 'All I want you to do is unlock it.'

His eyes flicked both ways, far more panicky than they should be. 'You can't do this.'

'I might be a girl, but I'm pretty sure I can pop this plastic head off.'

'I'll complain, I'll—'

'You can do what you want – but it'll be too late for head-less Yoda.'

They stood at an impasse, Dean's gaze flickering towards the bobblehead and back again.

Eventually, he reached for his belt and then edged around her, sideways, country-dance-style. He pressed a key into the lock and turned it, stepping away and holding out his hand. Jessica placed Yoda into it and then swung open the locker door.

'I don't care if you are police,' Dean fumed, 'you can't come in here and—' He cut himself off as Jessica stepped away.

There was a rucksack at the bottom of the locker, caked with muddy dark soil. Crocodile clips secured a series of wires from the bag to a small mobile phone sitting on the metal beside it.

'Is that—?' Dean started.

Jessica took another step backwards, barely able to gasp the words. 'I'm pretty sure it's a bomb.'

FORTY-FIVE

Manchester knew bombs. The IRA one had ended up being one big middle finger back to the terrorists, as the city had been rejuvenated and rebuilt around the destruction.

Then there was the Arena and all those poor people...

Men and women, old and young, white, black, and brown shuffled around the streets close to the hospital. Some were draped in blankets, others huddled in unflattering gowns. There were gurneys and drips being wheeled across the road, with scores of doctors, nurses and police officers doing all they could to help out.

That was *inside* the cordon that had been created on the park opposite the hospital. Wheelchairs were being lined up on the playground of the primary school next to the park as if it was an official parking area.

It could have been chaos, *should* have been, and yet the local community had come together in a time of crisis. They'd done it before and they were doing it again. Everyone from temporary students to residents who'd been living in the same houses all their lives had opened their doors. Beds and sofas were being lent, blankets shared, garden gates left open. Kettles were being boiled at such a rate that the National Grid would likely be putting out some advisory about the potential for power cuts. The grocery shop across from the park was handing out free water and even the solicitors' firm next door had proved themselves not to be the complete scum Jessica suspected by allowing their offices to be used as a temporary sick ward.

The sickest patients had been rushed away in ambulances and paramedic cars, with other hospitals squeezing in as many people as they could.

On the other side of the cordon, bemused shoppers were lining up to gawp at and speculate about what on earth was going on.

When it came to complete shambles, it was among the better ones in which Jessica had been involved.

Through the chaos, Jessica took a few moments to stop and watch everything that was unfurling around her. So many people helping out strangers reminded her that, despite the troublemakers that came naturally with the job, *most* people were ultimately kind-hearted.

Jessica had been evacuated from the hospital along with everyone else. With the bomb squad inside and uniformed officers busy keeping everyone away, she was something of a spare part.

There was still one thing she could do…

She started to walk along the looping pathway around the park where the atmosphere was relentlessly upbeat. It felt like the early stages of a summer carnival, before the party got going and the beer tent was swamped. Some goon was on a bench murdering an Oasis song with an acoustic guitar. As if the patients weren't having a bad enough day.

Somehow they were maintaining the cordon and Jessica nodded at various officers as she remained inside the park. In the meantime, she was scanning the faces of the crowds at the barriers.

After completing a lap, Jessica crossed the barriers and headed to one of the new-build houses close to the school. It was owned by a young woman who was busy shuttling trays of fizzy pop outside to anyone who wanted one. Caroline was inside, on the sofa by herself, an untouched pair of chocolate digestives on the table at her side. She was dressed in a hospital gown and borrowed trainers. When Jessica walked in, she peered up and then looked back down almost immediately.

'They wouldn't let me go with my baby,' she said.

'They moved all the children first,' Jessica replied. 'They'll all be safer at a different hospital.'

'Someone could've told me first.'

'I don't think there was time to lay down a proper plan. Hugo's on his way to the Salford Royal now. It'll be fine.'

'I want to go, too.'

'I'm not sure that's—'

Caroline didn't want to listen – but the moment she tried to stand, Jessica saw her friend's eyes cloud over. She hurried forward to support her, but Caroline flopped back onto the sofa, holding her hands over her face.

'I want to know he's okay,' Caroline said quietly.

Jessica sat on the sofa, rubbing her friend's back. 'You need to be okay yourself first.'

'Will you wait with me?'

Jessica's fingers tensed inadvertently and Caroline already knew the answer.

'You've got the world to save, right?' she added.

Without meaning to, Jessica found herself staring towards the window. The outside, where the action was. It was too close to the truth. 'A small corner of Manchester, but close enough.' She laughed softly, making it a joke. Caroline didn't join in. 'Will you be okay here by yourself?'

Caroline nodded lamely but didn't reply. Jessica stood and removed her hand from her friend's back. She didn't want to leave, but there was still work to do.

'I'll be back,' she said.

Caroline said nothing.

In the time Jessica had been in the house, a few more carloads of police officers had shown up. The cordon around the park wasn't quite a ring of steel, but it was probably a fairly thin aluminium. Jessica headed for a group of officers who were busy ordering a group of picture-taking kids to get back. Nothing to see here and all that.

She described Guy's height and thin, patchy hair – but it was far too broad a depiction for anyone to know who she was talking about. The priority had been getting people out of the hospital and, in truth, Jessica didn't really remember what Guy looked like – not properly. She'd only met him once, but she knew she'd recognise him if she saw him again.

Jessica was on her second lap of the park when she was distracted by the growl of an exhaust. She spotted a sporty dark chav-mobile pulling onto a side road. There was a pair of large howling exhausts on the back, which could only mean one thing.

Archie slammed his door closed and swaggered his way towards the park in what Jessica knew was his most expensive suit. The one with thin cream pinstripes on the dark grey material.

'I don't think you should be here,' Jessica said.

Archie reached into his pocket and held up his warrant card. 'Guess who's back, baby!'

'*Baby*? Have you lost your mind?'

Archie repocketed the card. 'Too much?'

'A hospital's being evacuated – so, yeah – too much.' His puppy-dog eyes sank slightly. 'You're back on the job?' she added.

'Got the call. Some sort of emergency, bodies needed, get your arse out to the hospital. Should've known you'd be at the centre of it. Anyway, what are we up to?'

He sounded far too excited for Jessica's liking.

'We're looking for someone,' she said, adding the briefest of descriptions for Guy and telling Archie there was a possible bomb inside the hospital.

'I reckon he's probably fluffed it,' she said. 'It'd have gone off already otherwise – but I reckon he'll be somewhere nearby. He'll be enjoying the chaos, if nothing else.'

Archie puffed out a long breath and turned in a circle. Aside from the park, it was a concrete jungle of houses and community blocks. They decided to split up. He set off in one direction around the outside park, with Jessica heading in the other. She walked as casually as she could, but the streets were crowded with people trying to watch, take photos and tell everyone they knew on social media that something major was going on. At one time it was, 'look at me, I'm at a gig'; now it was, 'look at me, I might get blown up! LOL ;)'.

There were also a *lot* of men with thinning hair. Jessica had never paid too much attention in the past, but blokes were so creative when it came to covering bald spots. There were the comb forwards and the comb backwards, not to mention the classic comb-over. Some shaved the whole lot off, presumably thinking it was a losing battle anyway. She also spent a lot of time looking at people in hats, concluding that she didn't really trust hat-wearers. If it was particularly hot or cold, then fair enough – but otherwise, what was the point?

On a couple of occasions, she crossed the road, sidling close to someone who might have been Guy. Some bloke in a flat cap turned out to be a regular nobody; a balding man turned out to be a woman with a shaved head.

By the time Jessica reached the front of the park, action was picking up outside the hospital. Someone had set up a TV camera on a tripod as close to the building as they were allowed. A woman in a suit was doing a piece to camera, looking earnest and sincere. Day one of media training, probably – look serious even when you have no idea what's going on.

Archie had reached the front of the park at the same time as Jessica but shrugged and shook his head.

And then Jessica saw him.

Guy was standing directly behind Archie. No hat, no weird comb-job. He was wearing a thin jacket and jeans, hands in his pockets, casual-as-you-like. An anonymous face in the crowd, listening to the reporter speculate about what was going on inside the hospital.

She took half a step forward, but that was all it took. She'd seen Guy – but he'd seen her, too. Their eyes met and he knew the game was done.

So he ran.

FORTY-SIX

Jessica had done too much running over the years. Why did nobody ever stand still, offer their wrists for cuffing and admit the game was up? Oh no, it was head for the nearest alley, Fosbury flop over a fence, do some trail-running through the woods, play real-life *Crossy Road*. Where were all these people when the Olympics came around?

Guy had a head start of fifteen metres or so, but he was quicker off the mark than Jessica – and had longer legs. By the time she'd rounded the crowd, he was already across Oxford Road and into the mangled maze of alleys that made up Moss Side.

Archie caught on soon enough, but he was even slower to start than she was.

'That him?' he shouted from behind.

If she wasn't running, Jessica would have pointed out that she wasn't chasing some bloke for her health, or because she was particularly desperate for a boyfriend. Instead, she galloped up over the pavement and raced towards the alley. Archie got the message, having the audacity to sprint past her now. A week off had done him good and his Scrappy-Doo legs whirred with motion.

Guy bounded through the alley, not pausing at the end as he blasted across the road. As well as the tight ginnels, the roads were packed with parked cars that were half on the pavement. Long rows of red-fronted terraces skimmed both sides, and within a street or two, Jessica was feeling the familiar sense of oppressive claustrophobia she felt whenever she had to visit.

Archie seemingly had no such worries – but he had to skid to a halt a moment before he was run over by a bright pink Mini. The car horn farted a loud beep of annoyance, but the dreadful dance music blaring from the speakers drowned out the driver's accompanying swearing.

Guy was further ahead than at the start and had the time to risk a peek over his shoulder as he skipped into a parallel lane. Archie didn't wait for Jessica to catch up, sprinting across the road and sliding across the bonnet of a sporty Toyota before running along the road parallel to the direction in which Guy had gone.

He'd obviously done the bonnet slide for show. The prick.

Jessica thought about stopping and calling for help – but Guy might be long gone by the time she managed to get the message across. Besides, a large portion of the on-duty officers were already enforcing a perimeter at the park. She bounded on, heading in the direction Guy had gone and trying to pretend the stabbing stitch in her stomach wasn't there.

She turned left to follow Guy's route but there was no sign of him or Archie. The lane lining the rear of two terraced rows was narrow, probably not enough to get a car through. Head-high red walls flanked both sides, with gravelly grit underfoot, just waiting to send her flying.

Bins were resting against the graffitied walls on both sides and Jessica lifted the flap of the nearest. She instantly reeled away from the rotting smell and risked a peep inside as she held her breath. There was a pile of dirtied nappies but no escaping suspect.

Jessica took a deep breath before trying the next bin. The inside was just as pleasant – someone had dumped a dead cat or something similar. Jessica slammed the lid and continued along the ginnel. Guy could easily be hiding in one of the back yards, or perhaps one of the houses was actually his – it wasn't like she knew his address.

'Arch?' Jessica called loudly but there was no reply.

She could hear the faint buzz of a television somewhere. Perhaps some kids playing as well. Jessica continued to the next intersection, crossing the road and heading into the alley. Still no sign.

Guy was gone – and there was no sign of Archie, either. He'd probably keeled over, thinking he was Mo Farah and then dying around the corner. Serves him right.

She unclipped her radio and walked along the lane with it in her hand, not quite ready to admit defeat. They'd have to get a helicopter and either reassign officers from the park or magic a few up from thin air.

Then she realised the noise she'd heard on the breeze wasn't a television with the volume up. It was the sound of people breathing too loudly, of an elbows-out grunt-and-shunt rumble. Jessica followed the sounds to where the ginnel intersected with another – and there, just around the bend, was Archie and Guy.

Guy was face down on the floor, his hands now cuffed in place. Archie was on his knees and spun around as Jessica said his name. There was a scuff across his chin, dirt across the front of his shirt, mud and grit on the knees. The arm of his suit jacket had been ripped away from the rest of it.

'He was trying to double back behind us,' Archie huffed.

He was out of breath as he turned to Guy, who was wriggling underneath him. 'I invented that trick, pal.'

'Your suit's a goner,' Jessica replied. 'Cheap one, was it?'

Archie glanced to the arm of the suit that was hanging around his wrist. 'Balls,' he said.

'Serves you right for sliding across car bonnets.'

FORTY-SEVEN

'Not bad, was it?'

Archie was bouncing as they walked back towards the park. Guy had been picked up in a van and was on his way to the station for questioning. Jessica figured he could wait for now. It was Easter bloody Sunday – a day of rest if ever there was one – and he'd made her run.

'I'd probably give it a four or five out of ten,' Jessica replied.

'*Five?*'

'More likely a four. Points off for ripped clothing, more for grazed knees. Sliding across bonnets is a definite no-no – and you get a big markdown for making it look like you were trying to sexually assault a suspect. What were you doing on your knees, for Christ's sake?'

Jessica bit away a grin.

'You're just annoyed that you couldn't catch him.'

'Dead wrong. I held back, figuring I'd let you do the chasing. When he looked over his shoulder, I guessed he'd try to double back around us, which is why I let you do the donkey work in cutting him off. While you were busy crawling around on your knees with your pants around your ankles, I did the hard graft of chasing him directly into your path.' Jessica paused. 'That's what the report's going to say in any case. Perhaps not the bit about pants-round-the-ankles.'

Archie was shaking his head. 'I don't know why I rushed back to work. I could've had the day off, feet up with the footy on.'

Jessica nudged him with her elbow. 'You love it really.'

He grinned. 'Aye.'

They retraced their steps through the alleys until they were back on Oxford Road. Patients were being helped up the steps towards the hospital and much of the watching crowd had dissipated. A member of the bomb squad was three steps up at the front of the hospital alongside some sort of hospital official talking to the media. Jessica and Archie slotted in towards the back of the small group of onlookers as the official talked about 'finding a viable device' and 'thanking our lucky stars' that there had been no explosion. From what Jessica could gather, the mobile phone in the locker had no reception, meaning it couldn't be reached.

A dodgy phone reception was the only thing that had saved the hospital.

Journalists asked questions about potential suspects, oblivious to the fact that the person who'd likely assembled it was currently on his way to Longsight Police Station. They wanted to know about motives, but the officer sensibly said that was information for another time. There'd be a police press officer somewhere, waking up late after an Easter lie-in, wondering what the hell was going on. For now, the reporters were more interested in how many people could have died rather than the number of sick people who'd been lucky. In the end, it *was* luck. Jessica had found the bomb, but it was only ineptitude that meant it hadn't gone off. That and the usual technical incompetence and banditry of mobile phone companies.

The hospital official finished by thanking the local community and saying there was 'no one quite like Mancs'. It was, of course, true – but perhaps not in the way he'd meant it. Jessica was sure she saw Archie's chest puff with pride.

'What now?' he asked.

'I've got a suspect to question. You can probably go home now the day has been saved. Either that or go and buy a new jacket. I suspect the guv will want a word. He'll be happy at having his Easter interrupted.' She paused and then added: 'Again.'

Officers were mooching around at the edge of the park, probably wondering if they had time to nick off down the road to Hulme for a quick burger and fries before work came calling again. That was until something came through on the radios that made them all head for the phalanx of police cars parked on the side streets opposite the hospital. Archie noticed it, too, switching on his own radio. They listened together as the first sets of flashing lights raced towards the junction on the far side of the park.

'I think this might take some explaining,' Archie said.

FORTY-EIGHT

Police cars and riot vans were double-parked outside the flank of shops close to the Lees Estate. Officers were massing close to the road, wondering if they'd need the full riot gear and tear gas. Either that, or speculating on whether they'd be back to the wife, kids and pile of Easter eggs anytime soon.

The reason was immediately obvious.

A large group of youngsters were gathered in the furthest corner. They were banging on windows, throwing stones and generally getting ready to tear the place down.

They were directly outside Jefferson's flat.

This time, there were no empty windows above – residents were watching with fear and interest. Some were outside their flats, arms crossed, eyeing the scene from the recesses of the estate. Jessica wondered how many of them had been there on the night she and Archie had been chased into the boiler room.

No one was intervening now.

Jessica was about to ask what was going on – aside from the obvious – when she spotted a familiar face. Pete was wearing a bulletproof vest as he spoke to an officer she didn't recognise. When he saw Jessica, he waved her across towards the riot vans. The introductions were brief as Pete pointed towards the assembled youth.

'I got a call about forty-five minutes ago,' he said. 'I was only a few streets away, but, when I got here, they were already banging on the windows.'

The officer in charge of the riot squad was called Kennaugh. He looked between them and asked if there was anything he needed to know. Jessica wasn't sure where to start, let alone figure out what was relevant. She'd not told Pete about Jefferson being an undercover officer – and had little intention of telling anyone about how she and Archie had broken into his flat to find out what he was hiding.

'Who called you?' Jessica asked, looking to Pete.

He wriggled slightly. 'Jefferson Cass.'

'He called you himself?'

'Right.'

'What does he want?'

'Protection. A safe way off the estate. He said kids had barricaded him in his flat. He didn't want to call 999. I don't know why.'

Jessica had a good idea why – he'd hoped Pete could get things done quietly. She wasn't looking forward to the potential questions if the riot squad did go in – but Jefferson would be looking forward to them even less.

There was a loud splintering of glass and they all turned to see that one of Jefferson's windows had been put through. The youths surged towards the flat, but something unseen stopped them from a full-on siege.

Kennaugh tensed, ready to give the dispersal order. That'd be it then. Internal inquests and too many uncomfortable questions about her role in things.

'Can you get me closer?' Jessica asked.

The officer shook his head. 'No chance.'

Jessica nodded towards one of the youths at the edge of the

group. He was standing next to a bike, not getting involved. 'That kid's named Thomas Adlington,' she said. 'I know him. Let me talk to him and find out what's going on. If it's not a good answer…' She nodded towards the suited and booted ninja squad next to the van.

Kennaugh scratched his chin. On the one hand, he could accompany her to have a word with a bunch of kids seemingly intent on rioting; on the other, there'd be a shedload of paperwork if he sent his officers in. The dilemma was all too familiar.

'I'll walk you over,' he said, before nodding towards Archie. '*Just* you. If anything happens that I don't like, I'll give the order.'

He didn't specify what the order meant – but Jessica guessed it would mean blokes with batons and bloody big boots arresting everyone in a half-mile radius.

Jessica slotted in behind Kennaugh as he walked calmly towards the group on the furthest side of the plaza. Since smashing Jefferson's window, they'd backed off slightly, seemingly forming some sort of plan. Jessica doubted it involved them heading home quietly.

Her hands were held wide to her sides as she matched the other officer's pace. His arms were similarly spread to indicate he was no immediate threat, despite the baton on his belt.

'All right, lads,' he said.

One of the bigger teens started marching towards them, features snarled in anger. There was a broken snooker cue in his hand. The rest of the group were a few steps behind, creating a wall between Jessica and Jefferson's flat.

'Hey!' Kennaugh snapped, stopping the lad in his tracks. He seemed surprised himself.

'I just want to talk,' Jessica said, peeping her head around. She nodded towards Thomas. 'We know each other, don't we?'

It was a push, to say the least. She'd seen him slapped

through a window and then asked him about it. He'd sworn at her and then pedalled away on his bike as if he was the new Bradley Wiggins.

There were around two dozen lads who all turned to look at Thomas. There was still a mark on his lip from where Jefferson had slapped him and made him bleed. He was ridiculously skinny, even given his youth, his ribs rippling against his top. His spots seemed to spark as one as he blushed. For a moment, Jessica thought he was going to deny all knowledge that they'd ever exchanged words.

'She tried to spike me,' he said.

Jessica wasn't entirely sure what that meant. 'I only want a word,' she said.

'What about?'

'About whatever's going on here.'

One of the kids she vaguely recognised took a step forward. 'He's nicked our fuckin' money.' The teenager turned towards Jefferson's flat and, for a moment, Jessica thought he was going to rush it. Thankfully, he stuck to spitting on the ground.

'What money?' Jessica asked.

None of them replied – which wasn't a surprise.

'Look, lads—' Kennaugh began, but he was quickly interrupted by the group's apparent leader.

'No, you look.' He turned and hurled a rock towards Jefferson's flat. It cannoned into the brickwork next to the front door and then bounced clear, sending a spray of cement with it.

Kennaugh took a step back, angling towards the radio on his shoulder.

Jessica thrust a hand across him. 'What if you let me in?' she said quickly.

Her colleague tried to pull her away, but Jessica took a step towards the group. She hoped her voice was even, not trembling.

'I'll talk to Jefferson,' she added. 'See if I can get him to come out, or work out what's happened.'

'He's got our fuckin' money – that's what's happened.'

Jessica jabbed a thumb towards the riot vans. 'I get that, but you're not going to get anything back if that lot get involved, are you?' She motioned towards the riot squad near the shops.

The leader with the snooker cue didn't seem concerned, but a lad with sandy hair stepped forward and said something that Jessica didn't catch. At that, the one with the cue started nodding. He stepped to the side, providing a clear route to Jefferson's flat. 'All right,' he said. 'Just you.'

Jessica turned to Kennaugh and shrugged. Her stomach was performing all sorts of tricks. At the present moment, it felt like there was some sort of loop the loop going on.

Kennaugh started to argue but Jessica's mind was made up. She didn't turn back as she walked slowly through the group, feeling the fury around her. They were all boys, probably between fourteen and nineteen. Some were thin like drainpipes, others tall and bulky. Fully-grown adults. One of them flinched towards her as if he was going to attack. He started laughing as she recoiled, but that was as bad as it got. Thomas was staring at the floor.

When Jessica reached Jefferson's front door, she suddenly realised that she didn't know what to do. She could sense the crowd behind her, the teenagers and ultimately the riot squad in the distance. Residents were above, too. All eyes on her.

Jessica knocked on the door and cleared her throat.

She waited and then counted the bolts as the clunked open. All six, including the one that blocked the hinge side. For a moment, she thought the lads behind might rush the door, that this was the opening they'd been waiting for.

The door edged inwards a centimetre or two – and then she saw Jefferson's eye. 'Come on then,' he hissed.

Jessica did as she was told, bundling herself into the flat as quickly as she could and then moving past Jefferson as he clunked the locks back into place.

He wasn't the only thing hissing: wrapped around Jefferson's shoulders was the albino snake.

No wonder the group hadn't barged in after smashing the window. No wonder they were regrouping.

Jefferson was no longer set for the beach in flip-flops and loose clothing. He was in trainers, jeans and a jacket, ready to go.

'You took your time,' he said. 'Is Nina out there? I know she spoke to you.'

'Not that I've seen. There's a riot squad.'

'Damn.'

Jessica headed into the living room, where a half-brick was lying in the middle of the carpet surrounded by a splintering of glass. The curtains were pulled and the snake tank was covered with a large sheet.

Jefferson headed into the room and slipped the sheet to one side, ushering the snake back inside and then recovering it.

'What's with the tank?' Jessica asked.

'What about it?'

'Why's it covered?'

Jefferson glanced towards the front window but didn't answer.

'The kids outside reckon you've nicked their money,' Jessica said.

Jefferson was shaking his head. 'I'm not saying anything until I've seen Nina. She said she was on her way.'

'There's only two ways she's going to be allowed anywhere near this place. One is if you voluntarily leave – which I wouldn't advise – the other is if the riot squad cross that square and arrest everyone in sight. I'm guessing neither way is going to work out well for you.'

Jefferson's swagger was gone and it was like he'd shrunk a few inches since Jessica last saw him. His skin was grey.

'What's with the tank?' she tried again.

Jefferson continued shaking his head but his attention was elsewhere, so Jessica stepped across to it and whipped the sheet aside.

It was obvious what was wrong. There was no paper at the bottom of the tank. The snakes were writhing on a thin sprinkling of some sort of sand or sawdust atop the bare glass.

The money had gone.

Jefferson noticed what she was doing far too late to stop it. He didn't bother to pretend he was mad.

'What was in the tank?' Jessica asked. She wanted to hear him say it.

'Nothing.'

'How about the money you apparently owe those kids...? Where's it gone?'

'If I knew that...'

He spat the reply, but then tailed off and flopped onto the armchair, head cradled in his hands.

'It's all got out of hand,' he said.

'What has?'

'Some little... *shit*. Someone had the actual nerve.' Jefferson spoke through grinding teeth, barely able to conceal his mix of anger and bemusement.

'What happened?' Jessica asked once more.

'I woke up feeling sick,' he said. 'I *was* sick. Over and over.'

'Bad prawn? I stay away from seafood nowadays.'

'I woke up on the sofa. Slept like a log. Like you do when you're a kid. Don't even remember falling asleep. One minute I watching TV, the next...'

'Are you pregnant?'

Jefferson looked at her and sneered. 'Oh, ha ha. Aren't you the funny one?'

Jessica resisted the urge to smile at finally cracking his previously unbreakable front.

'Someone poisoned me,' Jefferson said quietly. 'Must've done. What other answer is there? Someone spiked my drink and then came in overnight and robbed me.'

Jessica nodded towards the television. 'That's still here,' she said. 'Funny sort of robber who leaves all the valuables.'

'It must've been one of them,' Jefferson added.

'The kids?'

He didn't elaborate, so Jessica added: 'How would someone have spiked your drink?'

Jefferson glanced irritably towards the kitchen, where there were upturned glasses on the draining board. He clearly thought it had happened in his flat, not at some pub. He jabbed a finger towards the window at the back of the room. 'Someone was in here.'

'Why would a bunch of normal kids from an everyday estate want to rob you? And what would they rob?'

She waited but the reply didn't come.

'What have you got yourself into?' Jessica added, sitting opposite him. 'Drugs? Stolen goods? Bit of this, bit of that?'

No reply. Jefferson was staring at the brick on the floor.

'Nina's not going to be able to get you out of this,' Jessica said. 'You're done.'

'Don't you think I know that?'

'Do you? Do you really? You must've known something like this was going to happen sooner or later.'

'You're so smart, aren't you?'

'If you say so.'

'I'd like to see you do something like this.' He clicked his fingers. 'You'd fold like that.'

She couldn't help it. Jessica remembered the manor house out in the countryside. If only Jefferson knew who he was talking to.

He must have noticed something about the way she reacted because he nodded towards her. 'What?' he said.

Jessica fixed him with a stare. 'I'm not the issue here,' she said.

'What are you going to do to get me out?'

'Why do you think that's what I'm here for?'

He started to sound panicky: 'Why else are you here?'

'I wanted to hear what you had to say about why those kids think you owe them money. About why you had so much control over them.'

Jefferson turned away once more, not willing to answer.

'Why did you stop them?' Jessica asked.

'When?'

'When I was surrounded that night. You made them walk away. Without that...'

Jefferson forced a smile, narrow-lipped and humourless. 'I guess I'm a sucker for a chick in a suit.'

Jessica's radio sounded and she unclipped it, holding the device in her lap. It was the voice of Kennaugh. He didn't say much – and he didn't sound happy. Someone from on high had ordered him to escort Jefferson Cass off the estate. He told Jessica everything was now in position but that she should get away from the windows.

Then the shouting started.

FORTY-NINE

As it was, the kids outside Jefferson's flat decided they didn't fancy a ruck with a bunch of police officers kitted out with pads, helmets and sodding big truncheons. As soon as Kennaugh's men started their march, the teenagers scattered, shouting abuse and threats they clearly had no intention of carrying out. Jefferson was marched away from his apartment with a riot squad member on either side, and bundled into the back of a van as if he was a common crook. Someone was coming for his snakes, apparently.

Jessica wondered what might happen to him. She doubted it would be anything official and she was certain nobody would go out of their way to tell her. When undercover operations went wrong, the usual policy – which wasn't an official policy – was to get the man or woman out and pretend nothing had happened. If anyone came asking questions, there was only a missing person.

There was no sign of Nina and Jessica doubted they'd run into one another again. The only major thing she had going in her favour was that when everything was inevitably swept under that massive great carpet they kept at HQ, no one would come to her for answers. They'd be too busy covering their own arses and trying to figure out when and why Jefferson went rogue.

It occurred to her that Jefferson wasn't even his name. She'd probably never know the truth about who he was and what he was supposed to be doing. What she did know, what she'd seen in his broken face, was that he'd forgotten who he was.

Where did the undercover begin and end?

After Kennaugh and his team had left, it was down to Jessica, Archie and Pete. Pete had his hands in his pockets and was leaning on a battered phone box close to the shops.

'I think this whole experiment is probably over,' he said.

Jessica offered her hand. 'I think you're probably right.'

They shook and he stood staring at the estate for a moment before spinning on his heels and heading back to his office. At least he'd be doing the paperwork.

'Going to start any more riots today?' Archie asked when it was just them.

'Thinking about it.'

He nodded towards the plaza. 'D'you think we should check in on Roly?'

Jessica agreed and so they headed for the plaza for what she told herself would be the final time. She'd seen enough of this housing block to last more than one career.

Archie led the way up the echoing steps and headed along the balcony until they were outside Roly's door. He knocked and then stepped back. When there was no answer, Archie tried again, before kneeling and peering through the letter box.

'Roly?'

No answer.

'Can you see anything?' Jessica asked.

'Not much. The hallway.' Archie stood and straightened his already scuffed trousers. 'What d'you think?'

Jessica pressed against the window and tried to peep through the gap in the curtains.

'Bingo,' Archie said.

Jessica turned to see that the front door was open. 'What did you do?' she asked.

'It was unlocked.'

He shrugged and led the way into the familiar smell of stale fags and air freshener. Jessica checked the door to the bedroom as Archie headed towards the kitchen. The bed was made: neatly tucked, with plumped pillows. There was a Manchester United poster on the wall and little else of note except for a pair of slippers next to the bed.

'Jess...?'

Archie's voice brought Jessica into the kitchen, where she followed his eyeline to a single envelope on the table. Her name was written on the front in messy black handwriting.

'Admirer?' Archie said. He was teasing but Jessica knew. She'd probably known earlier but hadn't let herself believe it. Her fingers were trembling as she picked up the envelope and opened it with her nail.

The words on the card inside were easy enough to take in despite the shaky handwriting. Jessica read it twice and then offered it to Archie.

'Five words,' she said.

Dearest Jessica,
    Nothing personal.
    Roly

She removed the crumpled twenty-pound note from the envelope and placed it on the table. Archie read the note one more time and then looked to the money.

'He nicked the money?' Archie said.

Jessica sat at the table and rubbed her temples. It was too

much to take. The deathtrap heater no longer had the hose dangling through the window, instead there was a coil of plastic tubing piled on top.

A long coil.

'The old sod,' Jessica said.

'How did he do it?'

Jessica pursed her lips and thought about telling him about how Jefferson had fallen asleep unexpectedly; how he'd been sick when he woke up. He didn't know how lucky he was to still be alive, given the noxious muck that would have been pouring out of Roly's heater directly through Jefferson's window. Perhaps that'd teach him to close the damned thing.

'I have no idea,' Jessica replied.

Archie sat at the table opposite Jessica. He'd not put the pieces together but nodded towards the flat below. 'What do you think Jefferson was up to?'

'Some sort of Fagin gang. He had people nicking or dealing for him on other estates. He paid the kids as if they were employees. They were happy because they had his protection – plus he probably supplied the drugs, if that's what they were doing. Meanwhile, people round here had put up with so much for so long that they were happy for a respite. They either had no idea what was going on or some turned a blind eye as long as they got a quiet life. I don't blame them, really. What would you think if your old nan was getting turned over at a bus stop and then someone made it all go away?'

Archie sighed. They both knew it was true – but that didn't make it right. He picked up Roly's note and read it once more, then asked the question she was dreading.

'What now?'

FIFTY

EASTER MONDAY

Manchester Royal Infirmary was back to normal – which meant it was a scene of organised chaos. The casualty unit was packed with people who'd either had too much to drink over the long weekend and fallen off something; or blokes who'd decided to spend the weekend doing DIY – and then fallen off something. Either that or nailed a finger or toe to something it shouldn't be nailed to.

With the friendly smile of Melissa on the front desk, Jessica had bypassed all of that, heading along the corridors.

Perhaps unexpectedly, Guy had told them about how it was Francine's idea to 'cleanse' the hospital. He'd not done it to help them, as such, more to double down. He wanted to confess his own 'sins' of the years he'd spent as a hospital porter aiding those who committed the gravest crime of wanting to live. God's plan should be sacrosanct and all that. He'd taken a flyer from Francine at some point and, in his muddled brain, one thing had led to another.

The earlier victims, Henry, Lucy and Tiffany, had been in the wrong place at the wrong time. They had all gone into the hospital while Guy was on shift and their stories had been given too much attention in the media.

Francine had done the tracking down and then Guy had struck. Sons did what their mothers told them to, after all. Henry was pushed in front of the car, which could have been any vehicle. Archie just happened to be driving. Lucy had been shoved off the car park roof and then Tiffany had been barricaded in that food truck.

Even Guy's 'brother', Ezra, had defied God's will by having the blood transfusion. Francine could only stand for that for so long.

As for Mark ending up in the canal... Guy wasn't confessing to that. Maybe he did it, maybe not.

Jessica continued walking along the hospital corridors, wondering what might have been had Guy's device gone off. There were more questions to be asked about times and places; the who, what, when and why. Those were for another day.

As it was, for now, all Jessica cared about was that everyone here was safe.

Her thoughts flipped back to the now as she realised Caroline's room was empty.

Jessica asked a passing nurse if she knew where Caroline had gone but got a blank shake of the head in response.

Caroline's dressing gown was still hooked across the bedpost, so she hadn't checked herself out – which meant she was either on a trip to the ladies', or...

Jessica found Caroline and Hugo in the newborn unit. Not the intensive care area, the standard newborn unit.

Caroline squealed with delight as Jessica stepped inside.

'Look who's here,' she said in a girlish high-pitched voice.

Jessica smiled sheepishly, suddenly self-conscious about being the momentary centre of attention. She didn't need to worry for long – there was only one person on whom everyone's eyes were focused.

The baby was no longer in the incubator Jessica had previously seen him in. There was no mass of tubes and wires. He was lying in a crib, breathing all by himself.

'It's Auntie Jessica,' Caroline cooed.

She looked and sounded much more like her old self, her cheeks flushed with colour, her hair clean and tied back. Her thumb was almost as big as her baby's tiny hands. The child's matchstick-thin fingers creased and bent as he tried to figure out what to do with them.

Hugo was sitting at the side, watching Caroline and the baby, not saying much. He still looked as tired as when Jessica had met him at the airport and she wondered how many hours he'd slept. He had at least changed his clothes.

'Got your bags back?' Jessica asked.

Hugo nodded. He had one hand on Caroline's back but was playing with a coin with the other, apparently unaware he was doing it.

Caroline was staring at the baby. 'You can hold him if you want,' she said.

'Hugo?'

Caroline looked up at Jessica, confused and not getting it. They'd all missed too much sleep.

'He wants to say hello,' she added. 'He wants to hear how you helped him out of mummy's tummy.'

Jessica winced. 'I'm pretty sure he doesn't. Does he have a name yet?'

'Not yet. We've narrowed it down to two – either Ace or Winter.'

Jessica glanced towards Hugo, who puffed out his cheeks, making it clear it wasn't 'we' who had narrowed it down.

For the moment, Jessica held her tongue. Conversations about child abuse through naming could come later.

The baby gurgled and Caroline leant further over the crib.

When it was clear her child was simply trying to blow a raspberry, or perhaps breathe, she pressed back.

'I've got something to ask you,' she said.

Jessica took a seat next to Hugo, expecting the whole, 'Can you be godmother?' conversation. Of course she would be... as long as she didn't have to actually do very much.

Except that wasn't the question.

'It's a bit of a weird one,' Caroline said. 'I wondered if I was dreaming, but I remembered it this morning and it felt so... real.'

'What?'

'Did you call me a hoebag?'

THE GIRL WHO CAME BACK

Thirteen years ago Olivia Adams went missing. Now she's back... or is she?

When six-year-old **Olivia Adams** disappeared from her back garden, the small community of Stoneridge was thrown into turmoil. How could a child vanish in the middle of a cosy English village?

Thirteen years on and Olivia is back. Her mother is convinced it's her but not everyone is sure. If this is the missing girl, then where has she been - and what happened to her on that sunny afternoon?

If she's an imposter, then who would be bold enough to try to fool a child's own mother – and why?

Then there are those who would rather Olivia stayed missing. The past is the past and some secrets *must* remain buried.

THE WIFE'S SECRET

Charley Willis was thirteen years old when her parents were killed in their family home and she was found hiding in a cupboard upstairs.

Fifteen years later, Charley is marrying Seth Chambers. It should be the happiest day of their lives, a chance for Charley to put her past behind her, but just hours after the ceremony, she is missing.

No one saw her leave. No one knows where she is.

One thing is for certain... Seth is about to discover he doesn't really know the woman he just married. And his nightmare is only just beginning.

Printed in Great Britain
by Amazon